THE GREEN-PEA PIRATES

*"Captain Scraggs threw his brown derby on the deck
and leaped upon it"*

THE
GREEN-PEA PIRATES

BY
PETER B. KYNE

Author of
"Cappy Ricks," "The Long Chance," "Webster—
Man's Man," "The Valley of the Giants," Etc.

Illustrated by Gordon Grant

Wildside Press Edition: MMIII

Published by
Wildside Press, LLC
P.O. Box 301
Holicong, PA 18928-0301 USA
www.wildsidepress.com

Wildside Press Edition: MMIII

ORIGINALLY PUBLISHED BY THE SUNSET MAGAZINE

LIST OF ILLUSTRATIONS

THE GREEN-PEA PIRATES

The Green-Pea Pirates

CHAPTER I

THEY had seen the fog rolling down the coast shortly after the *Maggie* had rounded Pilar Point at sunset and headed north. Captain Scraggs has been steamboating too many unprofitable years on San Francisco Bay, the Suisun and San Pablo sloughs and dogholes and the Sacramento River to be deceived as to the character of that fog, and he remarked as much to Mr. Gibney. "We'd better turn back to Halfmoon Bay and tie up at the dock," he added.

"Calamity howler!" retorted Mr. Gibney and gave the wheel a spoke or two. "Scraggsy, you're enough to make a real sailor sick at the stomach."

"But I tell you she's a tule fog, Gib. She rises up in the marshes of the Sacramento and San Joaquin, drifts down to the bay and out the Golden Gate and just naturally blocks the wheels of commerce while she lasts. Why, I've known the ferry boats between San Francisco and Oakland to get lost for hours on their twenty-minute run—and all along of a blasted tule fog."

"I don't doubt your word a mite, Scraggsy. I never did see a ferry-boat skipper that knew shucks about sailorizing," the imperturbable Gibney responded. "Me, I'll smell my way home in any tule fog."

"Maybe you can an' maybe you can't, Gib, although far be it from me to question your ability. I'll take it for granted. Nevertheless, I ain't a-goin' to run the risk o' you havin' catarrh o' the nose an' confusin' your smells to-night. You ain't got nothin, at stake but your job, whereas if I lose the *Maggie* I lose my hull fortune. Bring her about, Gib, an' let's hustle back."

"Don't be an old woman," Mr. Gibney pleaded. "Scraggs, you just ain't got enough works inside you to fill a wrist watch."

"I ain't a-goin' to poke around in the dark an' a tule fog, feelin' for the Golden Gate," Captain Scraggs shrilled peevishly.

"Hell's bells an' panther tracks! I've got my old courses, an' if I foller them we can't help gettin' home."

Captain Scraggs laid his hand on Mr. Gibney's great arm and tried to smile paternally. "Gib, my *dear* boy," he pleaded, "control yourself. Don't argue with me, Gib. I'm master here an' you're mate. Do I make myself clear?"

"You do, Scraggsy. But it won't avail you nothin'. You're only master becuz of a gentleman's agreement between us two, an' because I'm man enough to figger there's certain rights due you as owner o' the *Maggie*. But don't you forget that accordin' to the records o' the Inspector's office, I'm master of the *Maggie*, an' the way I figger it, whenever there's any call to show a little real seamanship, that gentleman's agreement don't stand."

"But this ain't one o' them times, Gib."

"You're whistlin' it is. If we run from this here fog, it's skiffs to battleships we don't get into San Francisco

Bay an' discharged before six o'clock to-morrow night. By the time we've taken on coal an' water an' what-all, it'll be eight or nine o'clock, with me an' McGuffey entitled to mebbe three dollars overtime an' havin' to argue an' scrap with you to git it—not to speak o' havin' to put to sea the same night so's to be back in Halfmoon Bay to load bright an' early next mornin'. Scraggsy, I ain't no night bird on this run."

"Do you mean to defy me, Gib?" Captain Scraggs' little green eyes gleamed balefully. Mr. Gibney looked down upon him with tolerance, as a Great Dane gazes upon a fox terrier. "I certainly do, Scraggsy, old pepper-pot," he replied calmly. "What're you goin' to do about it?" The ghost of a smile lighted his jovial countenance.

"Nothin'—now. I'm helpless," Captain Scraggs answered with deadly calm. "But the minute we hit the dock you an' me parts company."

"I don't know whether we will or not, Scraggsy. I ain't heeled right financially to hit the beach on such short notice."

"That ain't no skin off'n my nose, Gib."

"Well, you can fire all you want, but you won't fire me. I won't go."

"I'll get the police to remove you, you blistered pirate," Scraggs screamed, now quite beside himself.

"Yes? Well, the minute they let go o' me I'll come back to the S. S. *Maggie* and tear her apart just to see what makes her go." He leaned out the pilot house window and sniffed. "Tule fog, all right, Scraggs. Still, that ain't no reason why the ship's company should fast, is it? Quit bickerin' with me, little one, an' see if you can't wrastle up some ham an' eggs. I want my eggs sunny side up."

Sensing the futility of further argument, Captain Scraggs sought solace in a stream of adjectival opprobrium, plainly meant for Mr. Gibney but delivered, nevertheless, impersonally. He closed the pilot house door furiously behind him and started for the galley.

"Some bright day I'm goin' to git tired o' hearin' you cuss my proxy," Mr. Gibney bawled after him, "an' when that fatal time arrives I'll scatter a can o' Kill-Flea over you an' the shippin' world'll know you no more."

"Oh, go to—glory, you pig-iron polisher," Captain Scraggs tossed back at him over his shoulder—and honour was satisfied. In the lee of the pilot house Captain Scraggs paused, set his infamous old brown derby hat on the deck and leaped furiously upon it with both feet. Six times he did this; then with a blow of his fist he knocked the ruin back into a semblance of its original shape and immediately felt better.

"If I was you, skipper, I'd hold my temper until I got to port; then I'd git jingled an' forgit my troubles inexpensively," somebody advised him.

Scraggs turned. In a little square hatch the head and shoulders of Mr. Bartholomew McGuffey, chief engineer; first, second and third assistant engineer, oiler, wiper, water-tender, and coal-passer of the *Maggie*, appeared. He was standing on the steel ladder that led up from his stuffy engine room and had evidently come up, like a whale, for a breath of fresh air. "The way you ruin them bonnets o' yourn sure is a scandal," Mr. McGuffey concluded. "If I had a temper as nasty as yourn I'd take soothin' syrup or somethin' for it."

Without waiting for a reply, Mr. McGuffey dropped back into his department and Captain Scraggs, his soul filled with rage and dire forebodings, repaired to the galley, and "candled" four dozen eggs. Out of the four dozen he found nine with black spots in them and carefully set them aside to be fried, sunny side up, for Mr. Gibney and McGuffey.

CHAPTER II

BEFORE proceeding further with this narrative, due respect for the reader's curiosity directs that we diverge for a period sufficient to present a brief history of the steamer *Maggie* and her peculiar crew. We will begin with the *Maggie*.

She had been built on Puget Sound back in the eighties, and was one hundred and six feet over all, twenty-six feet beam and seven feet draft. Driven by a little steeple compound engine, in the pride of her youth she could make ten knots. However, what with old age and boiler scale, the best she could do now was six, and had Mr. McGuffey paid the slightest heed to the limitations imposed upon his steam gauge by the Supervising Inspector of Boilers at San Francisco, she would have been limited to five. Each annual inspection threatened to be her last, and Captain Scraggs, her sole owner, lived in perpetual fear that eventually the day must arrive when, to save the lives of himself and his crew, he would be forced to ship a new boiler and renew the rotten timbers around her deadwood. She had come into Captain Scraggs's possession at public auction conducted by the United States Marshal, following her capture as she sneaked into San Francisco Bay one dark night with a load of Chinamen and opium from Ensenada. She had cost him fifteen hundred hard-earned dollars.

Scraggs—Phineas P. Scraggs, to employ his full name, was precisely the kind of man one might expect to own and operate the *Maggie*. Rat-faced, snaggle toothed and furtive, with a low cunning that sometimes passed for great intelligence, Scraggs' character is best described in a homely American word. He was "ornery." A native of San Francisco, he had grown up around the docks and had developed from messboy on a river steamer to master of bay and river steamboats, although it is not of record that he ever commanded such a craft. Despite his "ticket" there was none so foolish as to trust him with one—a condition of affairs which had tended to sour a disposition not naturally sweet. The yearning to command a steamboat gradually had developed into an obsession. Result—the "fast and commodious S. S. *Maggie*," as the United States Marshal had had the audacity to advertise her.

In the beginning, Captain Scraggs had planned to do bay and river towing with the *Maggie*. Alas! The first time the unfortunate Scraggs attempted to tow a heavily laden barge up river, a light fog had come down, necessitating the frequent blowing of the whistle. Following the sixth long blast, Mr. McGuffey had whistled Scraggs on the engine room howler; swearing horribly, he had demanded to be informed why in this and that the skipper didn't leave that dod-gasted whistle alone. It was using up his steam faster than he could manufacture it. Thereafter, Scraggs had used a patent foghorn, and when the honest McGuffey had once more succeeded in conserving sufficient steam to crawl up river, the tide had turned and the *Maggie*

could not buck the ebb.   McGuffey declared a few new
tubes in the boiler would do the trick, but on the other
hand, Mr. Gibney pointed out that the old craft was
practically punk aft and a stiff tow would jerk the tail
off the old girl.   In despair, therefore, Captain Scraggs
had abandoned bay and river towing and was prepared
to jump overboard and end all, when an opportunity
offered for the freighting of garden truck and dairy
produce from Halfmoon Bay to San Francisco.

But now a difficulty arose.   The new run was an
"outside" one—salt water all the way.   Under the
ruling of the Inspectors, the *Maggie* would be running
coastwise the instant she engaged in the green pea and
string bean trade, and Captain Scraggs's license provided for no such contingency.   His ticket entitled
him to act as master on the waters of San Francisco
Bay and the waters tributary thereto, and although
Scraggs argued that the Pacific Ocean constituted
waters "tributary thereto," if *he* understood the
English language, the Inspectors were obdurate.   What
if the distance was less than twenty-five miles? they
pointed out.   The voyage was undeniably coastwise
and carried with it all the risk of wind and wave.   And
in order to impress upon Captain Scraggs the weight
of their authority, the Inspectors suspended for six
months Captain Scraggs's bay and river license for having dared to negotiate two coastwise voyages without
consulting them.   Furthermore, they warned him that
the next time he did it they would condemn the fast
and commodious *Maggie*.

In his extremity, Fate had sent to Captain Scraggs a
large, imposing, capable, but socially indifferent person

who responded to the name of Adelbert P. Gibney. Mr. Gibney had spent part of an adventurous life in the United States Navy, where he had applied himself and acquired a fair smattering of navigation. Prior to entering the Navy he had been a foremast hand in clipper ships and had held a second mate's berth. Following his discharge from the Navy he had sailed coastwise on steam schooners, and after attending a navigation school for two months, had procured a license as chief mate of steam, any ocean and any tonnage.

Unfortunately for Mr. Gibney, he had a failing. Most of us have. The most genial fellow in the world, he was cursed with too much brains and imagination and a thirst which required quenching around pay-day. Also, he had that beastly habit of command which is inseparable from a born leader; when he held a first mate's berth, he was wont to try to "run the ship" and, on occasions, ladle out suggestions to his skipper. Thus, in time, he had acquired a reputation for being unreliable and a wind-bag, with the result that skippers were chary of engaging him. Not to be too prolix, at the time Captain Scraggs made the disheartening discovery that he had to have a skipper for the *Maggie*, Mr. Gibney found himself reduced to the alternative of longshore work or a fo'castle berth in a windjammer bound for blue water.

With alacrity, therefore, Mr. Gibney had accepted Scraggs's offer of seventy-five dollars a month—"and found"—to skipper the *Maggie* on her coastwise run. As a first mate of steam he had no difficulty inducing the Inspectors to grant him a license to skipper such an abandoned craft as the *Maggie*, and accordingly he hung up his ticket in her pilot house and was registered as her master, albeit, under a gentlemen's agreement with Scraggs he was not to claim the title of captain and was known to the world as the *Maggie's* first mate, second mate, third mate, quartermaster, purser, and freight clerk.   One Neils Halvorsen, a solemn Swede with a placid, bovine disposition, constituted the fo'-castle hands, while Bart McGuffey, a wastrel of the Gibney type but slower-witted, reigned supreme in the engine room.   Also his case resembled that of Mr. Gibney in that McGuffey's job on the *Maggie* was the first he had had in six months and he treasured it accordingly.   For this reason he and Gibney had been inclined to take considerable slack from Captain Scraggs until McGuffey discovered that, in all probability, no engineer in the world, except himself, would have the courage to trust himself within range of the *Maggie's* boilers, and, consequently, he had Captain Scraggs more or less at his mercy.   Upon imparting this suspicion to Mr. Gibney, the latter decided that it would be a cold day, indeed, when his ticket would not constitute a club wherewith to make Scraggs, as Gibney expressed it, "mind his P's and Q's."

It will be seen, therefore, that mutual necessity held this queerly assorted trio together, and, though they quarrelled furiously, nevertheless, with the passage of time their own weaknesses and those of the *Maggie* had aroused in each for the other a curious affection. While Captain Scraggs frequently "pulled" a monumental bluff and threatened to dismiss both Gibney and McGuffey—and, in fact, occasionally went so far as to order them off his ship, on their part Gibney and

McGuffey were wont to work the same racket and resign. With the subsidence of their anger and the return to reason, however, the trio had a habit of meeting accidentally in the Bowhead saloon, where, sooner or later, they were certain to bury their grudge in a foaming beaker of steam beer, and return joyfully to the *Maggie*.

Of all the little ship's company, Neils Halvorsen, colloquially designated as "The Squarehead," was the only individual who was, in truth and in fact, his own man. Neils was steady, industrious, faithful, capable, and reliable; any one of a hundred deckhand jobs were ever open to Neils, yet, for some reason best known to himself, he preferred to stick by the *Maggie*. In his dull way it is probable that he was fascinated by the agile intelligence of Mr. Gibney, the vitriolic tongue of Captain Scraggs, and the elephantine wit and grizzly bear courage of Mr. McGuffey. At any rate, he delighted in hearing them snarl and wrangle.

However, to return to the *Maggie* which we left entering the tule fog a few miles north of Pilar Point:

CHAPTER III

CAPTAIN SCRAGGS and The Squarehead partook first of the ham and eggs, coffee and bread which the skipper prepared. Scraggs then prepared a similar meal for Mr. Gibney and McGuffey, set it in the oven to keep warm, and descended to the engine room to relieve McGuffey for dinner. Neils at the same time took the course from Mr. Gibney and relieved the latter at the wheel. By this time, darkness had descended upon the world, and the *Maggie* had entered the fog; following her custom she proceeded in absolute silence, although as a partial offset to the extreme liability to collision with other coastwise craft, due to the non-whistling rule aboard the *Maggie*, Mr. Gibney had laid a course half a mile inside the usual steamer lanes, albeit due to his overwhelming desire for peace he had neglected to inform his owner of this; the honest fellow proceeded upon the hypothesis that what people do not know is not apt to trouble them.

Mr. McGuffey was already seated and disposing of his meal when Mr. Gibney entered. "Gib," he declared with his mouth full, "rinse the taste o' chewin' tobacco out o' your mouth before startin' to eat, an' then tell me, as man to man, if them eggs is fit for human consumption."

Mr. Gibney conformed with the engineer's request. "Eatable but venerable," was his verdict. "That

infernal Scraggs is tryin' to make the *Maggie* pay
dividends at the expense of our stomachs."

"*And* at the risk of our lives, Gib. I move we declare
a strike until Scraggs digs up the money to overhaul the
boiler. Just before we slipped into the fog I saw two
steam schooners headed south—so they must 'a' seen
us headed north. Jes' listen at them a-bellerin' off
there to port. They're a-watchin' and a-listenin',
expectin' to cut us down at every turn o' the screw.
First thing you know, Gib, you'll be losin' your ticket
for failin' to be courteous on the high seas."

"Six o' one an' half a dozen o' the other, Bart. If I
whistle I'll use up all your steam, an', then if we should
find ourselves in the danger zone we won't be able to get
out of our own way."

"Let's refuse to take her out again until Scraggsy
spends some money on her. 'Tain't Christian the way
he acts."

"Got to get in another pay day before I start the high
an' mighty, Bart. But I'll speak to the old man about
them eggs. They taste like they'd been laid by a
pelican before the Civil War. Somehow I can't eat
an egg that's the least bit rotten."

"It's gettin' so," McGuffey mourned, "that I don't
have no more time off in port. When I ain't standin'
by I'm repairin', an' when I ain't doin' either I'm
dreamin' about the danged old coffee mill. For a can-
celled postage stamp I'd jump the ship."

He gulped down his coffee, loaded his pipe, and went
below to relieve Scraggs, for although experience in
acting as McGuffey's relief had given Captain Scraggs
what might be termed a working knowledge of the

Maggie's engine, McGuffey was never happy with Scraggs in charge, even for five minutes. The habit of years caused him to cast a quick glance at the steam gauge, and he noted it had dropped five pounds.

"Savin' on the coal again," he roared. "Git out o' my engine room, you doggoned skinflint." He seized a slice bar, threw open the furnace door, raked the fire, and commenced shovelling in coal at a rate that almost brought the tears of anguish to his owner's eyes. "There! The main bearin's screamin' again," he wailed. "Oil cup's empty. Ain't I drilled it into your head enough, Scraggsy, that she'll cry her eyes out if you don't let her swim in oil?" He grasped the oil can and, in order to test the efficacy of its squirt, shot a generous stream down Captain Scraggs's collar.

"That for them rotten eggs, you miser," he growled. "Heraus mit 'em!"

Captain Scraggs fled, cursing, and sought solace in the pilot house.

"It's as black," quoted Mr. Gibney as he entered, "as the Earl of Hell's riding boots."

"And as thick," snarled Scraggs, "as McGuffey's head. Lordy me, Gib, but it's thick. You'd think every bloomin' steam pipe in the universe had busted."

"If they was all like the *Maggie's,*" Mr. Gibney retorted drily, "we wouldn't need to worry none. Not wishin' to change the conversation, Scraggsy, but referrin' to them eggs you slipped me and Bart for supper, all I gotta say is that the next time you go marketin' in ancient Egypt, me an' Mac's goin' to tell the real story o' the S.S. *Maggie* to the Inspectors. Now, that goes. Scatter along aft, Scraggs, and let me know what that taffrail log has to say about it."

Captain Scraggs read the log and reported the mileage to Mr. Gibney, who figured with the stub of a pencil on the pilot house wall, wagged his head, and appeared satisfied. "Better go for'd," he ordered, "an' help The Squarehead on the lookout. At eight o'clock we ought to be right under the lee o' Point San Pedro; when I whistle we ought to catch the echo thrown back by the cliff. Listen for it."

Promptly at eight o'clock, Mr. McGuffey was horrified to see his steam gauge drop half a pound as the *Maggie's* siren sounded. Mr. Gibney stuck his ingenious head out of the pilot house and listened, but no answering echo reached his ears. "Hear anything?" he bawled.

"Heard the *Maggie's* siren," Captain Scraggs retorted venomously.

Mr. Gibney leaped out on deck, selected a small head of cabbage from a broken crate and hurled it forward. Then he sprang back into the pilot house and straightened the *Maggie* on her course again. He leaned over the binnacle, with the cuff of his watch coat wiping away the moisture on the glass, and studied the instrument carefully. "I don't trust the danged thing," he muttered. "Guess I'll haul her off a coupler points an' try the whistle again."

He did. Still no echo. He was inclined to believe that Captain Scraggs had not read the taffrail log correctly, and when at eight-thirty he tried the whistle again he was still without results in the way of an echo from the cliff, albeit the engine room howler brought him several of a profuse character from the perspiring McGuffey.

"We've passed Pedro," Mr. Gibney decided. He ground his cud and muttered ugly things to himself, for his dead reckoning had gone astray and he was worried. The fog, if anything, was thicker than ever. He could not even make out the phosphorescent water that curled out from the *Maggie's* forefoot.

Time passed. Suddenly Mr. Gibney thrilled electrically to a shrill yip from Captain Scraggs.

"What's that?" Mr. Gibney bawled.

"I dunno. Sounds like the surf, Gib."

"Ain't you been on this run long enough to know that the surf don't sound like nothin' else in life but breakers?" Gibney retorted wrathfully.

"I ain't certain, Gib."

Instantly Gibney signalled McGuffey for half speed ahead.

"Breakers on the starboard bow," yelled Captain Scraggs.

"Port bow," The Squarehead corrected him.

"Oh, my great patience!" Mr. Gibney groaned. "They're on both bows an' we're headed straight for the beach. Here's where we all go to hell together," and he yanked wildly at the signal wire that led to the engine room, with the intention of giving McGuffey four bells—the signal aboard the *Maggie* for full speed astern. At the second jerk the wire broke, but not until two bells had sounded in the engine room—the signal for full speed ahead. The efficient McGuffey promptly kicked her wide open, and the Fates decreed that, having done so, Mr. McGuffey should forthwith climb

the ladder and thrust his head out on deck for a breath
of fresh air. Instantly a chorus of shrieks up on the
fo'castle head attracted his attention to such a degree
that he failed to hear the engine room howler as Mr.
Gibney blew frantically into it.

Presently, out of the hubbub forward, Mr. McGuffey
heard Captain Scraggs wail frantically: "Stop her!
For the love of heaven, stop her!" Instantly the engineer dropped back into the engine room and set the
Maggie full speed astern; then he grasped the howler
and held it to his ear.

"Stop her!" he heard Gibney shriek. "Why in
blazes don't you stop her?"

"She's set astern, Gib. She'll ease up in a minute."

"You know it," Gibney answered significantly.

The *Maggie* climbed lazily to the crest of a long oily
roller, slid recklessly down the other side, and took the
following sea over her taffrail. She still had some head
on, but very little—not quite sufficient to give her
decent steerage way, as Mr. Gibney discovered when,
having at length communicated his desires to McGuffey,
he spun the wheel frantically in a belated effort to swing
the *Maggie*'s dirty nose out to sea.

"Nothin' doin'," he snarled. "She'll have to come
to a complete stop before she begins to walk backward
and get steerage way on again. She'll bump as sure as
death an' taxes."

She did—with a crack that shook the rigging and
caused it to rattle like buckshot in a pan. A terrible
cry—such a cry, indeed, as might burst from the lips
of a mother seeing her only child run down by the
Limited—burst from poor Captain Scraggs. "My

ship! my ship!" he howled. "My darling little
Maggie! They've killed you, they've killed you!
The dirty lubbers!"

The succeeding wave lifted the *Maggie* off the beach,
carried her in some fifty feet further, and deposited her
gently on the sand. She heeled over to port a little and
rested there as if she was very, very weary, nor could all
the threshing of her screw in reverse haul her off again.
The surf, dashing in under her fantail, had more power
than McGuffey's engines, and, foot by foot, the *Maggie*
proceeded to dig herself in. Mr. Gibney listened for
five minutes to the uproar that rose from the bowels of
the little steamer before he whistled up Mr. McGuffey.

"Kill her, kill her," he ordered. "Your wheel will
bite into the sand first thing you know, and tear the
stern off her. You're shakin' the old girl to pieces."

CHAPTER IV

MCGUFFEY killed his engine, banked his fires, and came up on deck, wiping his anxious face with a fearfully filthy sweat rag. At the same time, Scraggs and Neils Halvorsen came crawling aft over the deckload and when they reached the clear space around the pilot house, Captain Scraggs threw his brown derby on the deck and leaped upon it until, his rage abating ultimately, no power on earth, in the air, or under the sea, could possibly have rehabilitated it and rendered it fit for further wear, even by Captain Scraggs. This petulant practice of jumping on his hat was a habit with Scraggs whenever anything annoyed him particularly and was always infallible evidence that a simple declarative sentence had stuck in his throat.

"Well, old whirling dervish," Mr. Gibney demanded calmly when Scraggs paused for lack of breath to continue his dance, "what about it? We're up Salt Creek without a paddle; all hell to pay and no pitch hot."

"McGuffey's fired!" Captain Scraggs screeched.

"Come, come, Scraggsy, old tarpot," Mr. Gibney soothed. "This ain't no time for fightin'. Thinkin' an' actin' is all that saves the *Maggie* now."

But Captain Scraggs was beyond reason. "McGuffey's fired! McGuffey's fired!" he reiterated. "The dirty rotten wharf rat! Call yourself an engineer?" he continued, witheringly. "As an engineer you're a howling success at shoemakin', you slob. I'll fix your clock for you, my hearty. I'll have your ticket took away from you, an' that's no Chinaman's dream, nuther."

"It's all my fault runnin' by dead reckonin'," the honest Gibney protested. "Mac ain't to fault. The engine room telegraph busted an' he got the wrong signal."

"It's his business to see to it that he's got an engine room telegraph that won't bust——"

"You dog!" McGuffey roared and sprang at the skipper, who leaped nimbly up the little ladder to the top of the pilot house and stood prepared to kick Mr. McGuffey in the face should that worthy venture up after him. "I can't persuade you to git me nothin' that I ought to have. I'm tired workin' with junk an' scraps an' copper wire and pieces o' string. I'm through!"

"You're right—you're through, because you're fired!" Scraggs shrieked in insane rage. "Get off my ship, you maritime impostor, or I'll take a pistol to you. Overboard with you, you greasy, addlepated bounder! You're rotten, understand? Rotten! Rotten! Rotten!"

"You owe me eight dollars an' six bits, Scraggs," Mr. McGuffey reminded his owner calmly. "Chuck down the spondulicks an' I'll get off your ship."

Captain Scraggs was beyond reason, so he tossed the money down to the engineer. "Now git," he commanded.

Without further ado, Mr. McGuffey started across
the deckload to the fo'castle head. Scraggs could not
see him but he could hear him—so he pelted the engineer with potatoes, cabbage heads, and onions, the vegetables descending about the honest McGuffey in a
veritable barrage. Even in the darkness several of
these missiles took effect.

Upon reaching the very apex of the *Maggie's* bow,
Mr. McGuffey turned and hurled a promise into the
darkness: "If we ever meet again, Scraggs, I'll make
Mrs. Scraggs a widow. Paste that in your hat—when
you get a new one."

The *Maggie* was resting easily on the beach, with the
broken water from the long lazy combers surging well
up above her water line. At most, six feet of water
awaited the engineer, who stood, peering shoreward and
listening intently, oblivious to the stray missiles which
whizzed past. Presently, from out of the fog, he heard
a grinding, metallic sound and through a sudden rift in
the fog caught a brief glimpse of blue flame with sparks
radiating faintly from it.

That settled matters for Bartholomew McGuffey.
The metallic sound was the protest from the wheels of a
Cliff House trolley car rounding a curve; the blue flame
was an electric manifestation due to the intermittent
contact of her trolley with the wire, wet with fog. Mc-
Guffey knew the exact position of the *Maggie* now, so he
poised a moment on her bow; as a wave swept past him,
he leaped overboard, scrambled ashore, made his way
up the beach to the Great Highway which flanks the
shore line between the Cliff House and Ingleside,
sought a roadhouse, and warmed his interior with four

fingers of whiskey neat. Then, feeling quite content with himself, even in his wet garments, he boarded a city-bound trolley car and departed for the warmth and hospitality of Scab Johnny's sailor boarding house in Oregon Street.

CHAPTER V

CAPTAIN SCRAGGS continued to hurl other people's vegetables into the murk forward for at least two minutes after Mr. McGuffey had shaken the coal dust of the *Maggie* from his feet, and was only recalled tomore practical affairs by the bored voice of Mr. Gibney.

"The owners o' them artichokes expect to get half a dollar apiece for 'em in New York, Scraggsy. Cut it out, old timer, or you'll have a claim for a freight shortage chalked up agin you."

"Nothin' matters any more," Scraggs replied in a choked voice, and immediately sat down on the half-emptied crate of artichokes and commenced to weep bitterly—half because of rage and half because he regarded himself a pauper. Already he had a vision of himself scouring the waterfront in search of a job.

"No use boo-hooin' over spilt milk, Scraggsy." Always philosophical, the author of the owner's woe sought to carry the disaster off lightly. "Don't add your salt tears to a saltier sea until you're certain you're a total loss an' no insurance. I got you into this and I suppose it's up to me to get you off, so I guess I'll commence operations." Suiting the action to the word, Mr. Gibney grasped the whistle cord and a strange, sad, sneezing, wheezy moan resembling the expiring protest of a lusty pig and gradually increasing into a long-drawn

25

but respectable whistle rewarded his efforts. For once, he could afford to be prodigal with the steam, and while it lasted there could be no mistaking the fact that here was a steamer in dire distress.

The weird call for help brought Scraggs around to a fuller realization of the enormity of the disaster which had overtaken him. In his agony, he forgot to curse his navigating officer for the latter's stubbornness in refusing to turn back when the fog threatened. He clutched Mr. Gibney by the right arm, thereby inter rupting for an instant the dismal outburst from the *Maggie's* siren.

"Gib," he moaned, "I'm a ruined man. How're we ever to get the old sweetheart off whole? Answer me that, Gib. Answer me, I say. How're we to get my *Maggie* off the beach?"

Mr. Gibney shook himself loose from that frantic grip and continued his pull on the whistle until the *Maggie*, taking a false note, quavered, moaned, spat steam a minute, and subsided with what might be termed a nautical sob. "Now see what you've done," he bawled. "You've made me bust the whistle."

"Answer my question, Gib."

"We'll never get her off if you don't quit interferin' an' give me time to think. I'll admit there ain't much of a chance, because it's dead low water now an' just as soon as the tide is at the flood she'll drive further up the beach an' fall apart."

"Perhaps McGuffey will have heart enough to telephone into the city for a tug."

"'Tain't scarcely probable, Scraggsy. You abused him vile an' threw a lot of fodder at him."

"I wish I'd been took with paralysis first," Scraggs wailed bitterly. "You'd best jump ashore, Gib, an' 'phone in. We're just below the Cliff House and you can run up to one o' them beach resorts an' 'phone in to the Red Stack Tug Boat Company."

"'Twouldn't be ethics for me, the registered master o' the *Maggie*, to desert the ship, Scraggsy, old stick-in-the-mud. What's the matter with gettin' your own shanks wet?"

"I dassen't, Gib. I've had a touch of chills an' fever ever since I used to run mate up the San Joaquin sloughs. Here's a nickel to drop in the telephone slot, Gib. There's a good fellow."

"Scraggsy, you're deludin' yourself. Show me a tug-boat skipper that would come out here on a night like this to pick up the S. S. *Maggie*, two decks an' no bottom an' loaded with garden truck, an' I'll wag my ears an' look at the back o' my neck. She ain't worth it."

"Ain't worth it! Why, man, I paid fifteen hundred hard cash dollars for her."

"Fourteen hundred an' ninety-nine dollars an' ninety-nine cents too much. They seen you comin'. However, grantin' for the sake of argyment that she's worth the tow, the next question them towboat skippers'll ask is: 'Who's goin' to pay the bill?' It'll be two hundred an' fifty dollars at the lowest figger, an' if you got that much credit with the towboat company you're some high financier. Ain't that logic?"

"I'm afraid," Scraggs replied sadly, "it is. Still, they'd have a lien on the *Maggie*——"

"Steamer ahoy!" came a voice from the beach.

"Man with a megaphone," Mr. Gibney cried. "Ahoy! Ahoy, there!"

"Who are you an' what's the trouble?"

Captain Scraggs took it upon himself to answer: "American steamer *Mag*——"

Mr. Gibney sprang upon him tigerishly, placed a horny, tobacco-smelling palm across Scraggs's mouth and effectively smothered all further sound. "American steamer *Yankee Prince*," he bawled like a veritable Bull of Bashan, "of Boston, Hong Kong to Frisco with a general cargo of sandal wood, rice, an' silk. Where're we at?"

"Just outside the Gate. Half a mile south o' the Cliff House."

"Telephone in for a tug. We're in nice shape, restin' easy, but our rudder's gone an' the after web o' the crank shaft's busted. Telephone in, my man, an' I'll make it up to you when we get to a safe anchorage. Who are you?"

"Lindstrom, of the Golden Gate Life Saving Station."

"I'll not forget you, Lindstrom. My owners are Yankees, but they're sports."

"All right. I'll telephone. On my way!"

"God speed you," murmured Mr. Gibney, and released his hold on Captain Scraggs, who instantly threw his arms around the navigating officer's burly neck. "I forgive you, Adelbert," he crooned. "I forgive you freely. By the tail of the Great Sacred Bull, you're a marvel. She's an all-night fog or I'm a Chinaman, and if it only stays thick enough——"

"It'll hold," Gibney retorted doggedly. "It's a tule

fog. They always hold. Quit huggin' me. Your breath's bad. Them eggs, I guess."

Captain Scraggs, hurled forcibly backward, bumped into the pilot house, but lost none of his enthusiasm. "You're a jewel," he declared. "Oh, man, what a head! Whatever made you think of the *Yankee Prince?*"

"Because," Mr. Gibney answered calmly, "there ain't no such ship, this land of ours bein' a free republic where princes don't grow. Still, it's a nice name, Scraggs, old tarpot—more particular since I thought it up in a hurry. Eh, what?"

"Halvorsen," cried Captain Scraggs.

The lone deckhand emerged from a hole in the freight forward whither he had retreated to escape the vegetable barrage put over by Captain Scraggs when McGuffey left the ship. "Aye, aye, sir," he boomed.

"All hands below to the galley!" Scraggs shouted. "While we're waitin' for this here towboat I'll brew a scuttle o' grog to celebrate the discovery o' real seafarin' talent. Gib, my *dear* boy, I'm proud of you. No matter what happens, I'll never have no other navigatin' officer."

"Don't crow till you're out o' the woods," the astute Gibney warned him.

CHAPTER VI

IN THE office of the Red Stack Tug Boat Company, Captain Dan Hicks, master of the tug *Aphrodite;* Captain Jack Flaherty, master of the *Bodega,* and Tiernan, the assistant superintendent on night watch, sat around a hot little box stove engaged in that occupation so dear to the maritime heart, to-wit: spinning yarns. Dan Hicks had the floor, and was relating a tale that had to do with his life as a freight and passenger skipper.

"We was makin' up to the dock when I see the general agent standin' in the door o' the dock office—an' all of a sudden I didn't feel so chipper about havin' crossed Humboldt bar in a sou'easter. I saw the old man runnin' his eye along forty foot o' twisted pipe railin', a wrecked bridge, three bent stanchions an' every door an' window on the starboard side o' the ship stove in, while the passengers crowded the rail lookin' cold an' miserable, pea-green an' thankful. No need for me to do any explainin'. He knew. He throws his dead fish eye up to me on what's left o' the bridge an' I felt my job was vacant.

"'We was hit by a sea or two on Humboldt bar, sir,' I says, as if gettin' hit by a sea or two an' havin' the ship gutted was an every-day experience."

"'Is that so, Hicks?' says he sweetly. 'Well, now, if you hadn't told me that I'd ha' jumped to the conclu-

sion that a couple o' the mess boys had got fightin' an'
wrecked the ship before you could separate 'em. Why
in this an' that,' he says, 'didn't you stick inside when
any dumb fool could see the bar was breakin'?'

"'I wanted to keep the comp'ny's sailin' schedule un-
broken, sir,' I says, tryin' to be funny.

"'Well, Captain,' he says, 'it 'pears to me you've
broken damned near everything else tryin' to do it.'

"I was certain he was goin' to set me down, but the
worst I got was a three months' lay-off to teach me
common sense——"

The telephone rang and Tiernan answered. Hicks
and Flaherty hitched forward in their chairs to listen.

"Hello. . . . Yes, Red Stack office. . . .
Steamer *Yankee Prince*. . . . What's that? . . .
silk and rice? . . . Half a mile below the Cliff
House, eh? . . . Sure, I'll send a tug right away,
Lindstrom."

Tiernan hung up and faced the two skippers. "Gentlemen," he announced, "here's a chance for a little
salvage money to-night. The American steamer *Yankee Prince* is ashore half a mile below the Cliff House.
She's a big tramp with a valuable cargo from Hong
Kong, with her rudder gone and her crank shaft
busted."

"It's high water at twelve thirty-seven," Jack
Flaherty pleaded. "You'd better send me, Tiernan.
The *Bodega* has more power than the *Aphrodite*."

This was the truth and Dan Hicks knew it, but he
was not to be beaten out of his share of the salvage
by such flimsy argument. "Jack," he pleaded, "don't
be a hog all the time. The *Yankee Prince* is an eight

thousand ton vessel and it's a two-tug job. Better send us both, Tiernan, and play safe. Chances are our competitors have three tugs on the way right now."

"What a wonderful imagination you have, Dan. Eight thousand tons! You're crazy, man. She's thirteen hundred net register and I know it because I was in Newport News when they launched her, and I went out with her skipper on the trial trip. She's a long, narrow-gutted craft, with engines aft, like a lake steamer."

"We'll play safe," Tiernan decided. "Go to it—both of you, and may the best man win. She'll belong to you, Jack, if she's thirteen hundred net and you get your line aboard first. If she's as big as Dan says she is, you'll be equal partners——"

But he was talking to himself. Down the docks Hicks and Flaherty were racing for the respective commands, each shouting to his night watchman to pipe all hands on deck. Fortunately, a goodly head of steam was up in each tug's boilers; because of the fog and the liability to collisions and a consequent hasty summons, one engineer on each tug was on duty. Before Hicks and Flaherty were in their respective pilot houses the oil burners were roaring lustily under their respective boilers; the lines were cast off within a minute of each other, and the two tugs raced down the bay through the darkness and fog.

Both Hicks and Flaherty had grown old in the towboat service and the rules of the road rested lightly on their sordid souls. They were going over a course they knew by heart—wherefore the fog had no terrors for them. Down the bay they raced, the *Bodega*

leading slightly, both tugs whistling at half-minute
intervals. Out through the Gate they nosed their
way, heaving the lead continuously, made a wide de-
tour around Mile Rock and the Seal Rocks, swung a
mile to the south of the position of the *Maggie*, and
then came cautiously up the coast, whistling continuously to acquaint the *Yankee Prince* with their presence
in the neighbourhood. In anticipation of the necessity
for replying to this welcome sound, Captain Scraggs
and Mr. Gibney had, for the past two hours, busied
themselves getting up another head of steam in the
Maggie's boilers, repairing the whistle, and splicing the
wires of the engine room telegraph. Like the wise
men they were, however, they declined to sound the
Maggie's siren until the tugs were quite close. Even
then, Mr. Gibney shuddered, but needs must when the
devil drives, so he pulled the whistle cord and was rewarded with a weird, mournful grunt, dying away into a
gasp.

"Sounds like she has the pip," Jack Flaherty remarked to his mate.

"Must have taken on some of that dirty Asiatic
water," Dan Hicks soliloquized, "and now her tubes
have gone to glory."

Immediately, both tugs kicked ahead under a dead
slow bell, guided by a series of toots as brief as Mr.
Gibney could make them, and presently both tug look-
outs reported breakers dead ahead; whereupon Jack
Flaherty got out his largest megaphone and bellowed:
"*Yankee Prince*, ahoy!" in his most approved fashion.
Dan Hicks did likewise. This irritated the avaricious
Flaherty, so he turned his megaphone in the direction

of his rival and begged him, if he still retained any of the instincts of a seaman, to shut up; to which entreaty Dan Hicks replied with an acidulous query as to whether or not Jack Flaherty thought he owned the sea.

For half a minute this mild repartee continued, to be interrupted presently by a whoop from out of the fog. It was Mr. Gibney. He did not possess a megaphone so he had gone below and appropriated a section of stove-pipe from the galley range, formed a mouthpiece of cardboard and produced a makeshift that suited his purpose admirably.

"Cut out that bickerin' like a pair of old women an' 'tend to your business," he commanded. "Get busy there—both of you, and shoot a line aboard. There's work enough for two."

Dan Hicks sent a man forward to heave the lead under the nose of the *Aphrodite*, which was edging in gingerly toward the voice. He had a searchlight but he did not attempt to use it, knowing full well that in such a fog it would be of no avail. Guided, therefore, by the bellowings of Mr. Gibney, reinforced by the shrill yips of Captain Scraggs, the tug crept in closer and closer, and when it seemed that they must be within a hundred feet of the surf, Dan Hicks trained his Lyle gun in the direction of Mr. Gibney's voice and shot a heaving line into the fog.

Almost simultaneous with the report of the gun came a shriek of pain from Captain Scraggs. Straight and true the wet, heavy knotted end of the heaving line came in over the *Maggie's* quarter and struck him in the mouth. In the darkness he staggered back from the stinging blow, clutched wildly at the air, slipped and rolled over among the vegetables with the precious rope clasped to his breast.

"I got it," he sputtered, "I got it, Gib."

"Safe, O!" Mr. Gibney bawled. "Pay out your hawser."

They met it at the taffrail as it came up out of the breakers, wet but welcome. "Pass it around the main-mast, Scraggsy," Mr. Gibney cautioned. "If we make fast to the towin' bits, the first jerk'll pull the anchor bolts up through the deck."

When the hawser had been made fast to the main-mast, the leathern lungs of Mr. Gibney made due an-nouncement of the fact to the expectant Captain Hicks. "As soon as you feel you've got a grip on her," he yelled, "just hold her steady so she won't drive fur-ther up the beach when I get my anchor up. She'll come out like a loose tooth at the tip of the flood."

The *Aphrodite* forged slowly ahead, taking in the slack of the hawser. Ten minutes passed but still the hawser lay limp across the *Maggie's* stern. Presently out of the fog came the voice of Captain Dan Hicks.

"Flaherty! Flaher-tee! For the love of life, Jack, where are you? Chuck me a line, Jack. My hawser's snarled in my screw and I'm drifting on to the beach."

"Leggo your anchor, you boob," Jack Flaherty ad-vised.

"I want a line an' none o' your damned advice," raved Hicks.

"'Tain't my fault if you get in too close."

"I'm bumping, Jack. I'm bangin' the heart out of her. Come on, you cur, and haul me off."

"If I pull you off, Dan Hicks, will you leave that

steamer alone? You've had your chance and failed to smother it. Now let me have a hack at her."

"It's a bargain, Jack. I'm not badly snarled; if you haul me out to deep water I can shake the hawser loose. I'm afraid to try so close in."

"Comin'," yelled Flaherty.

"Now, ain't that a raw deal?" Scraggs complained. "That junk thief gets hauled off first."

"The first shall be last an' the last shall be first," Gibney quoted piously. "Don't be a crab, Scraggs. Pray that the fog don't lift."

Out of the fog there rose a great hubbub of engine room gongs, the banging of the *Bodega's* Lyle gun, and much profanity. Presently this ceased, so Scraggs and Gibney knew Dan Hicks was being hauled off at last. While they waited for further developments, Scraggs sucked at his old pipe and Mr. Gibney munched a French carrot. "If you hadn't canned McGuffey," the latter opined, "we might have been able to back off under our own power as soon as the tide is at flood. This delay is worryin' me."

Following some fifteen minutes of kicking and struggling out in the deep water, whither the *Bodega* had dragged her, the *Aphrodite* at length freed herself of the clinging hawser; whereupon she backed in again, cautiously reeving in the hawser as she came. Presently, Dan Hicks, true to his promise to abandon the prize to Jack Flaherty, turned his megaphone beachward and shouted:

"*Yankee Prince*, ahoy! Cast off my hawser. The other tug will put a line aboard you."

But Mr. Gibney was now master of the situation.

He had a good hemp hawser stretching between him and salvation and until he should be hauled off he had no intention of slipping that cable. "Nothin' doin'," he answered. "We're hard an' fast, I tell you, and I'll take no chances. It's you or both of you, but I'll not cast off this hawser. If you want to let go, cast the hawser off at your end." Sotto voce he remarked to Scraggs: "I see him slippin' a three hundred dollar hawser, eh, Scraggsy, old stick-in-the-mud?"

"But I promised Flaherty I'd let you alone," pleaded Hicks.

"What do you think you have your string fast to, anyhow? A bay scow? If you fellows endanger my ship bickerin' over the salvage I'll have you before the Inspectors on charges as sure as God made little apples. I got sixty witnesses here to back up my charges, too."

"You hear him, Jack?" howled Hicks.

"Wouldn't that swab Flaherty drive you to drink," Gibney complained. "Trumpin' his partner's ace just for the glory an' profit o' gettin' ahead of him?" Aloud he addressed the invisible Flaherty: "Take it or leave it, brother Flaherty."

"I'll take it," Flaherty responded promptly.

Twenty minutes later, after much backing and swearing and heaving of lines the *Bodega's* hawser was finally put board the *Maggie*. Mr. Gibney judged it would be safe now to fasten this line to the towing bitts.

Suddenly, Captain Scraggs remembered there was no one on duty in the *Maggie's* engine room. With a half sob, he slid down the greasy ladder, tore open the furnace doors and commenced shovelling in coal with a recklessness that bordered on insanity. When the indicator showed eighty pounds of steam he came up on deck and discovered Mr. Gibney walking solemnly round and round the little capstan up forward. It was creaking and groaning dismally. Captain Scraggs thrust his engine room torch above his head to light the scene and gazed upon his navigating officer in blank amazement.

"What foolishness is this, Gib?" he demanded. "Are you clean daffy, doin' a barn dance around that rusty capstan, makin' a noise fit to frighten the fish?"

"Not much," came the laconic reply. "I'm a smart man. I'm raisin' both anchors."

"Well, all I got to remark is that it takes a smart man to raise both anchors when we only got one anchor to our blessed name. An' with that anchor safe on the fo'castle head, I, for one, can't see no sense in raisin' it."

"You tarnation jackass!" sighed Gibney. "You forget who we are. Do you s'pose the steamer *Yankee Prince* can lay on the beach all night with both anchors out, an' then be got ready to tow off in three shakes of a lamb's tail? It takes noise to get up two anchors— so I'm makin' all the noise I can. Got any steam?"

"Eighty pounds," Scraggs confessed. Having for the moment forgotten his identity, he was confused in the presence of the superior intelligence of his navigating officer.

"Run aft, then, Scraggs, an' turn that cargo winch over to beat the band until I tell you to stop. With the drum runnin' free she'll make noise enough for a winch three times her size, but you might give the necessary yells to make it more lifelike."

Captain Scraggs fled to the winch. At the end of five minutes, Mr. Gibney appeared and bade him desist. Then, turning his improvised megaphone seaward he addressed an imaginary mate: "Mr. Thompson, have you got your port anchor up?"

Scraggs took the cue immediately. "All clear forward, sir," he piped.

"Send the bosun for'd an' heave the lead, Mr. Thompson."

"Very well, sir."

Here The Squarehead, who had been enjoying the unique situation immensely, decided to take a hand. Presently, in sing-song cadence he was reporting the depth of water alongside.

"That'll do, bosun," Gibney thundered. Then, in his natural voice to Scraggs: "All set, Scraggsy. Guess we're ready to be pulled off. Get down in the engine room and stand by for full speed ahead when I give the word."

"Quick! Hurry!" Scraggs entreated as he disappeared through the little engine-room hatch, for the tide was now at the tip of the flood and the *Maggie* was bumping wickedly and driving further up the beach. Mr. Gibney turned his stovepipe seaward and shouted: "Tugboats, ahoy!"

"Ahoy!" they answered in unison.

"All read-y-y-y! Let 'er go-o-o-o!"

The Squarehead stationed himself at the bitts with a lantern and Mr. Gibney hastened to the pilot house and took his place at the wheel. When the hawsers commence to lift out of the sea, The Squarehead gave a warning shout, whereupon Mr. Gibney called the engine room. "Give her the gun," he commanded Scraggs. "Pull against them tugs for all you're worth. Remember this is the steamer *Yankee Prince*. We must not come off too readily."

Captain Scraggs opened the throttle, and while the two tugs steadily drew her off into deep water, the *Maggie* fought valiantly to stick to the beach and even to continue her interrupted journey overland. She merely succeeded in stretching both hawsers taut; slowly she was drawn seaward, stern first, and at the expiration of fifteen minutes' steady pulling, Mr. Gibney could restrain himself no longer. He rang for full speed astern—and got it promptly. Then, calling Neils Halvorsen to aid him, he abandoned the wheel and scrambled aft.

With no one at the wheel the *Maggie* shot off at a tangent and the hawsers slacked immediately. In the twinkling of an eye Mr. Gibney had cast them off, and as the ends disappeared with a swish over the stern he ran back to the pilot house, rang for full speed ahead, put his helm hard over, and headed the *Maggie* in the general direction of China, although as a matter of fact he cared not what direction he pursued, provided he got away from the beach and placed distance between the *Maggie* and two soon-to-be-furious tugboat skippers.

CHAPTER VII

A S THE *Maggie* chugged blithely away, the navigating officer's soul expanded in song, and in the voice of a bull walrus he delivered himself of a deep sea chantey more popular than proper.

Presently, away off in the fog, he heard the *Bodega* whistle. The *Aphrodite* answered immediately. Adelbert P. Gibney smiled and bit a large crescent out of his navy plug, for his soul was at peace. When The Squarehead came into the pilot house presently and grinned at him, Mr. Gibney handed Neils an electric torch. "Prowl around below in the old ruin, Neils," he commanded, "and see if we're makin' any water."

A quarter of an hour later Neils Halvorsen returned to report the *Maggie* apparently undamaged, so Mr. Gibney changed his course and headed stealthily in the direction of the whistling tugs. He came up behind them presently—approaching so close under cover of the fog that he could hear Dan Hicks and Jack Flaherty, both under a dead-slow bell, felicitating each other through their megaphones.

"Where d'ye suppose that dirty scoundrel's gone?" Hicks was demanding.

"Out to sea, of course," Flaherty bellowed. "He'll stand off until the fog lifts and then come ramping in as proud as Lucifer and look amazed when we send him in a bill."

"Bill!" Hicks' voice dripped with sarcasm. "The Red Stack Company will libel him, and if the old man doesn't, me an' my crew will."

"I'll bet a ripe peach he's a Jap, with a scoundrelly white skipper and white mates. They'll all stick together for a five-dollar bill and swear they never was on the beach at all. If they do, how're we goin' to prove it?"

"That's logic," the eavesdropping Gibney murmured to the binnacle.

"Oh, hell's bells, shut up and let's go home," Dan Hicks cried wearily. "We can catch him when he comes in."

"Suppose he doesn't come in. Suppose he's bound for Seattle, Dan."

"We can libel him wherever he goes."

"I'll bet he gave us a fictitious name, Dan!"

"Stow that grief, Jack. Stow it, or I'll go mad. The *Bodega* has more speed than the *Aphrodite*, so poke ahead there and let's try to get in an hour's sleep before daylight. If you can't feel your way in I can."

"I'll just tag along silent and lazy-like after you two misfortunates," Mr. Gibney decided, "an' you'll do my whistlin' for me." He called Scraggs on the howler and explained the situation. "Regular Cook's tour," he exulted. "Personally conducted. Off again, on again, away again, Finnegan—and not a nickel's worth of loss unless you count them vegetables you hove at McGuffey. Ain't you proud o' your navigatin' officer, Scraggsy, old tarpot?"

"I am, Gib, but I'll be prouder'n ever if you can follow them towboats in without havin' to claw off Baker's beach or the Point Bonita rocks."

"Calamity howler," Gibney growled. Half an hour later he caught the echo of the *Bodega's* whistle as the sound was hurled back from the high cliffs at Land's End, off to starboard. A minute later he heard the hoarse growl of the siren from the fog station on Point Bonita, on the port beam. He knew where he was now with as much certainty as if he was navigating in broad daylight, so he loafed along a couple of hundred yards behind the *Bodega*, until the *Maggie* ceased pitching— when he knew he was in the still water inside the entrance. So he sheered over to starboard, with Neils Halvorsen heaving the lead, and dropped anchor in five fathoms under the lee of Fort Mason. He was quite confident of his ability to sneak along the waterfront and creep into the *Maggie's* berth at Jackson Street bulkhead, but having gone astray in his calculations once that night, a vagrant sense of consideration for Captain Scraggs decided him to take no more risks until the fog should lift. He could hear the *Bodega* and the *Aphrodite* tooting as they continued down the bay, so he knew they were headed for their berths at the foot of Broadway, fog or no fog.

When Captain Scraggs, having banked his fires, came up out of the engine room, Mr. Gibney laid a great paw paternally upon the skipper's shoulder. "Scraggsy, old salamander," he announced, "I think I've done enough to-night to entitle me to some sleep until this tule fog lifts. Am I right?"

"You certainly are, Gib, my dear boy."

"Very well, then. I'll turn in. As for you, old sailor, your night's work is not ended. Have The Squarehead row you ashore in the skiff; I'll stay up an'

work the patent foghorn so he can find his way back
to the *Maggie*, while you hike down town———"

"What for?" Scraggs demanded irritably. "I'm all
wore out."

"This adventure ain't ended," Mr. Gibney warned
him. "There's a witness to our perfidy still at large.
His name is B. McGuffey, esquire, an' I'll lay you ten
to one you'll find him asleep in Scab Johnny's boardin'
house. Go to him, Scraggsy, an' bring a pint flask
with you when you do; wake him up, beg his pardon,
take him to breakfast, and promise him you'll do somethin' for his boilers. Old Mac's got a heart as tender
as a infant's. You can win him over."

"Oh, Gib, use some common sense. Mac'll lay
abed until noon. It stands to reason he'll have to,
because he didn't take no change of clothin' with him,
so he'll just naturally have to wait till his wet clothes
get dry before venturin' forth an' spreadin' the news
that the *Maggie's* on the beach. He doesn't know
we're off, an' once we're tied up at the dock and we
hear Mac's been talkin' we'll just spread the word that
he was so soused he jumped overboard an' swum ashore
without waitin' to see if we could back off. Lordy, Gib,
don't work me to death. I'm that weary I could flop
on this wet deck an' be off to sleep in a pig's whisper."

"I dunno but what there's reason in what you say,"
Mr. Gibney agreed. "Well, turn in, Scraggsy, but the
minute we hit the dock you run up town and fix things
up with Bart."

And without further ado he set the alarm clock for
seven o'clock, kicked off his shoes, and climbed into his
berth with his clothes on.

CHAPTER VIII

THE crews of the *Aphrodite* and the *Bodega* slept late also, for they were weary, and fortunately, no calls for a tug came into the office of the Red Stack Company all morning. About ten o'clock Dan Hicks and Jack Flaherty breakfasted and about ten thirty both met in the office. Apparently they were two souls with but a single thought, for the right hand of each sought the shelf whereon reposed the blue volume entitled "Lloyd's Register." Dan Hicks reached it first, carried it to the counter, wet his tarry index finger, and started turning the pages in a vain search for the American steamer *Yankee Prince.* Presently he looked up at Jack Flaherty.

"Flaherty," he said, "I think you're a liar."

"The same to you and many of them," Flaherty replied, not a whit abashed. "You said she was an eight thousand ton tramp."

"I never went so far as to say I'd been aboard her on trial trip, though—and I did cut down her tonnage, showin' I got the fragments of a conscience left," Hicks defended himself.

He closed the book with a sigh and placed it back on the shelf, just as the door opened to admit no less a personage than Batholomew McGuffey, late chief engineer, first assistant, second assistant, third assistant,

wiper, oiler, water-tender, and stoker of the S. S.
Maggie. With a brief nod to Jack Flaherty Mr. Mc-
Guffey approached Dan Hicks.

"I been lookin' for you, captain," he announced.
"Say, I hear the chief o' the *Aphrodite's* goin' to take a
three months' lay-off to get shet of his rheumatism.
Is that straight?"

"I believe it is, McGuffey."

"Well, say, I'd like to have a chance to substitoot
for him. You know my capabilities, Hicks, an' if
it would be agreeable to you to have me for your
chief your recommendation would go a long way toward
landin' me the job. I'd sure make them engines behave."

"What vessel have you been on lately?" Hicks demanded cautiously, for he knew Mr. McGuffey's reputation for non-reliability around pay-day.

"I been with that fresh water scavenger, Scraggs, in
the *Maggie* for most a year."

"Did you quit or did Scraggs fire you?"

"He fired me," McGuffey replied honestly. "If
he hadn't I'd have quit, so it's a toss-up. Comin' in
from Halfmoon Bay last night we got lost in the fog an'
piled up on the beach just below the Cliff House——"

"This is interesting," Jack Flaherty murmured.
"You say she walked ashore on you, McGuffey? Well,
I'll be shot!"

"She did. Scraggs blamed it on me, Flaherty. He
said I didn't obey the signals from the bridge, one word
led to another, an' he went dancin' mad an' ordered
me off his ship. Well, it's his ship—or it *was* his ship,
for I'll bet a dollar she's ground to powder by now—so

all I could do was obey. I hopped overboard an'
waded ashore. I suppose all my clothes an' things is
gone by now. I left everything aboard an' had to
borrow this outfit from Scab Johnny." He grinned
pathetically. "So I guess you understand, Captain
Hicks, just how bad I need that job I spoke about a
minute ago."

"I'll think it over, Mac, an' let you know," Hicks
replied evasively.

Mr. McGuffey, sensing his defeat, retired forthwith
to hide his embarrassment and distress; as the door
closed behind him, Hicks and Flaherty faced each other.

"Jack," quoth Dan Hicks, "can two towboat men,
holdin' down two hundred-dollar jobs an' presumed to
have been out o' their swaddlin' clothes for at least
thirty years, afford to be laughed off the San Francisco
waterfront?"

"I know one of them that can't, Dan. At the same
time, can a rat like Phineas P. Scraggs and a beachcomber like his mate Gibney make a pair of star-spangled
monkeys out of said two towboat men and get away
with it?"

"They did that last night. Still, I've known monkeys that would fight an' was human enough to settle
a grudge. Follow me, Jack."

Together they repaired to Jackson Street bulkhead.
Sure enough there lay the *Maggie*, rubbing her blistered
sides against the bulkhead. Captain Scraggs was nowhere in sight, but Mr. Gibney was at the winch, swinging ashore the crates of vegetables which The Squarehead and three longshoremen loaded into the cargo net.

"We're outnumbered," Jack Flaherty whispered.

"Let's wait until she's unloaded an' Gibney an' Scraggs are aboard alone."

They retired without having attracted the attention of Mr. Gibney, and a few minutes later, Captain Scraggs came down the bulkhead and sprang aboard.

"Well?" his navigating officer queried.

"Couldn't find him," Scraggs confessed. "Scab Johnny says he loaned Mac a dry outfit an' the old boy dug out for breakfast at seven o'clock an' ain't been around since."

"Did you try the saloons, Scraggsy?"

"I did. Likewise the cigar stands an' restaurants, an' the readin' rooms of the Marine Engineers' Association."

"Guess he's out hustlin' a job," Mr. Gibney sighed. He was filled with vague forebodings of evil. "If you'd only listened to my advice last night, Scraggsy—if you'd only listened," he mourned.

"We'll cross our bridges when we come to them, Gib. Cheer up, my boy, cheer up. I got a new engineer. He won't last, but he'll last long enough for Mac to forget his grouch an' listen to reason," and with this optimistic remark Captain Scraggs dropped into the engine room to get up enough steam to keep the winch working.

Promptly at twelve o'clock, the longshoremen knocked off work for the lunch hour and Neils Halvorsen drifted across the street to cool his parched throat with steam beer. While waiting for Scraggs to come up out of the engine room, and take him to luncheon, Mr. Gibney sauntered aft and was standing gazing reflectively upon a spot on the *Maggie's* stern where the hawsers had chafed away the paint, when suddenly his forebodings of evil returned to him a thousand fold stronger than they had been since Scraggs's return to the little ship. He glanced up and beheld gazing down upon him Captains Jack Flaherty and Daniel Hicks. Battle was imminent and the valiant Gibney knew it; wherefore he determined instantly to meet it like a man.

"Howdy, men," he saluted them. "Glad to have you aboard the yacht," and he stepped backward to give himself fighting room.

"Here's where we collect the towage bill on the S. S. *Yankee Prince*," Dan Hicks informed him, and leaped from the bulkhead straight down at Mr. Gibney. Jack Flaherty followed. Mr. Gibney welcomed Captain Hicks with a terrific right swing, which missed; before he could guard, Dan Hicks had planted left and right where they would do the most good and Mr. Gibney went into a clinch to save himself further punishment.

"Scraggsy," he bawled, "Scraggsy-y-y! Help! Murder! It's Hicks and Flaherty! Bring an ax!"

He flung Dan Hicks at Jack Flaherty; as they collided he rushed in and dealt each of them a powerful poke. However, Messrs. Hicks and Flaherty were sizeable persons and while, individually, they were no match for the tremendous Gibney, nevertheless what they lacked in horsepower they made up in pugnacity—and the salt sea seldom breeds a craven. Capt'n Scraggs thrust a frightened face up through the engine-room hatch, but at sight of the battle royal taking place on the deck aft, his blood turned to water and he thought only of escape. To climb up to the bulkhead without being seen was impossible, however, so, not knowing what else to do, he stood on the iron ladder and gazed, pop-eyed with horror, at the unequal contest.

Backward and forward the tide of battle surged. For nearly three minutes all Scraggs saw was an indistinct tangle of legs and arms; then suddenly the combatants disengaged themselves and Scraggs beheld Mr. Gibney lying prone upon the deck with a gory face upturned to the foggy skies. When he essayed to rise and continue the contest, Flaherty kicked him in the ribs and Hicks cursed them; so Mr. Gibney, realizing that all was over, beat the deck with his hand in token of surrender. Hicks and Flaherty waited until the fallen gladiator had recovered sufficient breath to sit up; then they pounced upon him, lifted him to the rail, and dropped him overboard. Captain Scraggs shrieked in protest at this added touch of barbarity, and Dan Hicks, turning, beheld Scraggsy's white face at the hatch.

"You're next, Scraggs," he called cheerfully, and turned to peer over the rail. Mr. Gibney had emerged on the surface and was swimming slowly away toward an adjacent float where small boats landed. He climbed wearily up on the float and sat there, gazing across at Hicks and Flaherty without animus, for to his way of thinking he had gotten off lightly, considering the enormity of his offense. The least he had anticipated was three months in hospital, and so grateful was he to Hicks and Flaherty for their great forbearance that he strangled a resolve to "lay" for Hicks and Flaherty and thrash them individually—something he was fully able to do—and forgot his aches and pains in a lively interest as to the fate of Captain Scraggs at the hands of the towboat men. He was aware that

Captain Scraggs had failed ignominiously to rally to the Gibney appeal to repel boarders, and in his own expressive terminology he hoped that what the enemy would do to the dastard would be "a-plenty."

The enemy, meanwhile, had turned their attention upon Scraggs, who had dodged below like a frightened rabbit and sought shelter in the shaft alley. He had sufficient presence of mind, as he dashed through the engine room, to snatch a large monkey wrench off the tool rack on the wall, and, kneeling just inside the alley entrance he turned at bay and threatened the invaders with this weapon. Thereupon Hicks and Flaherty pelted him with lumps of coal, but the sole result of this assault was to force Scraggs further back into the shaft alley and out of range.

The towboat men held a council of war and decided to drown Scraggs out. Dan Hicks ran up on deck and returned dragging the deck fire hose behind him. He thrust the brass nozzle into the shaft alley entrance and invited Scraggs to surrender unconditionally or be drowned like a kitten. Scraggs, knowing his own fire hose, defied them, so Dan Hicks started the pump while Flaherty turned on the water. Instantly the hose burst up on deck and Scraggs's jeers of triumph filled the engine room. The enemy was about to draw lots to see which one of the two should crawl into the shaft alley and throw a cupful of chloride of lime (for they found a can of this in the engine room) in Captain Scraggs's face, when a shadow darkened the hatch and Mr. Bartholomew McGuffey demanded belligerently: "What's goin' on down there? Who the devil's takin' liberties in my engine room?"

Dan Hicks explained the situation and the just cause for drastic action which they held against the fugitive in the shaft alley. Mr. McGuffey considered a few moments and made his decision.

"If what you say is true—an' I ain't in position to dispute you, not havin' been present when you hauled the *Maggie* off the beach, I don't blame you for feeling sore. What I do blame you for, though, is carryin' the war aboard the *Maggie*. If you wanted to whale Gib an' Scraggsy you should ha' laid for 'em on the dock. Under the circumstances, you make this a pers'nal affair, an' as a member o' the crew o' the *Maggie* I got to take a hand an' defend my skipper agin youse two. Fact is, gentlemen, I got a date to lick him first for what he done to me last night. Howsumever, that's a private grouch. The fact remains that you two jumped my pal Bert Gibney an' licked him somethin' scandalous. Hicks, I'll take you on first. Come up out of there, you swab, and fight. Flaherty, you stay below until I send for you; if you try to climb up an' horn in on my fight with Hicks, Gibney'll brain you."

A faint cheer came from the shaft alley. "Good old Mac. At-a-boy!"

"You're on, McGuffey. Nobody ever had to beg me to fight him," Dan Hicks replied cordially, and climbed to the deck. To his great surprise, Mr. Mc-Guffey winked at him and drew him off to the stern of the *Maggie*.

"There'll be no fight," he declared, "although we'll thud around on deck an' yell a couple o' times to make Scraggs think we're goin' to it. He figgers that by the time I've fought you an' Flaherty I won't be fit for com-

bat with him, even if I lick you both; he's got it all figgered out that I'll wait a couple o' days before tacklin'
him, an' he thinks my temper'll cool by that time an'
he can argy me out o' my revenge. Savey?"

"I twig."

Mr. Gibney had returned to the *Maggie* by this time
and he now took his station at the engine-room hatch
and growled at Flaherty and abused him. "Keep up
your courage, Scraggsy," he called, as Hicks and Mc-
Guffey pranced around the deck in simulated combat.
"Mac's whalin' the whey out o' Hicks an' Hicks
couldn't touch him with a buggy whip."

At the conclusion of the three minutes of horse-play,
Mr. McGuffey came to the hatch again. "Up with you,
Flaherty," he called loud enough for Captain Scraggs
to hear, "up with you before I go down after you."

Flaherty was about to possess himself of a hatchet
when the face of his confrère, Dan Hicks, appeared over
McGuffey's shoulder and grinned knowingly at him.
Immediately, Flaherty hurled defiance at his enemies
and came up on deck, and once more to Captain Scraggs
came the dull sounds of apparent conflict overhead.

Suddenly a cheer broke from Mr. Gibney. "All off
an' gone to Coopertown, Scraggsy," he shouted. "Come
up an' take a look at the fallen."

Out of the shaft alley came Scraggs with a rush,
tossing his wrench aside the better to climb the ladder.
He was half way up when Mr. Gibney reached down a
great hand, grasped him by the collar, and whisked him
out on deck with a single jerk. Here, to his horror, he
found himself confronted by a singularly scathless trio
who grinned triumphantly at him.

"Seein' is believin', Scraggs," Dan Hicks informed him. "That's a lesson you taught me an' Flaherty last night, but evidently you don't profit by experience. You're too miserable to beat up, but just to show you it ain't possible for a dirty bay pirate like you to skin the likes o' me an' Flaherty we purpose hangin' the seat o' your pants up around your coat collar. Face him about, Gibney."

Jack Flaherty raised his voice in song:

> Glorious! Glorious!
> One kick a piece for the four of us!

With a quick twist, Mr. Gibney presented Captain Scraggs for his penance; Flaherty and McGuffey followed Dan Hicks promptly and Captain Scraggs screamed at every kick. And now came Mr. Gibney's turn. "For failin' to stand up like a man, Scraggsy, an' battle Hicks an' Flaherty," he informed the culprit, and tossed him over to McGuffey to be held in position for him.

"Don't, Gib. Please don't," Scraggs wailed. "It ain't comin' to me from you. I never heard you callin' a-tall. Honest, I never, Gib. Have mercy, Adelbert. You saved the *Maggie* last night an' a quarter interest in her is yours—if you don't kick me!"

Mr. Gibney paused, foot in mid-air; surveyed the *Maggie* from stem to stern, hesitated, licked his lower lip, and glanced at the common enemy. For an instant it came into his mind to call upon the valiant and able McGuffey to support him in a fierce counter attack upon Hicks and Flaherty. Only for an instant, however; then his sense of fair play conquered.

"No, Scraggsy," he replied sadly. "She ain't worth it, an' your duplicity can't be overlooked. If there's anything I hate it's duplicity. Here goes, Scraggsy—and get yourself a new navigatin' officer."

Scraggs twisted and flinched instantly, and Mr. Gibney's great boot missed the mark. "Ah," he breathed, "I'll give you an extra for that."

"Don't! Please don't," Scraggs howled. "Lay off'n me an' I'll put in a new boiler an' have the compass adjusted."

The words were no sooner out of his mouth than Mr. McGuffey swung him clear of Mr. Gibney's wrath. "Swear it," he hissed. "Raise your right hand an' swear it—an' I'll protect you from Gib."

Captain Scraggs raised a trembling right hand and swore it. "I'll get a new fire hose an' fire buckets; I'll fix the ash hoist and run the bedbugs an' cockroaches out of her," he added.

"You hear that, Gib?" McGuffey pleaded. "Have a heart."

"Not unless he gives her a coat of paint an' quits bickerin' about the overtime, Bart."

"I promise," Scraggs answered him. "Pervided," he added, "you an' dear ol' Mac promises to stick by the ship."

"It's a whack," yelled McGuffey joyfully, and whirling, struck Dan Hicks a mighty blow on the jaw. "Off our ship, you hoodlums." He favoured Jack Flaherty with a hearty thump and swung again on Dan Hicks. "At 'em, Scraggsy. Here's where you prove to Gib whether you're a man—thump—or a mouse—thump—or a—thump, thump—bobtailed—thump—rat."

Dan Hicks had been upset, and as he sprawled on his back on deck, he appeared to Captain Scraggs to offer at least an even chance for victory. So Scraggs, mustering his courage, flew at poor Hicks tooth and toenail. His best was not much but it served to keep Dan Hicks off Mr. McGuffey while the latter was disposing of Jack Flaherty, which he did, via the rail, even as the towboat men had disposed of Mr. Gibney. Dan Hicks followed Flaherty, and the crew of the *Maggie* crowded the rail as the enemy swam to the float, crawled up on it and departed, vowing vengeance.

"All's well that ends well, gentlemen," Mr. McGuffey announced. "Scraggsy's goin' to buy a drink an' the past is buried an' forgotten. Didn't old Scraggsy put up a fight, Gib?"

"No, but he tried to, Mac. I'll tell the world he did," and he thrust out the hand of forgiveness to Scraggsy, who, realizing he had come very handsomely out of an unlovely situation, clasped the hands of Mr. Gibney and McGuffey and burst into tears. While Mr. McGuffey thumped him between the shoulder blades and cursed him affectionately, Mr. Gibney retired to change into dry garments; when he reappeared the trio went ashore for the promised grog and a luncheon at the skipper's expense.

CHAPTER IX

A WEEK had elapsed and nothing of an eventful nature had transpired to disturb the routine of life aboard the *Maggie*, until Bartholomew McGuffey, having heard certain waterfront whispers, considered it the part of prudence to lay his information before Scraggs and Mr. Gibney.

"Look here, Scraggs," he began briskly. "It's all fine an' dandy to promise me a new boiler, but when do I git it?"

"Why, jes' as soon as we can get this glut o' freight behind us, Bart, my boy. The way it's pilin' up on us now, what with this bein' the height o' the busy season an' all, it stands to reason we got to wait a while for dull times before layin' the *Maggie* up."

"What's the matter with orderin' the new boiler now so's to have it ready to chuck into her over the week-end," McGuffey suggested. "There needn't be no great delay."

"As owner o' the *Maggie*," Scraggs reminded him with just a touch of asperity, "you've got to leave these details to me. You've managed with the old boiler this long, so it 'pears to me you might be patient an' bear with it a mite longer, Bart."

"Oh, I ain't tryin' to be disagreeable, Scraggs, only it sort o' worries me to have to go along without bein' able to use our whistle. We got a reputation for joggin'

57

right along, mindin' our business an' never replyin' to them vessels that whistle us they're goin' to pass to port or starboard, as the case may be. Of course when they whistle, we know what they're goin' to do, but the trouble is *they* don't know what we're goin' to do. Dan Hicks an' Jack Flaherty's been makin' a quiet brag that one o' these days or nights they'll take advantage o' this well-known peculiarity of ourn to collide with the *Maggie* an' sink us, and in that case we wouldn't have no defense an' no come-back in a court of law. Me, I don't feel like drownin' in that engine room or gettin' cut in half by the bow o' the *Bodega* or the *Aphrodite*. Consequently, you'd better ship that new boiler you promised me an' save funeral expenses. We just naturally got to commence whistlin', Scraggsy."

"We'll commence it when business slacks up," Scraggs decided with finality.

Mr. Gibney who, up to this moment, had said nothing, now fixed Captain Scraggs with a piercing glance and threatened him with an index finger across the cabin table. "We don't have to wait for the slack season to have that there compass adjusted an' paint the topsides o' the *Maggie*," he reminded Scraggs. "As for her upper works, I'll paint them myself on Sundays, if you'll dig up the paint. How about that program?"

"We'll do it all at once when we lay up to install the boiler," Scraggs protested. He glanced at his watch. "Sufferin' sailor!" he cried in simulated distress. "Here it's one o'clock an' I ain't collected a dollar o' the freight money from the last voyage. I must beat it."

When Captain Scraggs had "beaten it," Gibney and McGuffey exchanged expressive glances. "He's runnin' out on us," McGuffey complained.

"Even so, Bart, even so. Therefore, the thing for us to do is to run out on him. In other words, we'll work a month, save our money, an' then, without a word o' complaint or argyment, we'll walk out."

"Oh, I ain't exactly broke, Gib. I got eighty-five dollars."

"Then," quoth Gibney decisively, "we'll go on strike to-night. Scraggsy'll be stuck in port a week before he can get another engineer an' another navigatin' officer, me an' you bein' the only two natural-born fools in San Francisco an' ports adjacent, an' before three days have passed he'll be huntin' us up to compromise."

"I don't want no compromise. What I want is a new boiler."

"You'll git it. We'll make him order the paint an' the boiler an' pay for both in advance before we'll agree to go back to work."

The engineer nodded his approval and after sealing their pact with a hearty handshake, they turned to and commenced discharging the *Maggie*. When Captain Scraggs returned to the little steamer shortly after five o'clock, to his great amazement, he discovered Mr. Gibney and McGuffey dressed in their other suits—including celluloid collars and cuffs.

"The cargo's out, Scraggsy, my son, the decks has been washed down an' everything in my department is shipshape." Thus Mr. Gibney.

"Likewise in mine," McGuffey added.

"Consequently," Mr. Gibney concluded, "we're

quittin' the *Maggie* an' if it's all the same to you we'll
have our time."

"My *dear* Gib. Why, whatever's come over you
two boys?"

"Stow your chatter, Scraggs. Shell out the cash.
The only explanation we'll make is that a burned child
dreads the fire. You've fooled us once in the matter
o' that new boiler an' the paintin', an' we're not goin'
to give you a second chance. Come through—or take
the consequences. We'll sail no more with a liar an'
a fraud."

"Them's hard words, Mr. Gibney."

"The truth is allers bitter," McGuffey opined.

Captain Scraggs paused to consider the serious predicament which confronted him. It was Saturday
night. He knew Mr. McGuffey to be the possessor
of more money than usual and if he could assure himself
that this reserve should be dissipated before Monday
morning he was aware, from experience, that the strike
would be broken by Tuesday at the latest. And he
could afford that delay. He resolved, therefore, on
diplomacy.

"Well, I'm sorry," he answered with every appearance of contrition. "You fellers got me in the nine-
hole an' I can't help myself. At the same time, I
appreciate fully your p'int of view, while realizin' that
I can't convince you o' mine. So we won't have no
hard feelin's at partin', boys, an' to show you I'm a
sport I'll treat to a French dinner an' a motion picture
show afterward. Further, I shall regard a refusal of
said invite as a pers'nal affront."

"By golly, you're gittin' sporty in your old age," the

engineer declared. "I'll go you, Scraggs. How about you, Gib?"

"I accept with thanks, Scraggsy, old tarpot. Personally, I maintain that seamen should leave their troubles aboard ship."

"That's the sperrit I appreciate, boys. Come to the cabin an' I'll pay you off. Then wait a coupler minutes till I shift into my glad rags an' away we'll go, like Paddy Ford's goat—on our own hook."

"Old Scraggsy's as cunnin' as a pet fox, ain't he?" the new navigating officer whispered, as Scraggs departed for his statcroom to change into his other suit. "He's goin' to blow himself on us to-night, thinkin' to soften our hard resolution. We'll fool him. Take all he gives us, but stand pat, Bart."

Bart nodded. His was one of those sturdy natures that could always be depended upon to play the game, win, lose, or draw.

As a preliminary move, Captain Scraggs declared in favour of a couple of cocktails to whet their appetites for the French dinner, and accordingly the trio repaired to an adjacent saloon and tucked three each under their belts—all at Captain Scraggs's expense. When he proposed a fourth, Mr. Gibney's perfect sportsmanship caused him to protest, and reluctantly Captain Scraggs permitted Gibney to buy. Scraggs decided to have a cigar, however, instead of another Martini. The ethics of the situation then indicated that McGuffey should "set 'em up," which he did over Captain Scraggs's protest—and again the wary Scraggs called for a cigar, alleging as an excuse for his weakness that for years three cocktails before dinner had been

his absolute limit.   A fourth cocktail on an empty stomach, he declared, would kill the evening for him.

The fourth cocktail having been disposed of, the bar-
keeper, sensing further profit did he but play his part
judiciously, insisted that his customers have a drink on
the house.   Captain Scraggs immediately protested
that their party was degenerating into an endurance
contest—and called for another cigar.   He now had
three cigars, so he gave one each to his victims and forcibly dragged them away from the bar and up to a Pine
Street French restaurant, the proprietor of which was
an Italian.   Captain Scraggs was for walking the six
blocks to this restaurant, but Mr. McGuffey had acquired, on six cocktails, what is colloquially described
as "a start," and insisted upon chartering a taxicab.

But why descend to sordid and vulgar details?
Suffice that when the artful Scraggs, pretending to
be overcome by his potations and very ill into the
bargain, begged to be delivered back aboard the *Maggie*,
Messrs. McGuffey and Gibney loaded him into a taxicab and sent him there, while they continued their
search for excitement.   Where and how they found it
requires no elucidation here; it is sufficient to state that
it was expensive, for when men of the Gibney and Mc-
Guffey type have once gotten a fair start naught but
financial dissolution can stop them.

On Monday morning, Messrs. Gibney and McGuffey
awoke in Scab Johnny's boarding house.   Mr. Gibney
awoke first, by reason of the fact that his stomach
hammered at the door of his soul and bade him be up
and doing.   While his head ached slightly from the
fiery usquebaugh of the Bowhead saloon, he craved a

return to a solid diet, so for several minutes he lay su-
pine, conjuring in his agile brain ways and means of
supplying this need in the absence of ready cash. "I'll
have to hock my sextant," was the conclusion at which
he presently arrived. Then he commenced to heave
and surge until presently he found himself clear of the
blankets and seated in his underclothes on the side of
the bed. Here, he indulged in a series of scratchings
and yawnings, after which he disposed at a gulp of
most of the water designed for his matutinal ablutions.
Ten minutes later he took his sextant under his arm
and departed for a pawnship in lower Market Street.
From the pawnshop he returned to Scab Johnny's
with eight dollars in his pocket, routed out the contrite
McGuffey, and carried the latter off to ham and eggs.

They felt better after breakfast and for the space of
an hour lolled at the table, discussing their adventures
of the past forty-eight hours. "Well, there's one thing
certain," McGuffey concluded, "an' that thing is sure
a cinch. Our strike has petered out. I'm not busted,
but I ain't heeled to continue on strike very long, so
let's mosey along down to the *Maggie's* dock an' see
how Scraggsy's gettin' along. If he has our places filled
we won't say nothin', but if he hasn't got 'em filled he'll
say somethin'."

"That's logic, Bart," Gibney agreed, and forthwith
they set out to interview Captain Scraggs. The owner
of the *Maggie* greeted them cheerily, but after discussing generalities for half an hour, Scraggs failed to
make overtures, whereupon Mr. Gibney announced
casually that he guessed he and Mac would be on their
way. "Same here, boys," Captain Scraggs piped

breezily. "I got a new mate an' a new engineer comin' aboard at ten o'clock an' we sail at twelve."

"Well, we'll see you occasionally," Mr. Gibney said at parting.

"Oh, sure. Don't be strangers. You're always welcome aboard the old *Maggie*," came the careless rejoinder.

Somewhat crestfallen, the striking pair repaired to the Bowhead saloon to discuss the situation over a glass of beer. However, Mr. Gibney's spirits never dropped below zero while he had one nickel to rub against another; hence such slight depression as he felt was due to a feeling that Captain Scraggs had basely swindled him and McGuffey. He was disappointed in Scraggs and said as much. "However, Bart," he concluded, "we'll never say 'die' while our money holds out, and in the meantime our luck may have changed. Let's scatter around and try to locate some kind of a job; then when them new employees o' Scraggsy quit or get fired—which'll be after about two voyages—an' the old man comes round holdin' out the olive branch o' peace, we'll give him the horselaugh."

Three days of diligent search failed to uncover the coveted job for either, however, and on the morning of the fourth day Mr. Gibney announced that it would be necessary to "raise the wind," if the pair would breakfast. "It'll probably be a late breakfast," he added.

"How're we goin' to git it, Gib?"

"We must test our credit, Mac. You go down to the rooms o' the Marine Engineers' Association and kick somebody's eye out for five dollars. I'd get out an' do some rustlin' myself, but I ain't got no credit. When a man that's been a real sailor sinks as low as I've sunk —from clipper ships to mate on a rotten little bumboat —people don't respect him none. But it's different with a marine engineer. You might be first assistant on a P. M. boat to-day an' second assistant on a bay tug to-morrow but nothin's thought of it."

"What're we goin' to do with the five dollars?"

"Well, we might invest it in a lottery ticket an' pray for the capital prize—but we won't. Ain't it dawned on you, Mac, that it's up to you an' me to find the steamer *Maggie* an' git back to work quick an' no back talk? Scraggs has new men in our jobs an' these new men has got to be got rid of, otherwise there's no tellin' how long they'll last. Naturally, this here riddance can be accomplished easier an' without police interference on the dock at Halfmoon Bay. We got to walk twenty miles to Halfmoon Bay to connect with the *Maggie* an' the five dollars is to keep us from starvin' to death in case we miss him an' have to walk back or wait for the return trip o' the *Maggie*."

"But suppose, after we've walked all that distance, we find Scraggs won't take us back? Then what?"

"Why, of course he'll take us back, Bart. He'll be glad to after we've finished with them scabs that's took our jobs an' are doin' us out of an honest livin'. He won't be able to work the *Maggie* back to San Francisco alone, will he?"

McGuffey nodded his approbation, and set forth to borrow the needful five dollars. Whatever the reason, he was not successful, and when they met again at Scab Johnny's, Mr. Gibney employed his eloquence to obtain credit from that cold-hearted publican, but all in vain. Scab Johnny had been too long operating on a cash basis with Messrs. Gibney and McGuffey to risk adding to an old unpaid bill.

They retired to the sidewalk to hold a caucus and Mr. McGuffey located a dime which had dropped down inside the lining of his coat. "That settles it," Gibney declared. "We've skipped two meals but I'll be durned if we skip another. We'll ride out to the San Mateo county line on the trolley with that dime an' then hoof it over the hills to Halfmoon Bay. Scraggs won't git away from the dock here until after twelve o'clock, so we know he'll lie at Halfmoon Bay all night. If we start now we'll connect with him in time for supper. Eh, Bart?"

"A twenty-mile hike on a tee-totally empty stomach, with a battle royal on our hands the minute we arrive, weak an' destitoote, ain't quite my idea o' enjoyment, Gib, but I'll go you if it kills me. Let's up hook an' away. I'm for gittin' back to work an' usin' moral persuasion to git that new boiler."

They took a hitch in their belts and started. From the point at which they left the trolley to their journey's end was a stiff six-hour jaunt, up hill and down dale, and long before the march was half completed the unaccustomed exercise had developed sundry galls and blisters on the Gibney heels, while the soles of poor McGuffey's feet were so hot he voiced the apprehension that they might burn to a crisp at any moment and drop off by the wayside. Men less hardy and less desperate would have abandoned the trip before ten miles had been covered.

CHAPTER X

THE crew of the *Maggie* had ceased working cargo for the day and Captain Scraggs was busy cooking supper in the galley when the two prodigals, exhausted, crippled, and repentant, came to the door and coughed propitiously, but Captain Scraggs pretended not to hear, and went on with his task of turning fried eggs with an artistic flip of the frying pan. So Mr. Gibney spoke, struggling bravely to appear nonchalant. With his eyes on the fried eggs and his mouth threatening to slaver at the glorious sight, he said:

"Hello, there, Scraggsy, old tarpot. How goes it with the owner o' the fast an' commodious steamer *Maggie?* Git that consignment o' post-holes aboard yet?"

Mr. Gibney's honest face beamed expectantly, for he was particularly partial to fried eggs. As for his companion in distress, anything edible and which would serve to nullify the gnawing at his internal economy would be welcome. Inasmuch as Captain Scraggs did not readily reply to Mr. Gibney's salutation, McGuffey decided to be more emphatic and to the point, albeit in a joking way.

"Hurry up with them eggs, Scraggs," he rumbled. "Me an' Gib's walked down from the city an' we're hungry. Jawn D. Rockerfeller'd give a million dollars for my appetite. Fry mine hard, Scraggsy. I want somethin' solid."

Scraggs looked up and his cold green eyes were agleam with malice and triumph as they rested on the unhappy pair. However, he smiled—a smile reminiscent of a cat that has just eaten a canary—and cold chills ran down the backs of the exhausted travellers. "Hello, boys," he piped. He turned from them to toss a few strips of bacon into the grease with the eggs; then he peered into the coffee pot and set it on the back of the galley range to simmer, before facing his guests again. His attitude was so significant that Mr. Gibney queried mournfully:

"Well, Phineas, you old vegetable hound, ain't you glad to see us?"

"Certainly, Gib, certainly. I'm deeply appreciative of the honour o' this visit, although I'm free to say we're hardly prepared for company. The stores is kind o' low an' I did just figger on havin' enough, by skimpin' a little, to last me an' my crew until we get back to San Francisco. I'd hate to put 'em on short rations, on account of unexpected company, be- cause it gives the ship a bad name. On the other hand, it's agin my disposition to appear small over a few fried eggs, while on still another hand, I realize you two got to get fed." He stepped to the door and pointed. "See that little shack about two points to starboard o' the warehouse? Well, there's a Dago livin' there an' he'll fix you two boys up a bully meal for fifty cents each."

"Scraggsy, ol' hunks, if three-ringed circuses was sellin' for six bits a throw me an' Bart couldn't buy a whisker from a dead tiger." The dreadful admission brought a dull flush to Mr. Gibney's already rubicund countenance.

"Shell out a coupler bucks, Scraggsy," McGuffey pleaded. "Me an' Gib's so empty we rattle when we walk."

"I ain't got no money to loan you two that ups an' leaves me in the lurch, without no notice," Scraggs flared at them. "If you two stiffs ain't able to support yourselves you'd ought to apply for admission to the poorhouse or the Home For the Feeble-minded."

Mr. Gibney smiled fatly. "Scraggsy! You're kiddin' us."

"Not by forty fathom, I ain't."

"Phineas, we just *got* t' eat," McGuffey declared ominously.

"Eat an' be dog-goned," the skipper snarled. "I ain't a-tryin' to prevent you. Are you two suckin' infants that I got to *feed* you? There's plenty o' fresh vegetables out on deck. Green peas ain't to be sneezed at, an' as for French carrots, science'll tell you there's ninety-two per cent. more nutriment in a carrot than——"

Mr. Gibney halted this dissertation with upraised hand. "Scraggs, it's about time you found out I ain't no potato bug, an' if you think McGuffey's a coddlin' moth you're wrong agin. Fork over them eggs an' the coffee an' a coupler slices o' dummy an' be quick about it or I'll bust your bob-stay."

"Get off my ship, you murderin' pirates," Scraggs screamed.

"Not till we've et," the practical-minded engineer retorted. "Even then we won't get off. Me an' Gib ain't got any feet left, Scraggs. If we had to walk another step we'd be crippled for life. Fry my eggs hard, I tell you."

"This is piracy, men. It's robbery on the high seas, an' I can put you over the road for it," Scraggs warned them. "What's more, I'll do it."

"The eggs, Scraggsy," boomed Mr. Gibney, "the eggs."

Half an hour later as the pirates, replete with provender, sat dangling their damaged underpinning over the stern railing where the gentle wavelets laved and cooled them, Captain Scraggs accompanied by the new navigating officer, the new engineer, and The Squarehead, came aft. The cripples looked up, surveyed their successors in office, and found the sight far from reassuring.

"I've already ordered you two tramps off'n my ship," Scraggs began formally, "an' I hereby, in the presence o' reliable witnesses, repeats the invitation. You ain't wanted; your room's preferred to your comp'ny, an' by stayin' a minute longer, in defiance o' my orders, you're layin' yourselves liable to a charge o' piracy. It'd be best for you two boys to mosey along now an' save us all a lot o' trouble."

Mr. Gibney carefully laid his pipe aside and stood up. He was quite an imposing spectacle in his bare feet, with his trousers rolled up to his great knees, thereby revealing his scarlet flannel underdrawers. With a stifled groan, McGuffey rose and stood beside his partner, and Mr. Gibney spoke:

"Scraggs, be reasonable. We ain't lookin' for trouble; not because we don't relish it, for we do where a couple o' scabs is concerned, but for the simple reason that we ain't in the best o' condition to receive it, although if you force it on us we'll do our best. If you chuck us off the *Maggie* an' force us to walk back to San Francisco, we're goin' to be reported as missin'. Honest, now, Scraggsy, old side-winder, you ain't goin' to maroon us here, alone with the vegetables, are you?"

"You done me dirt. You quit me cold. Git out. Two can play at a dirty game an' every dog must have his day. This is my day, Gib. Scat!"

"Pers'nally," McGuffey announced quietly, "I prefer to die aboard the *Maggie*, if I have to. This ain't movin' day with B. McGuffey, Esquire."

"Them's my sentiments, too, Scraggsy."

"Then defend yourselves. Come on, lads. Bear a hand an' we'll bounce these muckers overboard." The Squarehead hung back having no intention of waging war upon his late comrades, but the engineer and the new navigating officer stepped briskly forward, for they were about to fight for their jobs. Mr. Gibney halted the advance by lifting both great hands in a deprecatory manner.

"For Heaven's sake, Scraggsy, have a heart. Don't force us to murder you. If we're peaceable, what's to prevent you from givin' us a passage back to San Francisco, where we're known an' where we'll have at least a fightin' chance to git somethin' to eat occasionally."

"You know mighty well what's to prevent me, Gib.

I ain't got no passenger license, an' I'll be keel-hauled an' skull-dragged if I fall for your cute little game, my son. I ain't layin' myself liable to a fine from the Inspectors an' maybe have my ticket book took away to boot."

"You could risk your danged old ticket. It ain't no use to you on salt water anyhow," McGuffey jeered insultingly.

"We can work our passage an' who's to know the difference, Scraggsy?"

"You for one an' McGuffey for two. You'd have the bulge on me forever after. You could blackmail me until I dassen't call my ship my own."

"Don't worry, you snipe. Nobody else will ever hanker to own her." Another insult from McGuffey. Having made up his mind that a fight was inevitable, the honest fellow was above pleading for mercy.

"Enough of this gab," Mr. Gibney roared. "My patience is exhausted. I'm dog-tired an' I'm goin' to have peace if I have to fight for it. Me an' Bart stays aboard the steamer *Maggie* until she gets back to Frisco town or until we're hove overboard in the interim by the weight of numbers. An' if any man, or set o' male bipeds that calls theirselves men, is so foolish as to try to evict us from this packet, then all I got to say is that they're triflin' with death." (Here Mr. Gibney thrust out his superb chest and thumped it with his horny fists, after the fashion of an enraged gorilla. This was sheer bluff, however, for while there was not a drop of craven blood in the Gibney veins, he realized that his footwork, in the event of battle, would be sadly deficient and he hesitated to wage a

losing fight.) "I got my arms left, even if my feet is
on the fritz, Scraggs," he continued, "an' if you start
anything I'll hug you an' your crew to death. I'm a
rip-roarin' grizzly bear once I'm started an' there's
such a thing as drivin' a man to desperation."

The bluff worked! Captain Scraggs turned to his
retainers and with a condescending and paternal smile,
said: "Boys, let's give the dumb fools their own way.
If they insist upon takin' forcible possession o' my ship
on the high seas, there's only one name for the crime—
an' that's piracy, punishable by hangin' from the yard-
arm. "We'll just let 'em stay aboard an' turn 'em over
to the police when we git back to the city."

He started for his cabin and the crew, vastly relieved, followed him. The pirates once more sat down
and permitted their hot feet to loll overboard.

"It's cold down here nights, Gib," McGuffey opined
presently. "Where're we goin' to sleep?"

"In our old berths, of course." The success of his
bluff had operated on Gibney like a tonic. "Hop
into your shoes, Bart, an' we'll snake them two scabs
out o' their berths in jig time."

"I'm dodgin' fights to-night, Gib. Let's borrow a
blanket or two from The Squarehead an' curl up on deck.
It'll be warm over the engine-room gratin'."

Mr. Gibney yawned. "I guess you're right, Bart.
While you're at it, make Scraggs come through with a
blanket an' an overcoat for a pillow. Run up an'
threaten him. He'll wilt."

So McGuffey staggered forward. What arguments he
used shall not be recorded here. Suffice it, he returned
with what he went after.

CHAPTER XI

THE pirates were early astir; so early, in fact, that long before Captain Scraggs and his crew appeared on deck, Messrs. Gibney and McGuffey had quietly cooked breakfast in the galley. They ate six eggs each and consumed the only loaf of bread aboard, for which act of vandalism they were rewarded half an hour later by the sight of Captain Scraggs dancing on a new brown derby.

"It's a wonder that bird wouldn't get him a soft hat to do his jumpin' on," McGuffey remarked. "He's ruined enough good hats to have paid for the new boiler. Yes, sir, whenever ol' Scraggsy gets mad he most certainly gets hoppin' mad."

"It'll soak into his head after a while that us two mean business, Mac, an' he'll get sensible an' fire them outsiders. I'm lookin' for him to make peace before noon."

About ten o'clock that morning the little vessel completed taking on her cargo, the lines were cast off, and the homeward voyage was begun. As she hauled away from the wharf, Messrs. Gibney and McGuffey might have been observed seated on the stern bitts smoking, the picture of contentment. Pirates under the law they might be, but of this they knew nothing and cared less. With them, self-preservation was, indeed, the first law of human nature.

74

They were still seated on the stern bitts as the *Maggie* came abreast the Point Montara fog signal station, when Mr. Gibney observed a long telescope poking out the side window of the pilot house. "Hello," he muttered, "Scraggsy's seein' things," and following the direction in which the telescope was pointing he made out a large bark standing in dangerously close to the beach. In fact, the breakers were tumbling in a long white streak over the reefs less than a quarter of a mile from her. She was lying stern on to the beach, with one anchor out.

In an instant all was excitement aboard the *Maggie*. "That looks like an elegant little pick-up. She's plumb deserted," Scraggs shouted to his navigating officer. "I don't see any distress signals flyin' an' yet she's got an anchor out while her canvas is hangin' so-so."

"If she had any hands aboard, you'd think they'd have sense enough to clew up her courses," the mate answered.

At this juncture, Mr. Gibney and McGuffey, unable to restrain their curiosity, and forgetful of the fact that they were pirates with very sore feet, came running over the deckload and invaded the pilot house. "Gimme that glass, you sock-eyed salmon, you," Gibney ordered Scraggs, and tore the telescope from the owner's hands. "There ain't enough real seamanship in the crew o' this craft to tax the mental make-up of a Chinaman. "Hum—m—m! American bark *Chesapeake*. Starboard anchor out; yards braced a-box; royals an' to'-gallan'-s'ls clewed up; courses hangin' in the bunt-lines an' clew garnets, Stars-an'-Stripes upside down."

He lowered the glass and roared at Neils Halvorsen, who was at the wheel, "Starboard your helm, Square-head. Don't be afraid of her. We're goin' over there an' hook on to her. I should say she is a pick-up."

Mr. Gibney had abdicated as a pirate and assumed command of the S. S. *Maggie*. With the memory of a scant breakfast upon him, however, Captain Scraggs was still harsh and bitter.

"Git out o' my pilot house an' aft where the police can find you when they come lookin' for you," he screeched. "Don't you give no orders to my deckhand."

"Stow it, you ass. Don't fly in the face of your own interests, Scraggsy, you bandit. Yonder's a prize, but it'll require imagination to win it; consequently you need Adelbert P. Gibney in your business, if you're contemplatin' hookin' on to that bark, snakin' her into San Francisco Bay, an' libelin' her for ten thousand dollars' salvage. You an' me an' Mac an' The Square-head here have sailed this strip o' coast too long to-gether to quarrel over the first good piece o' salvage we ever run into. Come, Scraggsy. Be decent, forget the past, an' let's dig in together."

"If I had a gun," Scraggs cried, "I do believe I'd shoot you. Git out o'my pilot house, I tell you, or I'll stick a knife in you. I'll carve your gizzard, you black-guardin' pirate."

Inasmuch as Scraggs really did produce a knife, Mr. Gibney backed prudently away. "You're mighty quick to let bygones be bygones when you see me with a fortune in sight with you wantin' to horn in on the deal, ain't you?" the owner jeered. "You must think I'm a born fool."

"I don't think it a-tall. I know it. You're worse'n a born fool. You're sufferin' from acquired idiocy, which is the mental state folks find themselves in when they refuse to learn by experience an' profit by example. I've always claimed you ain't got no more imagination than a chicken, an' I'll prove it to you right now. Here you are, braggin' about how you're goin' to salvage that bark but givin' no thought whatever to the means to be employed. How're you goin' to pull her off? If the *Maggie* ever had a towline aboard I never seen it. Perhaps, however, you're figgerin' on poolin' all the shoestrings aboard."

"Every ship that size has a steel towin' cable, wound up on a reel, nice an' handy," the new navigating officer reminded Mr. Gibney. "I can put the skiff out, get the bark's line, haul it back, an' make it fast on the bitts you two skunks has been occupyin' instead of a prison cell."

"Hello! There's another county gone Democratic. Your old man must ha' been to sea once an' told you about it. Them bitts won't hold."

"I'll make the towline fast to the mainmast."

"That'll hold, I admit. But has the *Maggie* got power enough, what with the load she's totin' now, to tow that big bark in to San Francisco Bay?"

"Oh, we'll take it easy an' get there some time," Scraggs chipped in.

"You bet you'll take it easy—easier'n you think. Before you start towin' that bark, you'll have to clew up her canvas a whole lot to make the towin' easier, an' who's goin' to do that? An' you got to have a man at her wheel."

"Neils an' my mate."

"If that new mate dares to leave you in command o' the *Maggie*, alone an unprotected on the high seas an' you with a fresh water license, I'll——"

"Then Neils an' I'll do it."

"You don't know how. Besides, you're afraid to go aboard that bark. You don't know what kind of a frightful disease she may have aboard. Do you know a plague ship when you see one?"

Captain Scraggs paled a little, but the prospect of the salvage heartened him. "I don't give a hoot," he declared. "I'll take a chance."

"All right. Consider it taken. How're you goin' to get aboard her?"

"In the skiff."

"Where's the skiff?"

Captain Scraggs glanced around wildly, and when McGuffey jeered him, he cast his hat upon the deck and started to leap upon it. The devilish Gibney was right. It appeared that owing to a glut of freight on the landing, Captain Scraggs had decided, in view of the fine weather prevailing, to take an unusually large cargo that trip. With this idea in mind, he had piled freight over every available inch of deck space until the cargo was flush with the top of the house. On top of the house, the skiff always rested, bottom up. Captain Scraggs had righted the skiff, piled it full of loose artichokes from half a dozen crates broken in the cargo net while loading, and then proceeded to pile more vegetables on top of it and around it until the *Maggie's* funnel barely showed through the piled-up freight, and the little vessel was so top heavy she was cranky. In order to get at the small boat, therefore, it would be necessary to shift this load off the house, and the question that now confronted Scraggs and his crew was to find a spot that would accommodate the part of the deckload thus shifted!

When Captain Scraggs had completed his hornpipe on his hat he threw an appealing glance at his new mate. "We'll jettison what freight proves an embarrassment," this astute individual advised. "The farmers that own it will soak you a couple o' hundred dollars for the loss, but what's that with thousands in sight waitin' to be picked up?"

"Hear that, Gib? Hear that, you swab?"

"I heard it. Did you hear that?"

"What?"

"A nice, brisk little nor'west trade wind that's only blowin' about thirty mile an hour. The *Maggie* ain't got power enough to tow the bark agin that wind. You'll haul her ahead two feet an', in spite o' you, she'll slip back twenty-five inches."

"That trade wind dies down after sunset," the devilish new mate informed him.

"Quite true. But in the meantime you're burning coal loafin' around here, an' before you get the bark inside you'll be plumb out o' coal," Mr. McGuffey reminded them. "I know this old coffin like I know the back o' my own hand. Why, she lives on coal! Oh-h-h, Scraggsy, Scraggsy, poor old Scraggy," he keened in a high falsetto voice and subsided on a crate of celery, the while he waved his legs in the air and affected to be overcome by his merriment. Scraggs turned the colour of a ripe old Edam cheese, while Mr. Gibney folded his hands and looked idiotic.

"Old Phineas P. Scraggs, the salvage expert!" Mc-
Guffey's falsetto would have maddened a sheep. "He
cast his bread upon the waters and lo, it returned to
him after many days—and made him sick. O-h-h-h-h,
Scraggsy—poor old Scraggsy! If he went divin' for
pearls in three feet o' water he'd bring up a clam shell.
Oh, dear, I'm goin' to die o' this, Gib."

"Don't, Bart. I'm goin' to have need o' your well-
known ability to help salvage this bark. Scraggs, you
old sinner, has it dawned on you that what this proposition needs to get it over is a dash o' the Adelbert
P. Gibney brand of imagination?"

The new navigating officer drew Captain Scraggs
aside and whispered in his ear: "Make it up with
these Smart Alecks, Scraggs. They got it on us, but
if we can send you an' Halvorsen, McGuffey and Gibney over to the bark, you can get some sail on her an'
what with the wind helpin' us along, the *Maggie* can
tow her all right."

Mr. Gibney saw by the hopeful, even cunning, look
that leaped to Scraggs's eyes that the problem was about
to be solved without recourse to the Gibney imagination, so he resolved to be alert and not permit himself
to be caught out on the end of a limb. "Well, Scraggsy?" he demanded.

"I guess I need you in my business, Gib. You're
right an' I'm always wrong. It's a fact. I *ain't* got
no more imagination than a chicken. Hence, havin' no
imagination o' my own I ask you, as man to man
an' appealin' to your generous instincts as an old
friend an' former valued employee, to let bygones
be bygones an' haul us out o' the hole that threatens

to make us the laughin' stock o' the whole Pacific coast."

"Spoken like a man—I do not think. Scraggs, for once in my life I have you where the hair is short. You find yourself up agin a proposition that requires brains, you ain't got 'em yourself an' at last you're forced to admit that Adelbert P. Gibney is the man that peddles 'em. Now, you been doin' a lot o' hollerin' about me an' Bart bein' pirates under the law an' liable to hangin' an' imprisonment, an' that kind o' guff don't go nohow. We're willin' to admit that mebbe we've been a little mite familiar an' forward, bankin' on the natural leanin' of friend for friend that you take it all for the joke it's intended to be, but when you go to carryin' the joke too far, we got to protect ourselves. Scraggsy, I'm willin' to dig in an' help out in a pinch, but it's gettin' so me an' Mac can't trust you no more. We're that leery of you we won't take your word for nothin', since you fooled him on the new boiler an' me on the paint; consequently, we're off you an' this salvage job unless you give us a clearance, in writin', statin' that we are not an' never was pirates, that we're good, law-abiding citizens an' aboard the *Maggie* as your guests, takin' the trip at our own risk. When you sign such a paper, with your crew for witnesses, I'll demonstrate how that bark can be salvaged without makin' you remove so much as a head o' cabbage to get at your small boat. My imagination's better'n my reputation, Scraggsy, an' I ain't workin' it for nothin!"

"Gib, my *dear* boy. You're the most sensitive man I ever sailed with. Can't you take a little joke?"

"Sure, I can take a little joke. It's the big ones that

stick in my craw an' stifle my friendship. Gimme a
fountain pen an' a leaf out o' the log book an' I'll draw
up the affydavit for your signature."

Scraggs complied precipitately with this request;
whereupon Mr. Gibney spread his great bulk over the
chart case and with many a twist and flip of his tongue
on the up and down strokes, produced this remarkable
document:

> At Sea, Off Point Montara, aboard
> S. S. *Maggie*, of San Francisco.
> June 4, 19—.
> This is to sertify that A. P. Gibney, Esq., and Bart McGuffey,
> Esq. is law-abidin' sitisens of the U. S. A. and the constitootion
> thereof, and in no way pirates or such; and be it further resolved that
> the said parties hereto are aboard said American steamer *Maggie*
> this date on the special invite of Phineas P. Scraggs, owner, as his
> guests and at their own risk.
> Witness my hand and seal:

Captain Scraggs signed without reading and the new
mate and Neils Halvorsen appended their signatures
as witnesses. Mr. Gibney thereupon folded this clearance paper into the tiniest possible compact ball, wrapped it in a piece of tinfoil torn from a package of tobacco, to protect it from his saliva, tucked it in his
cheek and with a sign for McGuffey to follow him,
started crawling over the cargo aft. By this time, the
Maggie was within a hundred yards of the distressed
bark and was ratching slowly backward and forward
before her.

"In all my born days," quoth Mr. Gibney, speaking
a trifle thickly because of the document in his mouth,
"I never got such a wallop as Scraggs handed me an'

you last night. I don't forget things like that in a hurry. Now that we got a vindication o' the charge o' piracy agin us, I'm achin' to get shet of the *Maggie* an' her crew, so if you'll kindly peel off all of your clothes with the exception, say, of your underdrawers, we'll swim off to that bark an' give Phineas P. Scraggs an exhibition of real sailorizin' an' seamanship."

"What's the big idee?" McGuffey demanded cautiously.

"Why, we'll sail her in ourselves—me an' you—an' glom all the salvage for ourselves. T'ell with Scraggs an' the *Maggie* an' that new mate an' engineer. I'm off'n 'em for life." ·

Pop-eyed with excitement and interest, B. McGuffey, Esquire, stood up and with a single twist shed his cap and coat. His shirts followed. Both he and Gibney were already minus their shoes and socks. To slip out of their faded dungarees was the work of an instant. Strapping their belts around their waists to hold up their drawers, the worthy pair stepped to the rail of the *Maggie.*

"Hey, there? Where you goin', Gib? I give you that clearance paper on condition that you was to tell me how to salvage that there bark without havin' to shift my cargo to get at the small boat." ·

"I'm just about to tell you, Scraggs. You don't touch a thing aboard the *Maggie.* You leave her out of it entirely. You just jump overboard, like me an' Mac will in a jiffy, swim over to the bark, climb aboard, and sail her in to San Francisco Bay. When you get there you drop anchor an' call it a day's work." He grinned broadly. "One o' these bright days, Scraggs, when me an' Mac is just wallerin' in salvage money, drop around to see us an' we'll give you a kick in the face. Farewell, you boobs," and he dove overboard.

"Ta-ta," McGuffey cried in his tantalizing falsetto voice, and followed his leader into the briny deep. As they came up and snorted, grampus-like, shaking the water out of their eyes, they glanced back at the *Maggie* and observed that Captain Scraggs was, for the third time that never-to-be-forgotten voyage, jumping on his hat.

"If I was that far gone in a habit," quoth Mr. Mc-Guffey as he hauled up alongside Mr. Gibney, "I'll be switched if I wouldn't go bareheaded an' save expenses."

CHAPTER XII

THE tide was still at the flood and the two adventurers made fast progress toward the *Chesapeake*. Choosing a favourable opportunity as the vessel dipped, they grasped her martingale, climbed up on the bowsprit, and ran along the bowsprit to the to'gallan'-fo'castle. On the deck below a dead man lay in the scuppers, and such a horrible stench pervaded the vessel that McGuffey was taken very ill and was forced to seek the rail.

"Scurvy or somethin'," Mr. Gibney announced quite calmly. "Here's the devil to pay. There should be chloride of lime in the mate's storeroom—I'll scatter some on these poor devils. Too close to port now to chuck 'em overboard. Anyhow, Bart, me an' you ain't doctors, nor yet coroners or undertakers, so you'd better skip along an' build a fire under the donkey aft. Matches in the galley, of course."

"I wish she was a schooner," McGuffey complained, edging over to the weather rail. "It'd be easier for us two to sail her then. I'm only a marine engineer, Gib, an' while I been goin' to sea long enough to pick up something about handlin' a vessel, still I'll get dizzy if I go aloft—an' I'm sure to get sick. You'll have to do all the high an' lofty tumblin'—an' how in blue blazes us two're goin' to sail a square-rigger into port is a mystery to me."

"Leave the worryin' to your Uncle Gib, Bart. You can take the wheel an' steer, can't you? She has enough sail practically set now to make her handle good. Look at them courses hangin' in the buntlines an' the yards braced a-box! All we got to do is to square 'em around—but never mind explanations. I'll show you how it's done after we get steam up in the donkey. I'd prefer a wind about two points aft her beam, but never let it be said that I turned up my nose at a good stiff nor'west trade. I've sunk pretty low, Mac, but I was a real sailor once an' I can sail this old hooker wherever there's water enough to float her. It's just pie—well, for heaven's sake, Mac, what are you standin' around for? Ain't I ordered you to get steam up in the donkey? Lively, you lubber. After you've got the fire goin', we'll place leadin' blocks along the deck, lead all the runnin' gear to the winch head, an' stand by to swing them yards when I give the word."

Mr. Gibney trotted down to the main deck and prowled aft. On the port side of her house he found two more dead men, and a cursory inspection of the bodies told him they had died of scurvy. He circled the ship, came back to the fo'castle, entered, and found four men alive in their berths, but too far gone to leave them. "I'll have you boys in the Marine Hospital to-night," he informed the poor creatures, and sought the master's cabin. Lying on his bed, fully dressed, he found the skipper of the *Chesapeake*. The man was gaunt and emaciated.

The freebooter of the green-pea trade touched his wet forelock respectfully. "My name is Gibney, sir, an' I hold an unlimited license as first mate of sail or steam.

I was passin' up the coast on a good-for-nothin' little bumboat, an' seen you in distress, so me an' a friend swum over to give you the double O.   You're in a bad way, sir."

"Two hundred and eighty-seven days from Hamburg, Mr. Gibney.   Our vegetables gave out and we drank too much rain water and ate too much fresh fish down in the Doldrums.   Our potatoes all went rotten before we were out two months.   Naturally, the ship's officers stuck it out longest, but when we drifted in here this morning, I was the only man aboard able to stand up.   I crawled up on the to'-gallan' fo'castle and let go the starboard anchor.   I'd had it cock-billed for three weeks.   All I had to do was knock out the stopper."

While Mr. Gibney questioned him and listened avidly to the horrible tale of privation and despair, McGuffey appeared to report a brisk fire under the donkey and to promise steam in forty minutes; also that the *Maggie* was hove to a cable length distant, with her crew digging under the deckload of vegetables for the small boat. "Help yourself to a belayin' pin, Bart, an' knock 'em on the heads if they try to come aboard," Mr. Gibney ordered nonchalantly.

"Do I understand there is a steamer at hand, Mr. Gibney?" the master of the *Chesapeake* queried.

"There's an excuse for one, sir.   The little vegetable freighter *Maggie*.   She'll never be able to tow you in, because she ain't got power enough, an' if she had power enough she ain't got coal enough.   Besides, Scraggs, her owner, is a rotten bad article an' before he'll put a rope aboard you he'll tie you up on a contract for a figger that'd make an angel weep.   The way your ship lies an' everything, me an' McGuffey can sail her in for you at half the price."

"I can't risk my ship in the hands of two men," the sick captain answered. "She's too valuable and so is her cargo. If this little steamer will tow me in I'll gladly give her my towline and let the court settle the bill."

"Not by a million," Mr. Gibney protested. "Beg pardon, sir, but you don't know this here Scraggs like I do. I couldn't think of lettin' him set foot on this deck."

"*You* couldn't think of it? Well, when did *you* take command of *my* ship?"

"You're flotsam an' jetsam, sir, an' practically in the breakers. You're sick, an,' for all I know, delirious, so for the sake o' protectin' you, the sick seaman in the fo'castle an' the owners, I'm takin' command."

The master of the *Chesapeake* reached under his pillow and produced a pistol. "Out of my cabin or I'll riddle you," he barked feebly.

Mr. Gibney departed without a word of protest and proceeded to make his arrangements, regardless of the master's consent. As he and McGuffey busied themselves, laying the leading blocks along the deck, they glanced toward the *Maggie* and observed Captain Scraggs hurling crates of vegetables overboard in an effort to get at the small boat quickly. "He'll die when the freight claims come in," Mr. McGuffey chortled. "Poor ol' Scraggsy!"

"How're we goin' to git that durned anchor up, Gib?"

"We ain't goin' to get it up. We're goin' to knock out a shackle in the chain an' let her go to glory."

"Anchors is expensive, Gib. Mebbe they'll deduct the price o' that anchor from our salvage."

"By Jupiter, you're talkin', Mac. We'll just save that anchor, come to think of it."

"How?"

"Just let Scraggsy an' The Squarehead come aboard an' put the ship's towin' cable aboard the *Maggie*. The *Maggie'll* just about be able to hold her while us four up with the anchor—*an' cockbill* it agin!"

"They got the skiff overside," McGuffey warned.

"Throw over the Jacob's ladder and help 'em aboard, Mac. Nothin' like bein' neighbourly. This here's a delicate situation, what with the old man declinin' our services in favour of a tow by the *Maggie*, an' it occurs to me if we oppose him our standin' in court will be impaired. I see I got to use my imagination agin."

When Captain Scraggs came aboard, Mr. Gibney escorted him around to the master's cabin, introduced him, and stood by while they bargained. The sick skipper glowered at Mr. Gibney when Scraggs, with a wealth of detail, explained their presence, but, for all his predicament, he was a shrewd man and instantly decided to use Gibney and McGuffey as a fulcrum wherewith to pry a very low price out of Captain Scraggs. Mr. Gibney could not forebear a grin as he saw the captain's plan, and instantly he resolved to further it, if for no other reason than to humiliate and infuriate Scraggs.

"The tow will cost you five thousand, Captain," Scraggs began pompously.

"Me an' McGuffey'll sail you in for four," Gibney declared.

"Three thousand," snarled Scraggs.

"Sailin's cheap as dirt at two thousand. As a matter of fact, Scraggsy, me an' Mac'll sail her in for nothin' just to skin you out o' the salvage."

"Two thousand dollars is my lowest figure," Scraggs declared. "Take it or leave it, Captain. Under the circumstances, bargaining is useless. Two thousand is my last bid."

The figure Scraggs named was probably one fifth of what the master of the *Chesapeake* knew a court would award; nevertheless he shook his head.

"It's a straight towing job, Captain, and not a salvage proposition at all. A tug would tow me in for two hundred and fifty, but I'll give you five hundred."

Remembering the vegetables he had jettisoned, Scraggs knew he could not afford to accept that price. "I'm through," he bluffed—and his bluff worked.

"Taken, Captain Scraggs. Write out an agreement and I'll sign it."

With the agreement in his pocket, Scraggs, followed by Gibney, left the cabin. "One hundred each to you an' Mac if you'll stay aboard the *Chesapeake*, steer her, an' help the *Maggie* out with what sail you can get on her," Scraggs promised.

"Take a long, runnin' jump at yourself, Scraggsy, old sorrowful. The best me an' Mac'll do is to help you cockbill the anchor, an' that'll cost you ten bucks for each of us—in advance." The artful fellow realized that Scraggs knew nothing whatever about a sailing ship and would have to depend upon The Squarehead for the information he required.

"All right. Here's your money," Scraggs replied and handed Mr. Gibney twenty dollars. He and Neils Halvorsen then went forward, got out the steel towing cable, and fastened a light rope to the end of it. The skiff floated off the ship at the end of the painter, so The Squarehead hauled it in, climbed down into the skiff, and made the light rope fast to a thwart; then, with Captain Scraggs paying out the hawser, Neils bent manfully to the oars and started to tow the steel cable back to the *Maggie*. Half way there, the weight of the cable dragging behind slowed The Squarehead up and eventually stopped him. Exerting all his strength he pulled and pulled, but the sole result of his efforts was to wear himself out, seeing which the *Maggie's* navigating officer set the little steamer in toward the perspiring Neils, while Captain Scraggs, Gibney, and McGuffey cheered lustily.

Suddenly an oar snapped. Instantly Neils unshipped the remaining oar, sprang to the stern, and attempted, by sculling, to keep the skiff's head up to the waves. But the weight of the cable whirled the little craft around, a wave rolled in over her counter, and half-filled her; the succeeding wave completed the job and rolled the skiff over and The Squarehead was forced to swim back to the *Chesapeake*. He climbed up the Jacob's ladder to face a storm of abuse from Captain Scraggs.

The cable was hauled back aboard with difficulty, owing to the submerged skiff at the end of it. Captain Scraggs and The Squarehead leaned over the *Chesapeake's* rail and tugged furiously, when the wreck came alongside, but all of their strength was unequal to the task of righting the little craft by hauling up on the light rope attached to her thwart.

"For ten dollars more each me an' Mac'll tail on to that rope an' do our best to right the skiff. After she's righted, I'll bail her out, borrow new oars from this here bark, an' help Neils row back to the *Maggie* with the cable," Mr. Gibney volunteered. "Cash in advance, as per usual."

"You're a pair of highway robbers, but I'll take you," Scraggs almost wailed, and paid out the money; whereupon Gibney and McGuffey "tailed" on to the rope and with raucous cries hauled away. As a result of their efforts, the thwart came away with the rope and the quartet sat down with exceeding abruptness on the hard pine deck of the *Chesapeake*.

"I had an idee that thwart would pull loose," Mr. Gibney remarked, as he got up and rubbed the seat of his dungarees. "If you'd had an ounce of sense, Scraggsy, you'd have saved twenty dollars an' rigged a watch-tackle, although even then the thwart would have come away, pullin' agin a vacuum that way. Well, you've lost a good skiff worth at least twenty-five dollars not to mention the two ash breezes that went with her. That helps some. What're you goin' to do now? Lay the *Maggie* alongside the bark? I wouldn't if I was you. The sea's a mite choppy an' if you bump the *Maggie* agin the bark she'll do one o' two things— stave in her topsides or bump that top-heavy deckload o' vegetables overboard. An' if that happens," he reminded Scraggs, "you'll be doin' your bookkeepin' with red ink for quite a spell."

"I ain't licked yet—not by a jugful," Scraggs

snapped. "Halvorsen, haul down that signal halyard from the mizzenmast, take one end of it in your teeth, an' swim back to the *Maggie* with it. We'll fasten a heavier line to the signal halyard, bend the other end of the heavy line to the cable, an' haul the cable aboard with the *Maggie's* winch."

"You say that so nice, Scraggsy, old hopeful, I'm tempted to think you can whistle it. Neils, he's only askin' you to risk your life overboard for nothing. 'Tain't in the shippin' articles that a seaman's got to do that. If he wants a swimmin' exhibition make him pay for it—through the nose. An' if I was you, I'd find out how much o' this two thousand dollars, towage he's goin' to distribute to his crew. Pers'nally I'd get mine in advance."

"Adelbert P. Gibney," Captain Scraggs hissed. "There's such a thing as drivin' a man to distraction. Halvorsen, are you with me?"

"Aye bane—for saxty dollars. Hay bane worth a month's pay for take dat swim."

"You dirty Scowegian ingrate. Well, you don't get no sixty dollars from me. Bear a hand and we'll drop the ship's work boat overboard. I guess you can tow a signal halyard to the *Maggie*, can't you, Neils?"

Neils could—and did. Within fifteen minutes the *Maggie* was fast to her prize. "Now we'll cockbill the anchor," quoth Captain Scraggs, so McGuffey reporting sufficient steam in the donkey to turn over the windlass, the anchor was raised and cockbilled, and the *Maggie* hauled away on the hawser the instant Captain Scraggs signalled his new navigating officer that the hook was free of the bottom.

"The old girl don't seem to be makin' headway in the right direction," McGuffey remarked plaintively, after the *Maggie* had strained at the hawser for five minutes. Mr. Gibney, standing by with a hammer in his hand, nodded affirmatively, while the skipper of the *Chesapeake*, whom Mr. Gibney had had the forethought to carry out on deck to watch the operation, glanced apprehensively ashore. Scraggs measured the distance with his eye to the nearest fringe of surf and it was plain that he was worried.

"Captain Scraggs," the skipper of the *Chesapeake* called feebly, "Mr. Gibney is right. That craft of yours is unable to tow my ship against this wind. You're losing ground, inch by inch, and it will be only a matter of an hour or two, if you hang on to me, before I'll be in the breakers and a total loss. You'll have to get sail on her or let go the anchor until a tug arrives."

"I don't know a thing about a sailin' ship," Scraggs quavered.

"I know it all," Mr. Gibney cut in, "but there ain't money enough in the world to induce me to exercise that knowledge to your profit." He turned to the master of the *Chesapeake*. "For one hundred dollars each, McGuffey an' I will sail her in for you, sir."

"I'll not take the risk, Mr. Gibney. Captain Scraggs, if you will follow my instructions we'll get some sail on the *Chesapeake*. Take those lines through the leading blocks to the winch——"

The engineer of the *Maggie* came up on deck and waved his arms wildly. "Leggo," he bawled. "I've blown out two tubes. It'll be all I can do to get home without that tow."

"Jump on that, Scraggsy," quoth McGuffey softly and cast his silken engineer's cap on the deck at Scraggs's feet. The latter's face was ashen as he turned to the skipper of the *Chesapeake*. "I'm through," he gulped. "I'll have to cast off. Your ship's drivin' on to the beach now."

"Oh, say not so, Scraggsy," said Mr. Gibney softly, and with a blow of the hammer knocked out the stopper on the windlass and let the anchor go down by the run. "Not this voyage, at least." The *Chesapeake* rounded up with a jerk and Mr. Gibney took Captain Scraggs gently by the arm. "Into the small boat, old ruin," he whispered, "and I'll row you an' The Squarehead back to the *Maggie*. If she drifts ashore with that load o' garden truck, you might as well drown your self."

Captain Scraggs was beyond words. He suffered himself to be taken back to the *Maggie*, after which kindly action Mr. Gibney returned to the *Chesapeake*, climbed aboard, and with the assistance of McGuffey, hauled the work boat up on deck.

CHAPTER XIII

"NOW," Mr. Gibney inquired, approaching the skipper of the *Chesapeake*, "what'll you give me an' Mac, sir, to sail you in? Has it dawned on you, sir, that if I hadn't had sense enough to cockbill that anchor again you'd be on the beach this minute?"

"One thousand dollars," the skipper answered weakly.

"You refused to let us do it for a hundred. Now it'll cost you two thousand, an' I'm lettin' you off cheap at that. Of course, you can take a chance an' wait until word o' your predicament sifts into San Francisco an' a tug comes out for you, but in the meantime the wind may increase an' with the tide at the flood how do you know your anchor won't drag an' pile you up on them rocks to leeward?"

"I'll pay two thousand, Mr. Gibney."

Without further ado, Mr. Gibney went to the master's cabin, wrote out an agreement, carried the skipper aft and got his signature to the contract. Then he tucked the skipper into bed and came dashing out on deck. The wind was from the northwest and luckily the foreyard was braced to starboard while the mainyard was braced to port, so his problem was a simple one.

"Come here till I introduce you to the jib halyards,"

he bawled to McGuffey, and they went forward. Under Gibney's direction, the jib halyards were taken
through the leading blocks to the winch head; Mc-
Guffey manned the winch and the jib was hauled up.
"St-eady-y-y! 'Vast heavin'," cried Mr. Gibney.
"Now then, we'll cast off them jib halyards an' make
'em fast. . . . Right-O . . . Now stand by
to brace the foreyard. Bart, for the love o' heaven,
help me with this foreyard brace."

With the aid of the winch, they braced the foreyard;
then McGuffey ran aft and took the wheel while Mr.
Gibney scuttled forward, eased up the compressor on
the windlass, and permitted the anchor chain to pay
out rapidly. With the hammer, he knocked out the
pin at the forty-five fathom shackle and leaving the
anchor to go by the board, for it worried him no longer,
the bark *Chesapeake* moved gently off on a west-sou'-
west course that would keep her three points off the
land. She had sufficient head sail on now to hold her up.

Mr. Gibney fell upon the main to'gallan'-s'l leads
like a demon, carried them through the leading block
to the winch head, turned over the winch and sheeted
home the main-to'-gallan'-s'l. The *Chesapeake* gathered speed and Mr. Gibney went aft and stood beside
Mr. McGuffey, the while he looked aloft and thrilled
to the whine of the breeze through the rigging. "This
is sailorizin'," he declared. "It sure beats bumboat-
in'. Here, blast you, Bart. You're spillin' the wind
out o' that jib. First thing you know we'll have her in
irons an' then the fat *will* be in the fire."

He took the wheel from McGuffey. When he was
two miles off the beach he brought her up into the wind

and made the wheel fast, a spoke to leeward. "Sheet home the fore-to'-gallan'-s'l," he howled and dashed forward. "Leggo them buntlines an' clewlines, my hearties, an' haul home that sheet."

The ship lay in the wind, shivering. Mr. Gibney was here, there, everywhere. One minute he was dashing along the deck with a leading line, the next he was laying out aloft. He ordered himself to do a thing and then, with the pent-up energy of a thousand devils, he did it. The years of degradation as navigating officer of the *Maggie* fell away from him, as he sprang, agile and half-naked, into the shrouds; a great, hairy demigod or sea-goblin he lay out along the yards and sprang from place to place with the old exultant thrill of youth and joy in his work.

"Overhaul them buntlines an' clewlines," he bawled to an imaginary crew. "Set that main-royal." With McGuffey's help the sheets came home, the halyards were taken to, the yards mast-headed, and the halyards belayed to their pin. The main-royal was now set so they fell to on the fore-royal. A word, a gesture, from Mr. Gibney, and McGuffey would pounce on a rope like a bull-dog. With the fore-royal set, Mr. Gibney ran back to the wheel and put it hard over. There being no after sail set the bark swung off readily on to her course, slipping through the water at a nice eight-knot speed. Ten miles off the coast, Mr. Gibney hung her up in the wind again, braced his yards with the aid of the winch and McGuffey, came about and headed north. At three o'clock she cleared the lightship and wore around to come in over the bar, steering east by south, half-south, for Point Bonita. She drew the full advantage of the wind now and over the bar she came, ramping full through the Gate with her yards squared, on the last of the flood tide.

As they passed Lime Point, Mr. Gibney prepared to shorten sail and like a clarion blast his voice rang through the ship.

"Clew up them royals." He lashed the wheel and they brought the clewlines again to the winch head. The ship was falling off a little before the fore-royal was clewed up, so Mr. Gibney ran back to the wheel and put her on her course again while McGuffey brought the main-royal clewlines to the winch. Again Gibney made the wheel fast and helped McGuffey clew up the main-royal; again he set her on her course while Mc-Guffey, following instructions, made ready to clew up the fore-to'-gallan'-s'l. They were abreast Black Point before this latter sail was clewed up, and then they smothered the lower top-s'ls; the bark was slipping lazily through the water and McGuffey took the wheel.

"Starboard a little! Steady-y-y! Keep her as she heads," Gibney warned and cast off the jib halyards. The jibs slid down the stays, hanging as they fell. They were well up toward Meiggs wharf now and it devolved upon Mr. Gibney to bring his prize in on the quarantine ground and let go his port anchor. Fortunately, the anchor was already cock-billed. Mr. Gibney sprang to the fore-top-sail halyards and let them go and the fore-top-sail came down by the run.

"Hard-a-starboard! Make her fast, Bart, an' come up here an' help me with the anchor. Let go the main-top-sail halyards as you come by an' stand by the compressor on the windlass."

The *Chesapeake* swung slowly, broadside to the first of the ebb and with the wind on her port beam, Mr. Gibney knocked out the stopper with his trusty hammer and away went the rusty chain, singing through the hawsepipe. "Snub her gently, Mac, snub her gently, an' give her the thirty-fathom shackle to the water's edge," he warned McGuffey.

The bark swung until her bows were straightened to the ebb tide and with a wild, triumphant yell Mr. Gibney clasped the honest McGuffey to his perspiring bosom. The deed was done!

It was dark, however, before they had all the sails snugged up shipshape, although in the meantime the quarantine launch had hove alongside, investigated, and removed those of the crew who still lived. Shortly thereafter the coroner came and removed the dead, after which Gibney and McGuffey hosed down the deck, located some hard tack and coffee, supped and turned in in the officers' quarters. In the morning, Scab Johnny arrived in a launch with their other clothes (Mr. Gibney having thoughtfully sent him ten dollars on account of their old board bill, together with a request for the clothes), and when the agents of the *Chesapeake* sent a watchman to relieve them they went ashore and had breakfast at the Marigold Café. After breakfast, they called at the office of the agents, where they were complimented on their daring seamanship and received a check for one thousand dollars each.

"Well, now," McGuffey declared, after they had cashed their checks, "Seein' as how I've become independently wealthy by following your lead, Adelbert, all I got to say is that I'm a-goin' to stick to you like a limpet to a rock. What'll we do with our money?"

For the first time in his checkered career Mr. Gibney had a sane, sensible, and serious thought. "Has it ever occurred to you, Mac, how much nicer it is to have a few dollars in the bank, good clothes on your back, an' a credit with your friends? Me, all my life I been a come-easy, go-easy, come-Sunday,-God'll-send-Monday sort o' feller, until in my forty-second year I'm little better'n a beachcomber. It sure hurt me to have to beg that ornery Scraggs for a job; if I ever sighed for independence it was the other night in Halfmoon Bay when, footsore an' desperate, we stood by an' let that little wart harpoon us. So now, when you ask me what I'm goin' to do with my money, I'll tell you I'm going to save it, after first payin' up about seventy-five bucks I owe here an' there along the Front. I'm through drinkin' an' raisin' hell. Me for a savings bank, Bart."

"I said I'd string with you an' I will. After we deposit our money suppose we drop down to Jackson Street wharf an' say hello to Scraggs. I got a great curiosity to see what that new engineer has done to my boiler."

CHAPTER XIV

WHEN Captain Scraggs, after abandoning all
hope of salving the bark *Chesapeake*, returned
to the *Maggie*, the little craft reminded him of
nothing so much as the ward for the incorrigible of an
insane asylum. Due to Captain Scraggs's stupidity and
the general inefficiency of the *Maggie*, the new navigating
officer was of the opinion that he had been swindled out
of his share of the salvage, while the new engineer, furious at having been engaged to baby such a ruin as the
Maggie's boiler turned out to be, blamed Scraggs's parsi-
mony for the loss of *his* share of the salvage. Therefore, both men aired with the utmost frankness their
opinion of their employer; even Neils Halvorsen was
peeved. Their depression and rage was nothing, however, compared with that of Captain Scraggs's. He had
recklessly jettisoned approximately two hundred dollars'
worth of vegetables; indeed the loss might go higher,
for all he knew. Also, he had lost his skiff, and Mc-
Guffey and Gibney had practically blackmailed him out
of forty dollars. Then, to cap the climax, he had been
forced to abandon two thousand dollars to his enemies;
and as the *Maggie* crept north at three knots an hour
the knowledge that he must, even against his desires,
install a new boiler, overwhelmed him to such an extent
that he found it impossible to submit silently to the
nagging of the navigating officer. One word borrowed

another until diplomatic relations were severed and, in the language of the classic, they "mixed it." They were fairly well matched, and, to the credit of Captain Scraggs be it said, whenever he believed himself to have a fighting chance Scraggs would fight and fight well, under the Tom-cat rules of fisticuffs.

Following a bloody battle in the pilot house, he subdued the mate; following his victory he was still war mad, so he went to the engine-room hatch and abused the engineer. As a result of the day's events, both men quit when the *Maggie* was tied up at Jackson Street wharf and once more Captain Scraggs was helpless. In his extremity, he wished he hadn't been so hard on Mr. Gibney and McGuffey, for he realized he could never hope to get them back until their salvage money should be spent.

He had other tortures in addition. He could not afford to await the construction of a new boiler, for if he did some other skipper would cut in on the vegetable trade he had worked up, for vegetables, being perishable, could not lie on the dock at Halfmoon Bay longer than forty-eight hours. It behooved Scraggs, therefore, to place an order for the new boiler and, in the meantime, to get a gang down aboard the *Maggie* immediately and put in at least ten new tubes. By working night and day this job might be accomplished in forty-eight hours, and, fortunately, Sunday intervened. Scraggs shuddered at thought of the expense, for in addition to being parsimonious he had very little ready cash on hand and no credit.

When Mr. Gibney and McGuffey, wrapped in the calm thrall of their new-found financial independence, arrived at the *Maggie's* berth, they were inclined to levity. Indeed, they had come for the express purpose of spoofing their late employer; to crow over him and grind his poor soul into the dirt. Fortunately for Scraggs, he was not aboard, but sounds of activity coming from the engine room aroused McGuffey's curiosity to such an extent that he descended thereto at great risk to a new suit of clothes and discovered four men at work on the boiler. They had cut the rivets and removed the head and at sight of the ruin disclosed within, Mr. McGuffey was truly shocked—and awed. Why he hadn't been blown to Kingdom Come months before was a profound mystery.

He came up and joined Mr. Gibney on a pile of old hemp hawser coiled on the bulkhead. "Danged if I don't feel sorry for old Scraggsy, for all his meanness," he declared. "It's goin' to cost him five hundred dollars to patch up the old boiler an' keep the *Maggie* runnin' until he can ship a new boiler. The ol' fool don't know a thing about the job himself an' there's four men down there, without a foreman, soldierin' on him an' soakin' him a dollar an' a half an hour overtime. He's in so deep now he might as well jump into bank-ruptcy entirely an' put in a set o' piston rings, repack the pumps an' the stuffin'-box, shim up the bearin's an' do a lot of little things the old *Maggie's* just hollerin' to have done."

"To err is human; to forgive divine," Mr. Gibney orated. "Come to think of it, Mac, we give the old man all that was comin' to him the other day—a little bit more, mebbe. He must be raw an' bleedin', an' it wouldn't be sporty to plague him some more."

"Durned if I don't feel like jumpin' into a suit of dungarees an' helpin' him out in that engine room, Gib."

"Troubles always comes in a flock, Bart. The Squarehead tells me his new navigatin' officer an' the new engineer has jumped their jobs. It's a dollar to a dime he asks us to come back if he sees us half way willin' to be friendly an' forget the past."

"Well," the philosophical McGuffey declared. "Seein' as how we've reformed, even with money in bank, we might just as well be workin' as loafin'. There's more money in it. An' if it wasn't that Scraggs is so ornery there's worse jobs than me an' you had on the old *Maggie*."

"I been wonderin' if we couldn't reform Scraggsy by heapin' coals of fire on his head, Bart."

"What d'ye mean?   Heapin' coals o' fire on Scraggs'd sure keep an ash hoist busy."

"Oh, I dunno, Bart. The old man has his troubles. There's Mrs. Scraggs a-peckin' at him every time he goes home, an' the *Maggie's* a worry, not to mention the fact that there ain't much more'n a decent livin' for him in the green-pea trade. An' he ain't gittin' any younger, Bart. You got to bear that in mind."

"Yes, an' he's been disapp'inted in his ambitions," McGuffey agreed. "On top o' that, the Ocean Shore Railroad is buildin' down the coast an' as soon as the roadbed is completed over the San Pedro Mountains them farmers'll haul their produce to the railhead in motor trucks—an' there won't be no more business for the *Maggie*. Three months more'll see the *Maggie* laid up."

Mr. Gibney nodded. "It's just the sweet tenderness of Satan we'll be flush when Scraggsy's broke, Bart."

"Dang it, Gib, I sure feel sorry for the old man after takin' a look at that engine room. She's a holy fright."

"Well, we'll make up with him when he comes back, Bart, an' if he shows a contrite sperrit—well, who knows? We might do somethin' for him."

"He's got to have some financial help to get that engine turnin' over again, that's a cinch."

"So I been thinkin'. We might lend him a coupler hundred bones at ten per cent., secured by a mortgage on the *Maggie*, if he's up agin it hard. Havin' money in bank is one thing but locatin' an investment for it is another. I've kidded the old man a lot about the *Maggie*, but she's worth two thousand dollars if somebody'd spend a thousand on her inner works an' give her a dab o' paint an' some new fire hose an' one thing an' another."

"We'll wait here until Scraggs shows up an' see what he says. If he still says 'Good mornin', boys,' we'll answer him civil an' see what it leads to, Gib."

Mr. Gibney grunted his approval and Mr. McGuffey, bringing out a pocket knife, fell to manicuring his terrible finger nails and paring the callous patches off his palms. Mr. Gibney lighted a Sailor's Delight cigar and puffed meditatively, the while he watched a gasoline tug kicking the little schooner *Tropic Bird* into an adjacent berth. From the *Tropic Bird* came an odour of copra and pineapple and Mr. Gibney sighed; evidently that South Sea fragrance aroused in him old memories, for presently he spat overboard, watched his spittle float away on the tide, sighed again, and declared, apropos of nothing:

"When I was a young man, Mac, I was a damned fine young man. I had a bunch o' red whiskers an' a pair o' fists like two picnic hams. I was a wonder."

Silently Mr. McGuffey nodded an endorsement of his comrade's indicated horsepower and peculiar masculine beauty in the days of the latter's vanished youth. He continued to prune his hands.

"I was six feet two in my socks, when I wore any, which wasn't often," Mr. Gibney continued. "I've shrunk half an inch since them days. I weighed a hundred an' ninety-seven pounds in the buff an' my chest bulged like a goose-wing tops'l. In them days, I was an evil man to monkey with. I could have taken two like Scraggsy an' chewed 'em up, spittin' out their bones an' belt buckles. I sure was a wonder."

"You must ha' been with them red whiskers on your face," McGuffey agreed. He refrained from saying more, for instinct told him Mr. Gibney was about to grow reminiscent and spin a yarn, and B. McGuffey had a true seaman's reverence for a goodly tale, whether true, half-true, or wholly fanciful.

Mr. Gibney sniffed again the subtle tang of the South Seas drifting over from the *Tropic Bird*, and when a Kanaka, scantily clad, came on deck, threw a couple of fenders overside and retired to the forecastle singing one of those Hawaiian ballads that are so mournfully sweet and funereal, Mr. Gibney sighed again.

"Gawd!" he murmured. "I've sure made a hash o' my young life."

"What's bitin' you, Gib?" Mr. McGuffey's voice was molten with sympathy.

"I was just thinkin'," replied Mr. Gibney, "just thinkin', Mac. It's the pineapples as does it—the smell of the South Seas. Here I am, big enough and old enough and ugly enough to know better, and yet every time the *City Of Papeete* or the *Tropic Bird* or the *Aorangi* come into port and I see the Kanaka boys swabbin' down decks and get a snifter o' that fine smell of the Island trade, my innards wilt down like a mess o' cabbage an' I ain't myself no more until after the fifth drink."

"Sorter what th' feller calls vain regrets," suggested McGuffey.

"Vain regrets is the word," mourned Mr. Gibney. "It all comes back to me what I hove away when I was young an' foolish an' didn't know when I was well off. If there'd only been some good-hearted lad to advise me, I wouldn't be a-settin' here on a hemp hawser, a blasted beachcombin' bucko mate and out of a job. No, siree. I'd 'a' still been King Gibney, Mac, with power o' life an' death over two thousand odd blackbirds, an' I'd 'a' had a beautiful wife an' a dozen kids maybe, with pigs an' chickens an' copra an' shell an' a big bungalow an' money. *That's* what I chucked away when I was young an' nobody to advise me."

McGuffey made no comment on Mr. Gibney's outburst. There are moments in life when silence is the greatest sympathy one can offer, and intuitively McGuffey felt that he was face to face with a tragedy. When a shipmate's soul lay bare it was not for the McGuffey to inspect it too closely.

"Yes, McGuffey, I was a king once. Some people might try to make out as how I was only a chief, but you take it from me, Mac, I was a king. I was King Gibney, the first, of Aranuka, in the Gilberts, with the seat of government at Nonuti, which is a blackbird village right under Hakatuea. No matter which way you approach, you can't miss it. Hakatuea's a dead volcano, with ashes on top and just enough fire inside to cast a glow against the sky at night. There's a fair anchorage inside the reef, but it takes a good man to land through the surf at high tide in a whaleboat. I used to do it regular. Aranuka was a nice place, with plenty of fresh water, and some of the Island schooners, and once in a while a British gunboat would stop there. Gawd, McGuffey, but when I was king, they used to pay dear for their fresh water, except the gunboats, which of course came on and helped themselves without askin' no questions of me and parliament—which was both the same thing. I was in Aranuka first in '88 and again in '89, and I was a fool for leavin' it."

"What was you doin' in this here Aranuka?" asked Mr. McGuffey.

"In '88 I was blackbirdin', and in '89 I was—why, what d'ye expect a king does, anyhow? You don't suppose I *worked*, do you? Because I didn't. I ate and drank and slept and went in swimmin' with the court officers and did a little fishin' an' fightin'; and on moonlight nights I used to sprawl in the grass out on the edge of Hakatuea with my head in my queen's lap, rubberin' up at the Southern Cross and watchin' the rollers breakin' white over the reef. And everything'd be as still as death except for that eternal swishin' of the surf on the beach, babblin' of 'Peace! Peace! Peace!' an' maybe once in a while the royal voice lifted in one of them sad slumber songs of the South Seas—creepy and dirgelike and beautiful. My girl could sing circles around a sky lark. I taught her how to sing 'John Brown's Body Lies A-Smoulderin' in th' Grave,' though she didn't have no more notion o' what she was singin' than a ring-tailed monkey."

"How d'ye come to pick up with her?" inquired McGuffey politely.

"I didn't come to pick up with her," answered Mr. Gibney. "She took a fancy to them red whiskers o' mine, and picked up with me. She used to stick hibiscus flowers in them red curtains and stand off and admire me by the hour. You can imagine how gay I used to feel with flowers in my whiskers. That was one of the reasons why I left her finally.

"But them was the days! Me an' Bull McGinty was the two finest men north or south of the Line. We was worth six ordinary white men each, and twenty blacks, and we was respected. I first met Bull McGinty in Shanghai Nelson's boarding house, over in Oregon Street, not three blocks from where we're settin' now. I was twenty years old an' holdin' a second mate's ticket, for I'd been battin' around the world on clipper ships since I was fourteen, an' I'd bit my way to the front quicker than most. Bull was a big dark man, edgin' up onto the thirty mark. His great grandmother'd been a half-breed Batavian nigger, and his father was Irish. Bull himself was nothin', havin' been born at sea, a thousand miles from the nearest land. However, that ain't got nothin' to do with the story.

Bull McGinty was skipper an' owner of the schooner *Dashin' Wave*, 258 tons net register, when I met him in Shanghai Nelson's place. Also he was broke, with the *Dashin' Wave* lyin' out in the stream off Mission Rock with a Honolulu Chinaman aboard as crew and watchman, while Bull hustled around shore tryin' to raise funds to outfit her for another trip to the Islands. He'd been beachcombin' ten days when I met him, and we took to each other right off.

"'Gib,' says Bull McGinty, 'I like you an' if I ever get money enough to provision the *Dashin' Wave*, pay the clearance fee, and put a thousand or two of trade aboard her, you must come mate with me and if you should have a little money by, enough to fix us up, I'll not only give you the mate's berth, but I'll put you in on half the lay.'

"'Done,' says I. 'I ain't got ten cents Mex to my name, but I'll outfit that vessel an' get her to sea inside two weeks, or my name ain't Adelbert P. Gibney.'

"To look at me now, McGuffey, you'd never think that in them days I was one of the smartest young bucks that ever boxed the compass. I was born with a great imagination, Mac. All my life my imagination's been my salvation. The ability to grab opportunity by the tail and twist it was my long suit, so after my talk with Bull McGinty I took a cruise along the docks, lookin' for an idea, until I come to Sheeny Joe's place. He used to keep a sailors' outfittin' joint at Howard and East streets, an' as I stood in his doorway, the Great Idea sails up to Sheeny Joe's an' lets go both anchors.

"What was this Idea? It was a waterfront reporter. It was three waterfront reporters, from three mornin' papers, an' all lookin' for news.

"'Joe,' says one little runt, all hair an' nose an' eyeglasses, 'there ain't enough news on the Front to-day to dust a hummin' bird's eyebrow. Give me a story, Joe. Somethin' new an' brimmin' with human interest. You must have somethin' up your sleeve, ain't yuh?'

"Sheeny Joe is sellin' a Panama paraqueet a pair o' six-bit dungarees for a dollar and a half, and he ain't got no time for reporters, but he looks up an' he sees me lingerin' in the doorway.

"'Gib,' says he, 'tell these reporter friends o' mine about the time you was wrecked in the Straits o' Magellan, an' the fight you had with them man-eatin' Patagonian cannibal savages.'

"Of course, I never was wrecked in no Straits o' Magellan, and as for man-eatin' Patagonian cannibal savages, I wouldn't know one if I met him in my grog. But seein' as how Sheeny Joe is busy an' me owin' him quite a little bill, I have to make good, so I tells them the most hair-raisin' story they ever listened to. I showed 'em an old scar on my left leg where I was vaccinated once, and told 'em that's where they shot me with a bow an' arrer. While I was tellin' my story Sheeny Joe has to run out in th' back yard an' roll over three times, he's that fascinated with what I'm tellin' his friends.

"Did them fellers eat it up? They did. The story comes out next day with trimmin's on th' front page, an' I'm a hero. Of course me an' Sheeny Joe knows I'm a liar, but what's a lie or two when you're helpin' out a

shipmate? But anyhow, the whole business gives me
the idee I'm lookin' for, an' I takes all three mornin'
papers down to Bull McGinty an' lets him read 'em.

" 'Now,' says I, when Bull is through readin', 'you
have a sample of what publicity does for a man. I'm
a hero. But that don't outfit the schooner *Dashin'
Wave*. A man don't get no wages as a hero, Bull.
Nevertheless,' says I, 'I have invented a story that
will bring in money,' an' I tell the story to Bull. I
don't leave him until I have that yarn drilled right inter
his soul, an' then I call on Sheeny Joe an' tell him to
pass the word to all of his reporter friends that if they
want a good story to go down to Shanghai Nelson's
boardin' house an' ask for Bull McGinty, skipper o' the
schooner *Dashin' Wave*.

"Did they come? Mac, they came a-runnin'. The
little nosy guy with the hair chartered a hack, he was
in such a hurry. An' when they arrive, there sits
Bull McGinty, smilin' an' affable, an' he spills his yarn
as easy an' graceful an' slick as a mess o' eels. There's
a island in the Society group, says Bull, which he discovers on his last trip, an' which ain't in none o' the
British Admiralty notes. It's a regular island, with
palms an' breadfruit an' tamarinds an' mangoes an'
such, fine an' fertile, fifteen miles around the middle,
an' plenty o' water. But th' surprisin' thing about
this here island is that it ain't got nothin' livin' on it
except the most beautiful women in all the South Seas.
Accordin' to Bull, there ain't a male man nowhere on
the horizon. Th' men has been fightin' among themselves until every man Jack has been killed off. Nothin' left but women with dreamy eyes an' long black hair

an pearly teeth. 'A man,' says Bull McGinty, 'is at a premium. Over fifteen different girls fell in love with him before he was ashore ten minutes, an' he had to pull back to the schooner to escape 'em. At that, says Bull, as much as a hundred an' twenty-seven of 'em, as near as he could count, came swimmin' after him and chased the schooner until she was hull down on the horizon, an' then they give up an' swam back to home, sobbin' like babies.

"Bull explains that he's so dead stuck on the place he's goin' back, just as soon as he can get together say a hundred smart young lads to come in with him on the lay, outfit his schooner, an' get to sea. Every man that wants to come in on th' deal must be not less than twenty-one years old and not more than thirty, an' must be examined by a doctor to see that he ain't afflicted with no contagious sickness, like consumption, which just raises fits with them natives, once it gets in amongst 'em. It's Bull's plan to start a ideal colony, governed on new an' different lines, an' every man must marry. He can have as many wives as he can support after each man has had his choice of the herd. The women are all beautiful, but in order that nobody will have a kick comin' the choice of wives is to be determined by drawin' lots. The island is to be fenced off an' each member o' the expedition is to have so much land.

"In order to do everything shipshape, Bull explains that he has formed a company to be known as the Brotherhood o' the South Seas, capitalized for two hundred shares at $500 a share. Bull, bein' owner o' th' schooner, an' possessin' the secret of the latitude an'

longitude o' the island, an' bein' the movin sperrit, so
to speak, declares himself in on fifty-one per cent. o'
the capital stock. Stocksellin' will commence just as
soon as the printer can deliver the certificates.

"In the course of a somewhat checkered career,
Mac, I've seen some suckers, an' I've told some lies,
but this here was th' crownin' event of my life. We
had applications for stock the next morning before me
an' Bull was out o' bed. Four hundred and thirty-
one would-be colonists comes flockin' around us, tryin'
to hand us $500 each. Bull questions 'em all very
closely, and outer the lot he selects the biggest damn
fools in evidence. He was careful to select little skinny
men whenever possible. They was a lot o' Willie
boys an' young bloods lookin' for adventure, an' me
an' Bull McGinty was just the lads to give it to 'em
in bucketfuls. The little nosy reporter with the hair
was fair crazy to come, but McGinty gets a jackleg
doctor to examine him an' swear that he's sufferin' from
spatulation o' the medulla oblongata, housemaid's knee,
and the hives. We're mighty sorry, but it's agin the
by-laws to bring him along. He felt heartbroken, so
just before we up hook with the expedition, I had Bull
give him an' the other newspaper boys a hundred dollars
each. They was fine lads, all three, an' give us lots
o' free advertisin'.

"Bull got greedy an' was for charterin' another
schooner an' givin' all comers a run for their money,
but I was wise enough to see the danger o' numbers,
an' argued him out of it. I went mate on the *Dashin'
Wave*, as per program, an' on a lovely summer day we
towed out, with half San Francisco crowdin' the wharves

an' wishin' us bon voyage, which is French for a profit-able trip.

"We had a nice lot o' sick children on our hands be-fore we was over th' Potato Patch. We didn't have a regular crew, exceptin' Bull McGinty an' me an' the Chinaman who shipped as cook. However, some of the brotherhood used to go yachting, an' they was all the crew we needed. We had a fair run to Honolulu, where we took on five thousand dollars in trade—beads, an' mouth organs, an' calico, an' juice harps, an' dollar watches, an' a lot of old army revolvers with the firin' pins filed off, and what not.

"From Honolulu, we clears for Pago Pago, where all hands went ashore an' enjoyed themselves visitin' the different points o' interest. From Pago Pago, we goes to Tahiti, and from Tahiti to Suva, and in general gives them adventurers as nice a little summer vacation as they could have wished for. Bull was for dumpin' the lot at Suva an' gettin' down to business—said he'd fooled away enough time on the gang—but I argued that we'd took their money—$50,000 of it, and they was entitled to some kind of a run, an' if we marooned them, like as not they'd send a gunboat after us, an' the fat'd be in the fire. Bull gave in to me finally, though he growled a lot about the profits bein' all et up by the brotherhood, appetites increasin' consider-able at sea, an' all that.

"Just after we leave Suva we butts into a mild little typhoon, an' Bull scuds before it under bare poles, with just a wisp o' a jib to steady her. An' when the brother-hood was pea-green with seasickness I goes down into the bilges with a big auger an' scuttles the ship. In about two hours the brother at the wheel begins to complain that she's heavy an' draggin' like blazes, an' he fears maybe her seams has opened up under the strain.

"'I shouldn't wonder a bit,' says Bull McGinty, 'she's been jumpin' like a dolphin', and he goes below to investigate. Two minutes later he prances up on deck like a lunatic.

"'All hands to the pumps,' he yells; 'there's four feet o' water in the hold.' Aside he says to me, 'Gib, my boy, you're a jewel. Not a drop of water in that forward compartment where we piled the trade.'

"It was a terrible sad sight to see the seasick Brotherhood of the South Seas staggerin' below to the pumps. We had four pumps, an' feelin' that they might be able to pump her dry too soon, I had removed the suction leather from two of them. What a howl went up when Bull McGinty, roarin' like a sea lion, announces that all hands is doomed, because two of the pumps is nix comarous! Just about that time we ships a sea or two, and all hands lets go the pumps and starts to pray or weep or whatever they was minded to do under the circumstances. In the general excitement I slips below an' plugs up one hole, an' forces two men, at the point of a revolver that wasn't loaded, to pump ship. They just managed to hold the water level, while up on deck Bull is tearin' his hair an' cursin' somethin' frightful.

"Well, Mac, we kept that thing up for two days an' two nights, while the gale lasted, an' when we finally gets under the lee of an island, all hands are for throwin' up the sponge an' goin' back home. Somehow or

other, the expedition don't look so enticin' as it did at
first.   We cleared away both whaleboats and landed
the brotherhood on the island, where there was a
wharf an' a big tradin' station.   I forget what they
call the place, but steamers touch there regular.   Me
an' Bull McGinty and the Chinaman stayed aboard,
pumped out the ship, fixed the pumps, and plugged the
holes in her bottom so nobody could find out.   Then
we figures out the price of a passage back to Frisco,
second-class, for the whole bunch, an' me an' Bull goes
ashore with a big sack of Chili dollars an' fixes it up
with all hands to let go an' call it square for the ticket
home.   They wasn't feelin' as sore as much as you
might imagine.   None o' them had the brains or the
spunk of a mouse, and besides we'd give them a mighty
good time of it, all things considered.   So, to make a
long story short, we picks up a crew of half a dozen
black boys, pulls the two whaleboats back to the ship,
ups hook and sails away on our legitimate business.
We divides the spoils between us, an' my share is eleven
thousand cash an' a half interest in th' trade.

"We do a nice business in shell an' copra, an' such,
an' in Papeete we sell our cargo to a Jew trader an'
clean up fifteen hundred each additional on the voyage,
after which Bull declares he's tired of hucksterin'
around like any bloomin' peddler, an' we make up our
minds to do a little blackbirdin'.

"Was you ever a blackbirder, McGuffey? No?
Well, you didn't miss nothin'.   It's dirty business.
You drop in at a island, an' you invite the native chief
aboard an' get him drunk, and make a contract with
him for so many blackbirds to work for three years on

some other island, or on the coffee or henequen planta-
tions in Central America, and you promise them big
money and lots of tobacco, and a free trip back when
their time is up.   What labour you can't get by dealin'
with the chief, you shanghai 'em, and once in a while
you can make a bully good deal, particularly in the
New Hebrides and New Guinea, after a fight when
they have a lot of prisoners on hand which they're goin'
to eat until you come along an' buy 'em for a stick o'
tobacco.

"It ain't no fun, blackbirdin', McGuffey.   After
you've got 'em aboard, they may take a notion to jump
overboard and swim back, so you get 'em down below
an' clap the hatches on 'em until you're out of sight
o' land, an' the beggars howl an' there's hell to pay.

"Me an' Bull McGinty headed for the Gilberts that
first trip, an' managed to pick up a fair consignment of
labour.   We touched in at Nonuti the very last place,
which, as I says, is on the island o' Aranuka, right under
the Hakatuea volcano.   There was some strappin' big
buck native niggers there that would fetch $300 a head
Mex, an' so me an' Bull goes ashore to pow-wow with
the chief.   He was a fat old boy named Poui-Slam-
Bang, or some such name, an' he received us as nice as
you please.   Me an' Bull rubbed noses with Poui-Slam-
Bang an' all the head men, and they give a big feed in
our honour.   Roast pig an' roast duck an' stewed chicken
an' all the tropical trimmin's we had, Mac, including a
little barrel o' furniture polish that Bull brought ashore,
labelled Three Star Hennessy on the outside an' Three
Ply Deviltry inside.

"While we was at the feast, with everybody squattin'

around on their hind legs, pokin' their mits into a big
wooden bowl, Poui-Slam-Bang pipes up his only daugh-
ter, a lovely wench about seventeen years old with a
name that nobody can pronounce. I call her Pinky,
and of all the women I ever meets, black, white, brown,
red, or yellow, this Pinky is the loveliest, and has 'em all
hull down. She's wearin' a palm leaf petticoat and a
string o' shark's teeth around her neck with an empty
sardine box for a pendant. She has flowers in her hair,
which is braided in pig-tails, different from the other
girls. Her eyes—McGuffey, *them eyes!* Like a pair of
fireflies floatin' in sorghum. And as she stands there
working her toes in th' sand, she never takes her eyes
off them fine red whiskers o' mine.

"Bull gives her a cigar, and it's plain that he's taken
with her, but she never so much as looks at Bull. My
whiskers has done the trick—so bimeby, when all hands
is feeling jolly, including me an' McGinty, I sidles up to
Pinky an' sorter gives her to understand that she
wouldn't have to clap me in irons to fondle them red
whiskers o' mine. She sticks a flower in them, Mac,
s'help me, and then giggles foolish an' ducks into the
bush.

"Well, we rigs up a deal with Poui-Slam-Bang and
next afternoon stand out for the entrance with forty
odd head of labour in excess of what we had when we
arrived. We'd cleared the reef, and was comin' about
around Hakatuea Head, when what d'ye suppose we
sight? Nothin' more or less than Miss Pinky Poui-
Slam-Bang swimmin' right across our bows. She was
more than a mile out an' comin' like a shark, hand over
hand. Before I could yell to the boy at the wheel to

luff up, so we wouldn't run the girl down, we was right on top of her.

"'They'll have to revise the census of Aranuka,' says Bull McGinty. 'I do believe we hit that girl an' drove her under.'

"We was both rubberin' astern an' to starboard an' port, but not a sign o' the girl do we see. I got out my glasses an' searched around for full half an hour, an' by that time we was five miles out to sea, and it wasn't no use lookin' any more, an' besides I had work to attend to.

"We sailed along all the afternoon, over a sea as smooth as a dance-hall floor. Along about sunset I was up on the fo'castle head singin' 'Nancy Brown' when who should pop up onto the bowsprit but Pinky. She sat there a minute danglin' her legs an' smilin' an' s'help me, Mac, if it hadn't been daylight still, I'd a-swore she was a sperrit. I jumped two feet in the air an' came down with my mouth open. Pinky hops up on the bowsprit, and runs along to the fo'castle head, an' then I seen she was real. The little cuss! She'd swung herself up into the martingale, an' there she'd squatted all the afternoon until we was out o' sight o' land. Of course, she got a ducking every few minutes, but what's a duckin' to them kind o' people?

"I grabs hold o' Pinky, mighty glad to know we hadn't killed her, and brings her before Bull McGinty.

"'She's in love with some one of these black bucks aboard,' says Bull. "That's why she's followed. Isn't she the likely lookin' wench, Gib? I do believe I'll——"

"'No, you won't do no such thing, Bull,' says I. 'The fact o' the matter is the girl's in love with me, an' if anybody's to have her it'll be Adelbert P. Gibney.'

"'I'm not so sure o' that, Gib,' says Bull McGinty. "I'm skipper here.'

"'Well, I'm mate,' says I, 'with a half interest in this expedition.'

"'I'll fight you for her,' says Bull very pleasantly.

"'No,' says I, 'I'm opposed t' fightin' a shipmate under such circumstances, and moreover we're the only two white men aboard, an' if we fight I think I'll kill you, an' then I'd be lonesome. As a compromise, I'll tell you what we'll do. We'll give Pinky the freedom o' the ship, an' me an' you'll have a cribbage tournament from now until we drop anchor at Santa Maria del Pilar (that's a dog hole on the Guatemala coast). We'll play every chance we get, an' the lad that's ahead when we let go the anchor at Santa Maria del Pilar gets Pinky.'

"'Fair enough,' says Bull, 'an' here's my hand on it.'

"We had a smart passage o' fifteen days, and in that time me an' Bull McGinty plays just one hundred and eighteen games. We had to quit in the middle o' the last, with the score fifty-eight games to fifty-nine in Bull's favour, in order to let go the anchor at Santa Maria del Pilar. While we was up on deck, what do you suppose Pinky goes and does? She slips down to the cabin and fudges my peg three holes ahead. It seems that Bull, who talked the island lingo, has been braggin' to her an' tellin' her what we've been up to. The minute we have the anchor down, me an' Bull returns to the game. It's nip an' tuck to the finish an' I win by one point, Bull dyin' in the last hole, which makes the thing a draw.

"Says I to Bull McGinty: 'Bull, we can't both have her.'

"Says Bull to me: 'I hereby declare this tournament no contest, an' move that we sell the lady with the rest o' the herd, an' no hard feelin's between shipmates.'

"Nothin' could be fairer than that an' I tells Bull I'm willin'. So we sold Pinky for $200 Mex to Don Luiz Miguel y Oreña, an' sailed away for another flock o' blackbirds.

"We had busy times for the next six months until we found ourselves back at Santa Maria del Pilar with another cargo of savages. But all that time I'd been feelin' a little sneaky on account o' sellin' Pinky, an' as soon as we dropped anchor I had the boys pull me ashore, an' I chartered a white mule an' shapes my course for the hacienda of this Don Luiz Miguel y Oreña. I was minded to see how Pinky was gettin' on.

"It was comin' on dusk when I rides into Oreña's place, an' all th' hands was just in from the fields. The labour shacks was built in a kind of square along with the warehouses, an' in the centre o' this square was a snubbin' post, with bull rings, an' hangin' to this snubbin' post, with her hands triced up to the bull rings, was Pinky Poui-Slam-Bang with a little Colorado claro man standing off swingin' a rope's end on poor little Pinky's bare back.

"I'm not what you'd call a patient man, McGuffey, an' bein' o' th' sea and not used to ridin' horses, not to speak o' white mules, I was sore in more ways than one. I luffs up alongside o' this dry land bo'sum an' punches once. Then I jumps off my white mule, takes the swab by the heels, an' chucks him over the warehouse, into a cactus bush. Don Oreña was there an' he makes objections to me gettin' fresh with his help so, I tucks

Don Oreña under my arm, lays him acrosst my knee, and gives him a taste o' th' rope's end. He hollers murder, but I bats him around until he can't let out another peep, after which I grabs a machete that's handy an' chases the entire male population into the jungle. When I gets back, Pinky is hanging to the bull rings, about dead. I cuts her down, swings her on th' mule, an' makes for the coast. We was aboard th' *Dashin Wave* next mornin'.

"Bull was settin' up on top o' th' house eatin' an orange when me an' Pinky comes over th' rail.

"'Bull McGinty' says I, 'you're a sea captain. Come down off that house an' marry me to Pinky Poui-Slam-Bang.'

"'With pleasure,' says Bull, an' he done it, announcin' us man an' wife by all th' rules an' regulations o' th' Department o' Commerce an' Labour, th' *Dashin' Wave* being registered under th' American flag.

"Six weeks later I sets Pinky down on the beach at Nonuti, an' we both go up to her old man's shack for the parental blessin'. I expected Poui-Slam-Bang would slaughter th' roasted hog upon th' prodigal's return, but come t' find out, the old boy's been took in a scrap with one o' the hill tribes, an' speculation's rife as to his final disposition. Pinky allows that pa's been et up, an' she havin' no brothers is by all the rules o' the game queen o' Aranuka. Of course, me bein' her husband, I'm king. You can't get around my rights to the job nohow. For all that Pinky stands in with me, however, a big wild-eyed beggar makes up his mind that he'll make a better king than Adelbert P. Gibney, an' he comes at me with a four-foot war club, with two spikes drove crosswise through the business end o' it. As he swings, I soaks him between the eyes with a ripe breadfruit, with the result that his aim's spoiled an' he misses. So I took his club away an' hugged him until I broke three ribs, an' he was always good after that. I wanted t' be king, but I didn't believe in sheddin' no blood for the mere sake of office.

"Well, McGuffey, I was king of Aranuka for nearly six months. I was a popular king, too, an' there was never no belly-achin' at my decisions. I had a double-barrelled muzzle-loadin' shotgun, a present from Bull McGinty. Bull was all broke up at me desertin' the *Dashin' Wave,* but I promised to save all the Aranuka trade for him an' for nobody else, an' he stood off for Suva to get himself another mate.

"At first it was great business bein' king, an' I enjoyed it. I learned Pinky to speak a little English an' she learned me her lingo, an' we got along mighty fine. Pinky would lay awake nights, snoopin' around listenin' to what the rest o' the gang had to say about me, and twice she put me wise to uprisin's that threatened my throne. I used to get the ring leaders in my arms an' hug 'em, an' after one hug from Adelbert P. Gibney in them days——

"Well, as I was sayin', it was nice enough until the novelty wore off, an' there was nothin' to do that I hadn't done twenty times before. I thought some o' goin' to war with the wild niggers in the hills, an' avengin' my father-in-law's death, but I couldn't get my army more than three miles inland, so I had to give that up. Before three months had passed I wanted to abdicate the worst way. I wanted to tread a deck again,

an' rove around with Bull McGinty. I wanted th'
smell o' the open sea an' th' heave o' th' *Dashin' Wave*
underfoot. I was tired o' breadfruit an' guavas an'
cocoanuts an' all th' rest o' th' blasted grub that Pinky
was feedin' me, an' most of all I was gettin' tired o'
Pinky. She *would* put cocoanut oil in her hair. Yet
(here Mr. Gibney's voice vibrated with emotion as he
conjured up these memories of his lurid past) it never
occurred to me, at the time, I was that young an' foolish, that she was doin' it for *me*. She was as beautiful
as ever, an' Gawd knows nobody but a fool would get
tired o' such a fine woman, every inch a queen, but I was
just that foolish.

"I got so lonesome I wouldn't eat. I wished Mc-
Ginty would show up an' relieve me of my kingship. An'
one night sure enough he came. It was moonlight—
you've been in the tropics, McGuffey, you know what
real moonlight is—an' I was lyin' out on th' edge of
Hakatuea overlookin' the beach. I'd spotted a sail
at sunset an' somethin' told me it was the *Dashin'
Wave*. Pinky was with me, rubbin my head an' braid-
in' my whiskers an' cooin' over me like a baby, as happy
as any woman could be.

"Along about ten o'clock, I should say, here comes
the *Dashin' Wave* around the headland. I could see her
luff up an' come about with her bow headed straight
for the entrance between the reefs, an' th' water purlin'
under her forefoot. Everything was as still as the
grave, an' only the surf was swishin' up th' beach sobbin' 'Peace! Peace!' and there wasn't no peace for
King Gibney. Pretty soon I heard the creak of the
blocks an' the smash o' th' mast hoops as th' mains'l

came flutterin' down—then th' sound o' the cable
rushin' through the hawse-pipes as her hook took bottom.   In the moonlight I could see Bull McGinty
standin' by the port mizzen shrouds with a megaphone
up to his face, and his voice comes up to me like the
bugle blast of Kingdom Come.

"'O, Gib!   Are you there?'

"'Aye, aye, sir.'

"'Have ye et your full o' th' lotus?' says Bull.

"'Hard tack an' salt horse for King Gibney,' I yells
back.   'I ain't no vegetarian no more, Bull.   Do you
need a smart mate?'

"I could hear Bull McGinty chucklin' to himself.

"'You young whelp,' says Bull.   'I knew you'd out-
grow it.   They all do, when they're as young as you.
I'll send the whaleboat ashore.   Kiss Pinky good-bye
for me, too,' he adds.

"Two minutes later I heard the boat splash over the
stern davits an' the black boys raisin' a song as they
lay to their work.   I turns to Pinky, takes her in my
arms an' kisses her for the first time in three weeks, an'
she knows that th' jig is up.   She might 'a' slipped a dirk
in me, but she wasn't that kind.   Women is women,
McGuffey, the world over.   Pinky just kissed me half
a hundred times an' cries a little, holdin' on to me all
th' time, for naturally she don't like to see me go.   Finally I have to make her break loose, an' I climbs down
over the bluff an' wades out to my waist to meet the
boat.   I was aboard th' *Dashin' Wave* in two twos,
shakin' hands with Bull McGinty, an' ten minutes later
we had th' anchor up an' th' sails shook out, an' standin'
off for the open sea.   An' the last I ever saw of Mrs.

Pinky Gibney was a shadowy figger in th' moonlight standin' out on th' edge o' Hakatuea Head. The last I hear of her was a sob."

Mr. Gibney's voice was a trifle husky as he concluded his tale. He opened and closed his clasp knife and was silent for several minutes. Presently he sighed.

"When a feller's young, he never stops to think o' th' hurt he does," continued the erstwhile king of Aranuka. "Sometimes I lay awake at nights an' wonder whatever became o' Pinky. I can see her yet, standin' in th' moonlight, as fine a figger o' a woman as ever lived. Savage or no savage, she was true an' beautiful, an' I was a mighty dirty dawg." Mr. Gibney wiped away a suspicious moisture in his eyes and blew his nose unnecessarily hard.

"You was," coincided McGuffey. "You was all o' that. What became o' Bull McGinty?"

"He married a sugar plantation in Maui. He's all right for the rest o' his life. An' as for me as gave him his start, look at me. Ain't I a sight? Here I am, forty-two years old an' only a thousand dollars in my pocket. Instead of bein' master of a clipper ship, I'm mate on a dirty little bumboat. I fall asleep on deck an' dream an' somethin' drops on my face an' wakes me up. Is it a breadfruit, Mac? It is not. It's a head of cabbage. I grab something to throw at Scraggs's cat. Is it a ripe mango? No, it's a artichoke. In fancy I go to split open a milk cocoanut. What happens? I slash my thumb on a can o' condensed cream. Instead o' th' Island trade, I'm runnin' in th' green-pea trade, twenty miles of coast, freightin' garden truck! My Gawd!"

Mr. Gibney stood up and dusted the seat of his new suit. He was dry after his long recital and Captain Scraggs was too long putting in an appearance, so he decided not to wait for him. "Let's go an' stow away a glass of beer," he suggested to McGuffey. "I'm thirstier'n a camel."

McGuffey was willing so they left the bulkhead for the more convivial shelter of the Bowhead saloon.

CHAPTER XV

HAD either Gibney or McGuffey glanced back as they headed for their haven of forgetfulness they might have seen Captain Scraggs poking his fox face up over the edge of a tier of potato boxes piled on the bulkhead not six feet from where Gibney and McGuffey had been sitting. Upon his return to the *Maggie*, about the time Mr. Gibney commenced spinning his yarn, he had almost walked into the worthy pair, and, wishing to avoid the jeers and jibes he felt impending, he had merely stepped aside and hidden behind the potato boxes in order to eavesdrop on their plans, if possible. Had Mr. Gibney been less interested in his past or Mr. McGuffey less interested in the recital of that past they would have seen Scraggs.

The owner of the *Maggie* shook his fist in impotent rage at their retreating backs. "You think you've suffered before," he snarled. "But I'll make you suffer some more, you big brute. I'll hurt you worse than if I caved in your head with a belayin' pin. I'll break your heart, that's what I'll do to you. You wait."

In the course of an hour Gibney and McGuffey returned, and Scraggs met them as they leaped down on to the deck of the *Maggie*. "Gentlemen," he remarked—"an' at that I'm givin' you two all the best of it, even if you two have got a quit-claim deed that you ain't pirates—I wish to announce that if you two have come

aboard my ship for the puppose o' havin' a little fun
at my expense, I'm a-goin' to call the police an' have
you arrested for disturbin' the peace. On the other
hand an' futher, if your mission's a peaceful one, you're
welcome aboard the *Maggie*. I may have a temper an'
say things that sounds mighty harsh when I'm het
up, but in my calmer moments my natural inclination
is to be a sport."

"Scraggsy, old hard-luck," Mr. Gibney boomed,
"we won so we can afford to be generous in victory.
Like you, me an' Mac is inclined to be uppish at times,
particularly in the hour of triumph, an' say an' do
things we're apt to be ashamed of later."

"Them's my sentiments," McGuffey chimed in.

"We ain't comin' aboard to beg you for no job," Mr.
Gibney warned. "Git that idea out o' your head—if
you got it there. Me an' Bart each got close to a
thousand dollars in bank this minute an' we're as free
an' independent as two hogs walkin' on ice. Any ol'
time we can't stand up we can set down."

Captain Scraggs was frankly mystified. "If you
two got a thousand dollars each in bank—an' I ain't
disputin' it, for I hear on good authority you got that
much for salvin' the *Chesapeake*—what're you hangin'
around the *Maggie* for?"

Mr. Gibney approached and placed his great right
arm fraternally across Scraggs's skinny shoulder. Mr.
McGuffey performed a similar office with his brawny
left, and Captain Scraggs looked apprehensive, like a
man who is about to be kissed by another in public.

"Scraggsy, when all is lovely an' the goose honks
high, it's our great American privilege to fight like bear-

eats if we feel that way about it.   But when misfortune
descends on one of us, like a topmast in a typhoon, it's
time to stop bickerin'.   Me an' Bart, driftin' along the
docks for a constitootional this mornin', bears the
sorrerful tidin's that your new navigatin' officer an'
your new engineer has quit.   Judgin' from that shanty
on your left eye, at least one of 'em quit under protest.
Immediately, Scraggsy, me an' Mac decided you
might hate our innards but just the same you needed
us in your business.   Consequently, we're here to help
you if you'll let us an' for not another durned reason
in the world."

"There's four alleeged mechanics down in the engine
room loafin' on the job an' gettin' ready to soak you a
dollar an' a half an hour overtime to-night an' Sunday,"
McGuffey informed the skipper.   "An' that hurts me.
I don't mind takin' a poke at you myself but I'll be
shot if I'll stand idly by an' see somebody else do it.
With your kind permission, Scraggs, I'll climb into my
dungarees an' make things hum in that engine room."

Captain Scraggs was truly affected.   His weak chin
trembled and tears came to his little mean green eyes.
He could not speak; so Mr. Gibney hugged him and
patted him on the back and told him he was a good fellow away down low, if the truth were only known;
whereat Captain Scraggs commenced to sob aloud.
McGuffey coughed and tears as big as marbles cas-
caded down the honest Gibney's rubicund countenance.

"I ain't wuth your sympathy after the way I treated
you," Captain Scraggs cried brokenly.

"Shet up, you little bum," Mr. Gibney cried furi-

ously. "Or I'll bang you in that other eye that's
ready for bangin'."

"If you're shy a few bucks——" McGuffey began.

"I am," Captain Scraggs wailed. "I'm worried to
death. I don't know how I'm ever goin' to pay for
that bloody boiler an' git to sea with the *Maggie*——"

"Little sorrel-top," Mr. Gibney murmured, ruffling
Scraggs's thin blonde hair. "Forget them sordid mone-
tary considerations. I'm somethin' like forty jumps
ahead o' the devil an' ruination for the first time since
me an' Bull McGinty organized the Brotherhood o'
the South Seas——"

"Leggo me," snarled Captain Scraggs and springing
back, he bent and looked earnestly into Mr. Gibney's
happy countenance. "Good land o' Goshen, if you
ain't him!" Hate gleamed in his eyes.

"Ain't who, you shrimp!" Mr. Gibney was mystified
at this abrupt change of attitude.

Captain Scraggs blinked and passed his hand wearily
across his brow. "Forgive me, Gib," he answered
humbly. "I was sort o' took back, that's all."

"Took back at what?"

"We won't say nothin' more about it, Gib, except
that while I'd like to accept your kind offer an' put
you back on the job again, I—I just can't bring myself
to do it. I'll have to forget first."

"Forget what? Bart, is Scraggsy gone nutty?"

"Out with it, Scraggs," Mr. McGuffey urged. "Spit
it out, whatever it is."

"I'd rather not, but since you ask me I suppose I
might as well. Gib, ever since me an' you first hooked
up together, away back in the corner o' my head there's

been lurkin' a suspicion that once before, a long time ago, you an' me have had some business dealin's, but for the life o' me I couldn't place you.   One minute I'd just be a-staggerin' on the brink of memory, as the feller says, an' the next it'd slip away from me.   But just now, when you mentioned Bull McGinty an' the Brotherhood o' the South Seas—well, Gib, it all come back to me like a flash.   Bull McGinty an' the schooner *Dashin'. Wave!*"   Captain Scraggs shook his head as if his thoughts threatened to congeal in his brain and he desired to shake them up.   "Bull had a dash o' the tar-brush in his make up, if I don't disremember, an' you was his young mate.   Man, how funny you did look with them long red whiskers—an' you little more'n a boy."

"Jumpin' Jehosophat, Scraggsy!   Was you one o' the Brotherhood?"

Captain Scraggs came close and thrust his face up for Mr. Gibney's inspection.   "Gib," he said solemnly, "look at me!   Touch the cord o' memory an' think back.   D'ye remember that pore little feller you robbed of five hundred dollars twenty-odd year ago in the schooner *Dashin' Wave?*   D'ye remember that typhoon we was in an' how, when I was that tuckered out an' so seasick I couldn't stand up, you made me pump ship an' when I protested, you stuck a horse pistol under my nose an' *made* me?   That man, Adelbert P. Gibney was *me!   Me!   Me!*"   Scraggs's voice rose in a crashing crescendo; his teeth clicked together and he shook his skinny fist under the great Gibney nose. Gibney paled and drew away from him.

"How was I to know, Scraggsy?" he faltered.   "The

whole bunch was runts—sickly, measly little fellers. Nevertheless an' agin, you shouldn't ought to have any kick comin'. You had a fine trip an' a heap of adventure an' me an' Bull paid your passage back to San Francisco. Come, Scraggs. Be sensible. What's the use holdin' a grudge after twenty-five years?"

"Oh, I ain't holdin' a grudge, exactly, Gib, my boy. I admit I had a good run for my money an' it was a smart piece o' work, an' I got to admire the idea, same as I got to admire the seamanship you displayed sailin' the *Chesapeake* single-handed. It ain't what you done to me as makes my blood boil. It's what you went an' done afterward."

"What'd I do afterward? You can't hang nothin' on me, Phineas P. Scraggs. Bluffin' don't go. Cough it up."

"All right, since you drive me to it. How about that lovely, untootered savage that you lures into your foul clutches so's you can make yourself king of Aranuka? Hey? Hey? How about that little tropic wild flower you carelessly plucked an' thrun away? Oh, I'll admit she was a savage, but she was sweet an' human for all that an' she had feelin's. She had a heart to bust an' you busted it for fair."

Mr. Gibney attempted to hoot, but made a poor job of it. "Why, wherever do you get this wild tale, Scraggsy, old spell-binder? You're sure jingled or you wouldn't talk so vagrant."

"You can't git away with it like that, Gib. I trailed you. Gib, for two mortal years I follered you, after you dropped us at Suva, an' I was just a thirstin' for your blood. If I'd met up with you any time them first two years I'd have shot you like a dog. I got a whisper you was in Aranuka but when I got there you'd left. But I found your wife—her you called Pinky. She couldn't believe you'd slipped your cable for good an' there she was, a-waitin' an' a-waitin' for her king to come back. Gib, I'm free to tell you that piracy, barratry, murder an' homicide pales into insignificance compared with what you went an' done, for you broke an innercent an' trustin' heart an' hell's too good for a man that'll pull a trick like that."

"Scraggsy, Scragg y, Scraggsy," Mr. Gibney protested. "Them's awful hard words."

"I can't help it. You told me to speak out an' I'm a-doin' it. You hooks up w:th this unsophisticated, trustful woman—she ain't a woman; she's a young girl at the time—an' she ain't civilized enough to be on to your kind. So you finds it easy to make her love you. Not with the common sordid love of a white woman but with the fierce, undyin' passion o' the South Seas. An' when you get her in your clutches, her an' her whole possessions an' she's yours body an' bones, in the sight o' God an' the sight o' man—you ups an' leaves her! You throw her down like she's so much dirt an' leave her to die of a broken heart. An' she'd a-done it, too, if it hadn't a' been for the children."

Captain Scraggs was fairly thunderin' his denunciation as he concluded with: "You—you murderer! Ain't you ashamed of yourself?"

Mr. Gibney, thoroughly crushed, hung his head. "If there was kids, Scraggsy," he pleaded, "they wasn't mine, not that I knows on."

"I ain't sayin' you don't speak the truth there, Gib.

Maybe you don't know that part of it, because you left before they was born. Yes, sir, that gal had two twins—a boy an' a girl an' both that white, when I see them as yearlings, you'd never suspect they had a dab o' the tar-brush in 'em at all. The boy had red hair—provin' he was yourn, Gib."

Mr. Gibney could stand no more. He sat down on the hatch coaming and covered his face with his hard red hands. "If there was kids, Scraggsy," he sobbed, "I didn't know it. I had everything else, Scraggs, but heirs to my throne. Scraggsy, believe me or not, but if I'd had children I'd have stuck by Pinky. I wouldn't desert my own flesh an' blood, so help me."

"Well," Scraggs went on sorrowfully, "Pinky's dead an' so her troubles is over. I heard some years ago she'd passed on with consumption. But them two *hapahaole* kids o' yourn, Gib. Just think of it. Banged an' ragged around between decks, neither black nor white—too good for the natives an' not good enough for the whites. Princes on their mother's side, they been robbed o' their hereditary rights by a gang o' native roughnecks, while their own father loafs alongshore in San Francisco an' enjoys himself."

"Looky here, Scraggs," Mr. McGuffey struck in ominously. "Ain't you said about enough? Don't hit a feller when he's down."

"Well, he ain't down so low that he can't climb back. If he's got a spark o' manhood left in him he'll never rest until he goes back to Aranuka, looks up them progeny o' his, an' does his best to make amends for the past. Gib, you can't work for me aboard the *Maggie* —not if the old girl couldn't turn her screw until you

stepped aboard. Pers'nally you got a lot o' fine p'ints an' I like you, but now that I know your past——"
He threw out his hands despairingly. "It's your morals, Gib, it's your blasted morals."

"You're right, Scraggs," Mr. Gibney mumbled brokenly. "It's my duty to go look up them poor children o' mine. Bart, you stick by old Scraggsy. I owe him somethin' for showin' me my duty an' I'm lookin' to you to pay the interest on my bill till I get back with them poor kids o' mine. Until then I guess I ain't fit to 'sociate with white men."

Mr. McGuffey appeared on the point of weeping and put his arm around his old comrade in silent sympathy. Presently Mr. Gibney shook hands with him and Scraggs and, motioning them not to follow him, went ashore. Before him, in his mind's eye, there floated the picture of a South Sea Island with the nodding, tufted palms fringing the beach and the glow of a volcano against the moonlit sky. Standing on the headland, waving him a last farewell, stood the broken-hearted victim of his capricious youth, the lovely Pinky Poui-Slam-Bang. Every lineament of her beautiful features was tattooed indelibly on his memory; he knew she would haunt him forever.

He went up to the Bowhead saloon, had a drink, leaned on the end of the bar and thought it over. There was but one way to get back to Aranuka and that was to ship out before the mast on a South Sea trader—and with that thought came remembrance of the *Tropic Bird*, soon to be discharged and outward bound.

Five minutes later, Mr. Gibney was aboard the

Tropic Bird and had presented himself at her master's cabin. "Where're you bound for next trip, sir?" he inquired.

"General trading through the Marquesas, the Society Islands, and the Gilberts."

"Happen to be goin' to Aranuka, in the Gilberts?"

"You bet. Got a trading station there."

"How are you off for a good mate?"

"Got one."

"How about a second mate?"

"Got a crackerjack."

"Well, I'm not particular. I'll make a bully bo'sun, sir."

"Very well. We'll be sailing some day next week and you can sign up before the Commissioner any time you're ready. By the way, what's your name?"

"Gibney, sir. Adelbert P. Gibney."

"Any experience in the South Seas?"

"Heaps of it. I was mate for three years with Bull McGinty in the old *Dashin' Wave* more'n twenty years ago."

The master of the *Tropic Bird* blinked. "Gibney! Gibney!" he murmured. "Why, I wonder if you're the same man. Are you the chap that was king of Aranuka for six months and then abdicated for no reason at all?"

"I was, sir," Mr. Gibney confessed shamefacedly. "I'm King Gibney of Aranuka."

"What was your wife's name?"

"I called her Pinky for short."

"By Neptune, what a coincidence! Why, Gibney, I saw Her Majesty on our last trip, less than two

months ago, and she was telling me all about you.
Great old girl, Pinky, and mighty proud of the fact
that once she had a white husband. So you're King
Gibney, eh? Well, well! The world is certainly
small." The skipper chuckled, nor noticed Mr. Gibney's bulging eyes and hanging jaw. "Going back to
take over your kingdom again, Gibney?" he demanded
jocosely.

"You say you saw her *two months ago?*" Mr. Gibney bellowed. "D'ye mean to tell me she's alive?"

"I did and she's very much so."

"An' the twins. How about them?"

"There are no twins. Pinky never had any children
until after Bull McGinty took up with her, which was
after you left her. They say she doesn't think quite
as much of McGinty as she did of you. He has a dash
of dark blood and it shows up strong."

"The dog wrote me he'd married a sugar plantation
in Maui."

"Perhaps he did. If the plantation didn't produce,
though, you can bet Bull McGinty wouldn't stay put.
By the way, I have a photograph of Queen Pinky.
Snapped her with my kodak on the last trip." He
searched around in the drawer of his desk and brought
the picture forth. "Think you'd recognize Her Majesty after all these years?" he asked.

Mr. Gibney seized the picture, gazed upon it a moment, and emitted one horrified ejaculation which in
itself would have been sufficient to bar him forever from
polite society. For what he gazed upon was not the
lovely Pinky of other days, but a very fat, untidy,
ugly black woman in a calico Mother Hubbard dress.

The face, while good-natured, was wrinkled with age and dissipation; indeed, worldling that he was, Mr. Gibney saw at a glance that Pinky had grown fond of her gin. From the royal lips a huge black cigar protruded.

"I guess I won't take that bo'sun job after all," he gasped—and fled. Two minutes later, Captain Scraggs and Mr. McGuffey, were astonished to find Mr. Gibney waiting for them on deck. His face was terrible to behold; he fixed Scraggs with a searching glance and advanced upon the *Maggie's* owner with determination in every movement.

"Why—why, Gib, we thought you was headed south by this time," Scraggs sputtered, for something told him great events portended.

"You dirty dawg! You little fice! You figgered on breakin' my heart an' sendin' me off on a wild-goose chase, didn't you?" Mr. Gibney leaped and his great hand closed over Captain Scraggs's collar. "Own up," he bellowed. "Where'd you git this dope about me an' Pinky? Lie to me agin an' I'll toss you overboard," and in order to impress Captain Scraggs with the seriousness of his intentions he cuffed the latter vigorously with his open left palm.

"I was behind the potato crates this mornin' whilst you an' Mac was yarnin'," Scraggs hastened to confess. "Ow! Wow! Leggo, Gib! Can't you take a little joke?"

"Was Mac here in on the joke? Was you let in on it after I went?" Mr. Gibney demanded of his Fidus Achates.

"I was not, Gib. I don't call it no joke to wring a feller's heart like Scraggsy wrung yourn."

"In addition to makin' a three-ply jackass o' me!" Captain Scraggs cowered under the rain of ferocious slaps and attempted to fight back, but he was helpless in the huge Gibney's grasp and was forced to submit to a boxing of the ears that would have addled his brains, had he possessed any. "Now, then," Mr. Gibney roared, as he cast the skipper loose, "let that be a lesson to you to let the skeletons in my closet alone hereafter. Mac, you're not to lend Scraggsy a cent to help him out on expenses, added to which me an' you quit the *Maggie* here an' now."

"You're a devil," McGuffey growled at Scraggs, "an' sweet Christian thoughts is wasted on you."

Glowering ferociously, the worthy pair went over the rail.

CHAPTER XVI

GODLESS and wholly irreclaimable as Mr. Gibney and Mr. McGuffey might have been and doubtless were, each possessed in bounteous measure the sweetest of human attributes, to-wit: a soft, kind heart and a forgiving spirit. Creatures of impulse both, they found it absolutely impossible to nourish a grudge against Captain Scraggs, when, upon returning to Scab Johnny's boarding house that night, their host handed them a grubby note from their enemy. It was short and sweet and sounded quite sincere; Mr. Gibney read it aloud:

On Board the *Maggie*, Saturday night.

DEAR FRIENDS:

I am sorry. I apologize to you, Gib, because I hurt your fealings. I also apologize to Bart for hurting the fealings of his dear friend. Speeking of hurts you and Gib hurt me awful with your kidden when you took the *Chesapeake* away from me so I jest had to put one over on you. To er is human but to forgive is devine. After what I done I don't expect you two to come back to work ever but for God's sake don't give me the dead face when we meat agin. Remember we been shipmates once.

P. P. SCRAGGS.

"Why, the pore ol' son of a horse thief," Mr. Gibney murmured, much moved at this profound abasement. "Of course we forgive him. It ain't manly to hold a grouch after the culprit has paid his fair price for his sins. By an' large, I got a hunch, Bart, that old Scraggsy's had his lesson for once."

"If you can forgive him, I can, Gib."

"Well, he's certainly cleaned himself handsome, Bart. Telephone for a messenger boy," and Mr. Gibney sat down and wrote:

> Scraggsy, old fanciful, we're square. Forget it and come to breakfast with us at seven to-morrow at the Marigold Café. I'll order deviled lam kidneys for three. It's alright with Bart also.
>
> Yours,
>
> Gib.

This note, delivered to Captain Scraggs by the messenger boy, lifted the gloom from the latter's miserable soul and sent him home with a light heart to Mrs. Scraggs. At the Marigold Café next morning he was almost touched to observe that both Gibney and McGuffey showed up arrayed in dungarees, wherefore Scraggs knew his late enemies purposed proceeding to the *Maggie* immediately after breakfast and working in the engine room all day Sunday. Such action, when he knew both gentlemen to be the possessors of wealth far beyond the dreams of avarice, bordered so closely on the miraculous that Scraggs made a mental resolve to play fair in the future—at least as fair as the limits of his cross-grained nature would permit. He was so cheerful and happy that McGuffey, taking advantage of the situation, argued him into some minor repairs to the engine. The work was so far advanced by midnight Sunday that Scraggs realized he would get to sea by Tuesday noon, so he dismissed Gibney and McGuffey and ordered them home for some needed sleep.

McGuffey's heart was with the *Maggie's* internal economy, however, and on Monday morning he was up betimes, leaving Mr. Gibney to snore blissfully until eight o'clock.

About nine o'clock, as Mr. Gibney was on his way to the Marigold Café for breakfast, he was mildly interested, while passing the Embarcadero warehouse, to note the presence of fully a dozen seedy-looking gentlemen of undoubted Hebraic antecedents, congregated in a circle just outside the warehouse door. There was an air of suppressed excitement about this group of Jews that aroused Mr. Gibney's curiosity; so he decided to cross over and investigate, being of the opinion that possibly one of their number had fallen in a fit. He had once had an epileptic shipmate and was peculiarly expert in the handling of such cases.

Now, if the greater portion of Mr. Gibney's eventful career had not been spent at sea, he would have known, by the red flag that floated over the door, that a public auction was about to take place, and that the group of Hebrew gentlemen constituted an organization known as the Forty Thieves, whose business it was to dominate the bidding at all auctions, frighten off, or buy off, or outbid all competitors, and eventually gather unto themselves, at their own figures, all goods offered for sale.

In the centre of the group Mr. Gibney noticed a tall, lanky individual, evidently the leader, who was issuing instructions in a low voice to his henchmen. This individual, though Mr. Gibney did not know it, was the King of the Forty Thieves. As Mr. Gibney luffed into view the king eyed him with suspicion. Observing this, Mr. Gibney threw out his magnificent chest, scowled at the king, and stepped into the warehouse for all the world as if he owned it.

An oldish man with glasses—the auctioneer—was seated on a box making figures in a notebook. Him Mr. Gibney addressed.

"What's all this here?" he inquired, jerking his thumb over his shoulder at the group.

"It's an old horse sale," replied the auctioneer, without looking up.

Mr. Gibney brightened. He glanced around for the stock in trade, but observing none concluded that the old horses would be led in, one at a time, through a small door in the rear of the warehouse. Like most sailors, Mr. Gibney had a passion for horseback riding, and in a spirit of adventure he resolved to acquaint himself with the ins and outs of an old horse sale.

"How much might a man have to give for one of the critters?" he asked. "And are they worth a whoop after you get them?"

"Twenty-five cents up," was the answer. "You go it blind at an old horse sale, as a rule. Perhaps you get something that's worthless, and then again you may get something that has heaps of value, and perhaps you only pay half a dollar for it. It all depends on the bidding. I once sold an old horse to a chap and he took it home and opened it up, and what d'ye suppose he found inside?"

"Bots," replied Mr. Gibney, who prided himself on being something of a veterinarian, having spent a few months of his youth around a livery stable.

"A million dollars in Confederate greenbacks," replied the auctioneer. "Of course they didn't have any value, but just suppose they'd been U. S.?"

"That's right," agreed Mr. Gibney. "I suppose the swab that owned the horse starved him until the poor animal figgered that all's grass that's green. As the feller says, 'Truth is sometimes stranger than fiction.' If you throw in a saddle and bridle cheap, I might be induced to invest in one of your old horses, shipmate."

The auctioneer glanced quickly at Mr. Gibney, but noticing that worthy's face free from guile, he burst out laughing.

"My sea-faring friend," he said presently, "when we use the term 'old horse,' we use it figuratively. See all this freight stored here? Well, that's old horses. It's freight from the S. P. railroad that's never been called for by the consignees, and after it's in the warehouse a year and isn't called for, we have an old horse sale and auction it off to the highest bidder. Savey?"

Mr. Gibney took refuge in a lie. "Of course I do. I was just kiddin' you, my hearty." (Here Mr. Gibney's glance rested on two long heavy sugar-pine boxes, or shipping cases. Their joints at all four corners were cunningly dove-tailed and wire-strapped.) "I was a bit interested in them two boxes, an' seein' as this is a free country, I thought I'd just step in an' make a bid on them," and with the words, Mr. Gibney walked over and busied himself in an inspection of the two crates in question.

The fact of the matter was that so embarrassed was Mr. Gibney at the exposition of his ignorance that he desired to hide the confusion evident in his sun-tanned face. So he stooped over the crates and pretended to be exceedingly interested in them, hauling and pushing them about and reading the address of the consignee who had failed to call for his goods. The crates were both consigned to the Gin Seng Company, 714 Dupont Street, San Francisco. There were several Chinese characters scrawled on the top of each crate, together with the words, in English: "Oriental Goods."

As he ceased from his fake inspection of the two boxes, the King of the Forty Thieves approached and surveyed the sailor with an even greater amount of distrust and suspicion than ever. Mr. Gibney was annoyed. He disliked being stared at, so he said:

"Hello, Blumenthal, my bully boy. What's aggravatin' *you*?"

Blumenthal (since Mr. Gibney, in the sheer riot of his imagination elected to christen him Blumenthal, the name will probably suit him as well as any other) came close to Mr. Gibney and drew him aside. In a hoarse whisper he desired to know if Mr. Gibney attended the auction with the expectation of bidding on any of the packages offered for sale. Seeking to justify his presence, Mr. Gibney advised that it was his intention to bid in everything in sight; whereupon Blumenthal proceeded to explain to Mr. Gibney how impossible it would be for him, arrayed against the Forty Thieves, to buy any article at a reasonable price. Further: Blumenthal desired to inform Mr. Gibney that his (Mr. Gibney's) efforts to buy in the "old horses" would merely result in his running the prices up, for no beneficent purpose, since it was ever the practice of the Forty Thieves to permit no man to outbid them. Perhaps Mr. Gibney would be satisfied with a fair day's profit without troubling himself to hamper the Forty Thieves and interfere with their combination, and with the words, the king surreptitiously slipped Mr. Gibney a fifty-dollar greenback.

Mr. Gibney's great fist closed over the treasure, he having first, by a coy glance, satisfied himself that it was really fifty dollars. He shook hands with the king. He said:

"Blumenthal, you're a smart man. I am quite content with this fifty to keep off your course and give you a wide berth to starboard. I'm sensible enough to know when I'm licked, an' a fight without profit ain't in my line. I didn't make my money that way, Blumenthal. I'll cast off my lines and haul away from the dock," and suiting the action to the figure, Mr. Gibney departed.

He went first to the Seaboard Drug Store, where he quizzed the druggist for five minutes, after which he continued his cruise. Upon reaching the *Maggie*, he proceeded to relate in detail, and with many additional details supplied by his own imagination, the story of his morning's adventure.

"Gib," said McGuffey enviously, "you're a fool for luck."

"Luck," said Mr. Gibney, beginning to expand, "is what the feller calls a relative proposition——"

"You're wrong, Gib," interposed Captain Scraggs. "Relatives is unlucky an' expensive. Take, f'r instance, Mrs. Scraggs's mother——"

"I mean, you lunkhead," said Mr. Gibney, "that luck is found where brains grow. No brains, no luck. No luck, no brains. Lemme illustrate. A thievin' land shark makes me a present o' fifty dollars not to butt in on them two boxes I'm tellin' you about. Him an' his gang wants them two boxes. Fair crazy to get 'em. Now, don't it stand to reason that them fellers knows what's *in* them boxes, or they wouldn't give me fifty dollars to haul ship? Of course it does. However, in order to earn that fifty dollars, I got to back water. It wouldn't be playin' fair if I didn't. But that don't prevent me from puttin' two dear friends o' mine (here Mr. Gibney encircled Scraggs and McGuffey with an arm each) next to the secret which I discovers, an' if there's money in it for old Hooky that buys me off, it stands to reason that there's money in it for us three. What's to prevent you an' McGuffey from goin' up to this old horse sale an' biddin' in them two boxes for the use and benefit of Gibney, Scraggs, an' McGuffey, all share an' share alike? You can bid as high as a hundred dollars if necessary, an' still come out a thousand dollars to the good. I'm tellin' you this because I know what's n them two boxes."

McGuffey was staring fascinated at Mr. Gibney. Captain Scraggs clutched his mate's arm in a frenzied clasp.

"*What?*" they both interrogated.

"You two boys," continued Mr. Gibney with aggravating deliberation, "ain't what nobody would call dummies. You're smart men. But the trouble with both o' you boys is you ain't got no imagination. Without imagination nobody gets nowhere, unless it's out th' small end o' th' horn. Maybe you boys ain't noticed it, but my imagination is all that keeps me from goin' to jail. Now, if you two had read the address on

them two boxes, it wouldn't 'a' meant nothin' to you.
Absolutely nothin'. But with me it's different. I'm
blessed with imagination enough to see right through
them Chinamen tricks. Them two boxes is marked
"Oriental Goods" an' consigned (here Mr. Gibney
raised a grimy forefinger, and Scraggs and McGuffey
eyed it very much as if they expected it to go off at any
moment)—"them two boxes is consigned to the Gin
Seng Company, 714 Dupont Street, San Francisco."

"Well, that's up in Chinatown all right," admitted
Captain Scraggs, "but how about what's inside the
two crates?"

"Oriental goods, of course," said McGuffey.
"They're consigned to a Chinaman, an' besides, that's
what it says on the cases, don't it, Gib? Oriental
goods, Scraggs, is silks an' satins, rice, chop suey, punk,
an' idols an' fan tan layouts."

Mr. Gibney tapped gently with his horny knuckles
on the honest McGuffey's head.

"If there ain't Swiss cheese movements in that head
block o' yours, Mac, you an Scraggy can divide my
share o' these two boxes o' ginseng root between you.
Do you get it, you chuckleheaded son of an Irish potato? Gin Seng, 714 Dupont Street. Ginseng—a root
or a herb that medicine is made out of. The dictionary
says it's a Chinese panacea for exhaustion, an' I happen to know that it's worth five dollars a pound an'
that them two crates weighs a hundred and fifty pounds
each if they weighs an ounce."

His auditors stared at Mr. Gibney much as might a
pair of baseball fans at the hero of a home run with two
strikes and the bases full.

"Gawd!" muttered McGuffey.

"Great grief, Gib! Can this be possible?" gasped Captain Scraggs.

For answer, Mr. Gibney took out his fifty-dollar bill and handed it to—to McGuffey. He never trusted Captain Scraggs with anything more valuable than a pipeful of tobacco.

"Scraggsy," he said solemnly, "I'm willin' to back my imagination with my cash. You an' McGuffey hurry right over to the warehouse an' butt in on the sale when they come to them two boxes. The sale is just about startin' now. Go as high as you think you can in order to get the ginseng at a profitable figger, an' pay the auctioneer fifty dollars down to hold the sale; that will give you boys time to rush around to dig up the balance o' the money. Tack right along now, lads, while I go down the street an' get me some breakfast. I don't want Blumenthal to see me around that sale. He might get suspic'ous. After I eat I'll meet you here aboard th' *Maggie*, an' we'll divide the loot."

With a fervent hand-shake all around, the three shipmates parted.

After disposing of a hearty breakfast of devilled lamb's kidneys and coffee, Mr. Gibney invested in a ten-cent Sailor's Delight and strolled down to the *Maggie*. Neils Halvorsen, the lone deckhand, was aboard, and the moment Mr. Gibney trod the *Maggie's* deck once more as mate, he exercised his prerogative to order Neils ashore for the remainder of the day. Since Halvorsen was not in on the ginseng deal, Mr. Gibney concluded that it would be just as well to have him out of

the way should Scraggs and McGuffey appear unex-
pectedly with the two cases of ginseng.

For an hour Mr. Gibney sat on the stern bitts and
ruminated over a few advantageous plans that had
occurred to him for the investment of his share of the
deal should Scraggs and McGuffey succeed in landing
what Mr. Gibney termed "the loot." About eleven
o'clock an express wagon drove in on the dock, and the
mate's dreams were pleasantly interrupted by a gleeful
shout from Captain Scraggs, on the lookout forward
with the driver. McGuffey sat on top of the two
cases with his legs dangling over the end of the wagon.
He was the picture of contentment.

Mr. Gibney hurried forward, threw out the gang-
plank, and assisted McGuffey in carrying both crates
aboard the *Maggie* and into her little cabin. Captain
Scraggs thereupon dismissed the expressman, and all
three partners gathered around the dining-room table,
upon which the boxes rested.

"Well, Scraggsy, old pal, old scout, old socks, I see
you've delivered the goods," said Mr. Gibney, batting
the skipper across the cabin with an affectionate slap
on the shoulder.

"I did," said Scraggs—and cursed Mr. Gibney's
demonstrativeness. "Here's the bill o' sale all regular.
McGuffey has the change. That bunch o' Israelites
run th' price up to $10.00 each on these two crates o'
ginseng, but when they see we're determined to have
'em an' ain't interested in nothin' else, they lets 'em go
to us. McGuffey, my *dear* boy, whatever are you
a-doin' there—standin' around with your teeth in
your mouth? Skip down into th' engine room and

bring up a hammer an' a col' chisel. We'll open her up an' inspect th' swag."

Upon McGuffey's return, Mr. Gibney took charge. He drove the chisel under the lid of the nearest crate, and prepared to pry it loose. Suddenly he paused. A thought had occurred to him.

"Gentlemen," he said (McGuffey nodded his head approvingly), "this world is full o' sorrers an' disappointments, an' it may well be that these two cases don't contain even so much as a smell o' ginseng after all. It may be that they are really Oriental goods. What I want distinctly understood is this: no matter what's inside, we share equally in the profits, even if they turn out to be losses. That's understood an' agreed to, ain't it?"

Captain Scraggs and McGuffey indicated that it was.

"There's a element o' mystery about these two boxes," continued Mr. Gibney, "that fascinates me. They sets my imagination a-workin' an' joggles up all my sportin' instincts. Now, just to make it interestin' an' add a spice t' th' grand openin', I'm willin' to bet again my own best judgment an' lay you even money, Scraggsy, that it ain't ginseng but Oriental goods."

"I'll go you five dollars, just f'r ducks," responded Captain Scraggs heartily. "McGuffey to hold the stakes an' decide the bet."

"Done," replied Mr. Gibney. The money was placed in McGuffey's hands, and a moment later, with a mighty effort, Mr. Gibney pried off the lid of the crate. Captain Scraggs had his head inside the box a fifth of a second later.

"Sealed zinc box inside," he announced. "Get a can opener, Gib, my boy."

"Ginseng, for a thousand," mourned Mr. Gibney. "Scraggsy, you're five dollars of my money to the good. Ginseng always comes packed in air-tight boxes."

He produced a can opener from the cabin locker and fell to his work on a corner of the hermetically sealed box. As he drove in the point of the can opener, he paused, hammer in hand, and gazed solemnly at Scraggs and McGuffey.

"Gentlemen" (again McGuffey nodded approvingly), "do you know what a vacuum is?"

"I know," replied the imperturbable McGuffey. "A vacuum is an empty hole that ain't got nothin' in it."

"Correct," said Mr. Gibney. "My head is a vacuum. Me talkin' about ginseng root! Why, I must have water on the brain! Ginseng be doggoned! *It's opium!*"

Captain Scraggs was forced to grab the seat of his chair in order to keep himself from jumping up and clasping Mr. Gibney around the neck.

"Forty dollars a pound," he gasped. "Gib—Gib, my *dear* boy—you've made us wealthy——"

Quickly Mr. Gibney ran the can opener around the edges of one corner of the zinc box, inserted the claws of the hammer into the opening, and with a quick, melodramatic twist, bent back the angle thus formed.

Mr. Gibney was the first to get a peep inside.

"Great snakes!" he yelled, and fell back against the cabin wall. A hoarse scream of rage and horror broke from Captain Scraggs. In his eagerness he had driven his head so deep into the box that he came within an inch of kissing what the box contained—which happened to be nothing more nor less than a dead Chinaman! Mr. McGuffey, always slow and unimaginative, shouldered the skipper aside, and calmly surveyed the ghastly apparition.

"Twig the yellow beggar, will you, Gib?" said McGuffey; "one eye half open for all the world like he was winkin' at us an' enjoyin' th' joke."

Not a muscle twitched in McGuffey's Hibernian countenance. He scratched his head for a moment, as a sort of first aid to memory, then turned and handed Mr. Gibney ten dollars.

"You win, Gib. It's Oriental goods, sure enough."

"Robber!" shrieked Captain Scraggs, and flew at Mr. Gibney's throat. The sight reminded McGuffey of a terrier worrying a mastiff. Nevertheless, Mr. Gibney was still so unnerved at the discovery of the horrible contents of the box that, despite his gigantic proportions, he was well-nigh helpless.

"McGuffey, you swab," he yelled. "Pluck this maritime outlaw off my neck. He's tearin' my windpipe out by th' roots."

McGuffey choked Captain Scraggs until he reluctantly let go Mr. Gibney; whereupon all three fled from the cabin as from a pestilence, and gathered, an angry and disappointed group, out on deck.

"Opium!" jeered Captain Scraggs, with tears of rage in his voice. "Ginseng! You and your imagination, you swine, you! Get off my ship, you lout, or I'll murder you."

"'Great snakes,' he
yelled — and fell back
against the cabin wall"

Mr. Gibney hung his head.

"Scraggsy—an' you, too, McGuffey—I got to admit that this here is one on Adelbert P. Gibney. I—I——"

"Oh, hear him," shrilled Captain Scraggs. "One on him! It's two on you, you bloody-handed ragpicker. I suppose that other case contains opium, too! If there ain't another dead corpse in No. 2 case I hope my teeth may drop overboard."

"Shut up!" bellowed Mr. Gibney, in a towering rage. "What howl have you got comin'? They're my Chinamen, ain't they? I paid for 'em like a man, didn't I? All right, then. I'll keep them two Chinamen. You two ain't out a cent yet, an' as for this five I wins off you, Scraggs, it's blood money, that's what it is, an' I hereby gives it back to you. Now, quit yer whinin', or by the tail o' the Great Sacred Bull, I'll lock you up all night in th' cabin along o' them two defunct Celestials."

Captain Scraggs "shut up" promptly, and contented himself with glowering at Mr. Gibney. The mate sat down on the hatch coaming, lit his pipe, and gave himself up to meditation for fully five minutes, at the end of which time McGuffey was aware that his imagination was about to come to the front once more.

"Well, gentlemen" (again McGuffey nodded approvingly), "I bet I get my twenty bucks back outer them two Chinks," he announced presently.

"How'll yer do it?" inquired McGuffey politely.

"How'll I do it? Easy as fallin' through an open hatch. I'm a-goin' t' keep them two stiffs in th' boxes until dark, an' then I'm a-goin' to take 'em out, bend a rope around their middle, drop 'em overboard an' anchor 'em there all night. I see th' lad we opens up in No. 1 case has had a beautiful job o' embalmin' done on him, but if I let them soak all night, like a mackerel, they'll limber up an' look kinder fresh. Then first thing in th' mornin' I'll telephone th' coroner an' tell him I found two floaters out in th' bay an' for him to come an' get 'em. I been along the waterfront long enough t' know that th' lad that picks up a floater gets a reward o' ten dollars from th' city. You can bet that Adelbert P. Gibney breaks even on th' deal, all right."

"Gib, my *dear* boy," said Captain Scraggs admiringly. "I apologize for my actions of a few minutes ago. I was unstrung. You're still mate o' th' American steamer *Maggie*, an' as such, welcome to th' ship. All I ask is that you nail up your property, Gib, an' remove it from th' dinin' room table. I want to remind you, however, Gib, that as shipmates me an' McGuffey don't stand for you shoulderin' any loss on them two cases o'—Oriental goods. We was t' share th' gains, if any, an' likewise th' losses."

"That's right," said McGuffey, "fair an' square. No bellyachin' between shipmates. Me an' Scraggs each owns one-third o' them diseased Chinks, an' we each stands one-third o' th' loss, if any."

"But there won't be no loss," protested Mr. Gibney.

"Drayage charges, Gib, drayage charges. We give a man a dollar to tow 'em down t' th' ship."

"Forget it," answered Mr. Gibney magnanimously, "an' let's go over an' get a drink. I'm all shook up."

After the partners had partaken of a sufficient quantity of nerve tonic, Mr. Gibney suddenly recollected that he had to go over to Market Street and redeem the sextant which he had pawned several days before. And since McGuffey knew, from ocular evidence, that Mr. Gibney was "flush," he decided to accompany the mate and preserve him from temptation. There was safety in numbers, he reasoned. Captain Scraggs said he thought he'd go back to the *Maggie*. He had forgotten to lock the cabin door.

CHAPTER XVII

HAD either Mr. Gibney or McGuffey been watching Captain Scraggs for the next twenty minutes they would have been much puzzled to account for that worthy's actions. First he dodged around the block into Drumm Street, and then ran down Drumm to California, where he climbed aboard a cable car and rode up into Chinatown. Arrived at Dupont Street he alighted and walked up that interesting thoroughfare until he came to No. 714. He glanced at a sign over the door and was aware that he stood before the entrance to the offices of the Chinese Six Companies, so he climbed upstairs and inquired for Gin Seng, who presently made his appearance.

Gin Seng, a very nice, fat Chinaman, arrayed in a flowing silk gown, begged, in pidgin-English, to know in what manner he could be of service.

"Me heap big captain, allee same ship," began Captain Scraggs. "On board ship two China boys have got." (Here Captain Scraggs winked knowingly.) "China boy no speak English——"

"That being the case," interposed Gin Seng, "I presume that you and I understand each other, so let's cut out the pidgin-English. Do I understand that you are engaged in evading the immigration laws?"

"Exactly," Captain Scraggs managed to gasp, as soon as he could recover from his astonishment. "They

160

showed me your name an' address, an' they won't leave th' ship, where I got 'em locked up in my cabin, until you come an' take 'em away. Couple o' relatives of yours, I should imagine."

Gin Seng smiled his bland Chinese smile. He had frequent dealings with ship masters engaged in the dangerous though lucrative trade of smuggling Chinese into the United States, and while he had not received advice of this particular shipment, he decided to go with Captain Scraggs to Jackson Street bulkhead and see if he could not be of some use to his countrymen.

As Captain Scraggs and his Chinese companion approached the wharf the skipper glanced warily about. He had small fear that either Gibney or McGuffey would show up for an hour, for he knew that Mr. Gibney had money in his possession. However, he decided to take no chances, and scouted the vicinity thoroughly before venturing aboard the *Maggie*. These actions served but to increase the respect of Gin Seng for the master of the *Maggie* and confirmed him in his belief that the *Maggie* was a smuggler.

Captain Scraggs took his visitor inside the little cabin, carefully locked and bolted the door, lifted the zinc flap back from the top of the crate of "Oriental goods," and displayed the face of the dead Chinaman. Also he pointed to the Chinese characters on the wooden lid of the crate.

"What does these hen scratches mean?" demanded Scraggs.

"This man is named Ah Ghow and he belongs to the Hop Sing tong."

"How about his pal here?"

"That man is evidently Ng Chong Yip. He is also a Hop Sing man."

Captain Scraggs wrote it down. "All right," he said cheerily; "much obliged. Now, what I want to know is what the Hop Sing tong means by shipping the departed brethren by freight? They go to work an' fix 'em up nice so's they'll keep, packs 'em away in a zinc coffin, inside a nice plain wood box, labels 'em 'Oriental goods,' and consigns 'em to the Gin Seng Company, 714 Dupont Street, San Francisco. Now why are these two countrymen o' yours shipped by freight— where, by the way, they goes astray, for some reason that I don't know nothin' about, an' I buys 'em up at a old horse sale?"

Gin Seng shrugged his shoulders and replied that he didn't understand.

"You lie," snarled Captain Scraggs. "You savey all right, you fat old idol, you! It's because if the railroad company knew these two boxes contained dead corpses they'd a-soaked the relatives, which is you, one full fare each from wherever these two dead ones comes from, just the same as though they was alive an' well. But you has 'em shipped by freight, an' aims to spend a dollar an' thirty cents each on 'em, by markin' 'em 'Oriental Goods.' Helluva way to treat a relation. Now, looky here, you bloody heathen. It'll cost you just five hundred dollars to recover these two stiffs, an' close my mouth. If you don't come through I'll make a belch t' th' newspapers an' they'll keel haul an' skulldrag th' Chinese Six Companies an' the Hop Sing tong through the courts for evadin' th' laws o' th' Interstate Commerce Commission, an'

make 'em look like monkeys generally. An' then th'
police'll get wind of it. Savey, policee-man, you fat
old murderer? Th' price I'm askin' is cheap, Charley.
How do I know but what these two poor boys has been
murdered in cold blood? There's somethin' rotten
in Denmark, my bully boy, an' you'll save time an'
trouble an' money by diggin' up five hundred dollars."

Gin Seng said he would go back to Chinatown and
consult with his company. For reasons of his own he
was badly frightened.

Scarce had he departed before the watchful eye of
Captain Scraggs observed Mr. Gibney and McGuffey
in the offing, a block away. When they came aboard
they found Captain Scraggs on top of the house, seated
on an upturned fire bucket, smoking pensively and gazing across the bay with an assumption of lamblike inno-
cence on his fox face.

At the suggestion of Scraggs, Gibney and McGuffey
nailed up the box of "Oriental Goods," set both boxes
out on the main deck, aft, and covered them with a
tarpaulin. For about an hour thereafter all three sat
around the little cabin table, talking, and presently
it became evident, to Mr. Gibney's practiced eye, that
Captain Scraggs had something on his mind. Mr.
Gibney, suspecting that it could be nothing honest,
was surprised, to say the least, when Captain Scraggs
made a clean breast of his proposition.

"Gib—an' you, too, McGuffey. I been thinkin'
this thing over, an' as master o' this ship an' the one
who does the biddin' in o' these two Chinks at th' sale,
it's up to me t' try an' bring you both out with a profit,
an' I think th' sellin' should be left to me. I won't hide

nothin' from you boys. I'm a-willin' to take a chance that I can sell them two cadavers to some horsepital f'r dissection purposes, an' get more outer th' deal than you can, Gib, by passin' 'em off as floaters. I'm a-willin' to give you an' McGuffey a five-dollar profit over an' above your investment, an' take over th' property myself, just f'r a flyer, an' to sorter add a sportin' interest to an otherwise humdrum life. How about it, lads?"

"You can have my fraction," said McGuffey promptly; whereupon Captain Scraggs produced the requisite amount of cash and immediately became the owner of a two-thirds' interest.

Mr. Gibney was a trifle mystified. He knew Scraggs well enough to know that the skipper never made a move until he had everything planned ahead to a nicety. The mate was not above making five dollars on the day's work, but some sixth sense told him that Captain Scraggs was framing up a deal designed to cheat him and McGuffey out of a large and legitimate profit. Sooner than sell to Captain Scraggs, therefore, and enable him to unload at an unknown profit, Mr. Gibney resolved to retain his one-third interest, even if he had to go to jail for it. So he informed Captain Scraggs that he thought he'd hold on to his share for a day or two.

"But, Gib, my *dear* boy," explained Scraggs, "you ain't got a word to say about this deal no more. Don't you realize that I hold a controllin' interest an' that you must bow to th' vote o' th' majority?"

"Don't I, though," blustered Mr. Gibney. "Well, just let me catch you luggin' off my property without

my consent—in writin'—an' we'll see who does all th'
bowin', Scraggsy. I'll cut your greedy little heart out,
that's what I'll do."

"Well, then," said Scraggs, "you get your blasted
property off'n my ship, an' get yourself off an' don't
never come back." :

"F'r th' love o' common sense," bawled Mr. Gib-
ney, "what do you think I am? A butcher? How am
I to get away with a third o' two dead Chinamen?
Ain't you got no reason to you at all, Scraggs?"

"Very well, then," replied the triumphant Scraggs,
"if you won't sell, then buy out my interest an' rid
my ship o' this contaminatin' encumbrance."

"I won't buy an' I won't sell—leastways until I've
had time to consider," replied Mr. Gibney. "I smell a
rat somewheres, Scraggs, an' I don't intend to be beat
outer my rights. Moreover, I question McGuffey's
right to dispose o' his one-third without asking my
advice an' consent, as th' promoter o' this deal, f'r th'
reason that by his act he aids an' abets th' formation
o' a trust, creates a monopoly, an' blocks th' wheels o'
free trade; all of which is agin public policy an' don't
go in no court o' law. McGuffey, give Scraggs back
his money an' keep your interest. When any o' th'
parties hereto can rig up a sale o' these two Celestials,
it's his duty to let his shipmates in on th' same. He
may exact a five per cent. commission for his effort,
if he wants t' be rotten mean, an' th' company has t'
pay it t' him, but otherwise we all whacks up, share an'
share alike, on profits an' losses."

"Right you are, Gib, my hearty," responded Mc-
Guffey. "Scraggs, we'll just call that sale off, f'r th'

sake o' harmony. Here's your money. I ain't chokin'
off Gibney's steam at no time, not if I know it."

"You infernal river rats," snarled Scraggs, "I'll—
I'll——"

"Stow it," Mr. Gibney commanded. "I never did
see the like o' you, Scraggs. You're all right an' good
comp'ny right up until somebody declines to let you
have your own way—an' then, right off, you fly in a
rage an' git abusive. I'm gittin' weary o' bein' ordered off your dirty little scow an' then bein' invited
back agin. One o' these bright days, when you start
pulling for the fiftieth time the modern parable o' the
Prodigal Son an' the Fatted Calf, I'm goin' to walk out
o' the cast for keeps. Now, if I was you an' valued the
services of a good navigatin' officer an' a good engineer,
I'd just take a little run along the waterfront an' cool
off. Somethin' tells me that if you stick around here
argyin' with me you'll come to grief—which same is no
idle fancy, you snipe."

Captain Scraggs hastened to take advantage of this
invitation, for it stood him in hand to do so. His
plans, due to Mr. Gibney's inexplicable obstinacy, had
failed to mature and he was fearful that Gin Seng, after
consulting with his tong, might return to the *Maggie*
at any moment and ruin the deal by exposing it to
Gibney and McGuffey; therefore Scraggs resolved to
run up to 714 Dupont Street and warn Gin Seng to let
the matter lie in abeyance for a couple of days, alleging
as an excuse that he was being subjected, for some
unknown reason, to police surveillance. Scraggs decided that after three days the presence of the two dead
Chinamen aboard the *Maggie* would commence to

wear on the Gibney nerves and the deadlock over the final disposition of their gruesome purchase would result in Gibney and McGuffey harkening to reason and accepting a profitable compromise. If it should cost him a leg, Captain Scraggs was resolved to make those two corpses pay for the repairs in the *Maggie's* engine room.

Following his departure, Messrs. Gibney and McGuffey sat on deck smoking and striving to fathom the hidden design back of Scraggs's offer to buy them out. "He's got his lines fast somewhere—you can bank on that," was Mr. Gibney's comment, for he knew that Scraggs never made a move that meant parting with money until he was certain he saw that money, somewhat augmented, returning to him. "While we was away he rigged up some kind of a deal, Bart. It stands to reason it was a mighty profitable deal, too, otherwise old Scraggsy wouldn't have flew into such a rage when I blocked him. My imagination may be a bit off the course at times, Bart, but in general, if there's a deal whale floatin' around the ship I can smell it."

"What do you make out o' that fat Chinaman cruisin' down the bulkhead in an express wagon an' another Chinaman settin' up on the bridge with him?" McGuffey demanded. "Seems to me they're comin', bows on, for the *Maggie*."

"They tell me to deduct somethin', Bart. Wait a minute till we see if they're comin' aboard. If they are——"

"They're goin' to make a landin', Gib."

"—then I deduct that this body-snatchin' Scraggs——"

"They're boardin' us, Gib."

"—has arranged with yon fat Chinaman to relieve us o' the unwelcome presence of his defunct friends. *He's gone an' hunted up the relatives an' made 'em come across*—that's what he's done. The dirty, low, schemin' granddaddy of all the foxes in Christendom! Wasn't I the numbskull not to think of it myself?"

"'Tain't too late to mend your ways, Gib. I don't see Scraggs nowhere," Mr. McGuffey suggested promptly. "All that remains for me an' you to do, Gib, is to imagine the price, collect the money, an' declare a dividend. Quick, Gib! What'll we ask him?"

"I'll fish around an' see what figger Scraggs charged him," the cautious Gibney replied and stepped to the rail to meet Gin Seng, for it was indeed he.

"Sow-see, sow-see, hun-gay," Mr Gibney saluted the Chinaman in a facetious attempt to talk the latter's language. "Hello, there, John Chinaman. How's your liver? Captain he allee same get tired; he no waitee. Wha's mallah, John. Too long time you no come. You heap lazy all time."

Gin Seng smiled his bland, inscrutable Chinese smile. "You ketchum two China boy in box?" he queried.

"We have," boomed McGuffey, "an' beautiful specimens they be."

"No money, no China boy," Gibney added firmly.

"Money have got. Too muchee money you wantee. No can do. Me pay two hundred dollah. Five hundred dollah heap muchee. No have got."

"Nothin' doin', John. Five hundred dollars an' not a penny less. Put up the dough or beat it."

Gin Seng expostulated, lied, evaded, and all but wept, but Mr. Gibney was obdurate and eventually the China-man paid over the money and departed with the re-mains of his countrymen. "I knew he'd come through, Bart," Mr. Gibney declared. "They got to ship them stiffs to China to rest alongside their ancestors or be in Dutch with the sperrits o' the departed forever after."

"Do we have to split this swag with that dirty Scraggs?" McGuffey wanted to know. "Seein' as how he tried to give us the double cross——"

"We'll fix Scraggsy—all ship-shape an' legal so's he won't have no comeback. Quick, grab some o' them empty potato crates an' pile 'em here where the stiffs was lyin' an' cover 'em up with the tarpaulin. I don't want Scraggsy to think the corpses is gone until I've hooked him good and plenty."

The stage was set in a few minutes and the conspir-ators set themselves to await the return of Scraggs. They had not long to wait. Upon his arrival at Gin Seng's place of business Captain Scraggs had been in-formed that Gin Seng had gone out twenty minutes before, and further inquiry revealed the portentous fact that he had departed in an express wagon. Con-sumed with misgivings of disaster, Scraggs returned to the *Maggie* as fast as the California Street cable car and his legs could carry him; as he came aboard his anxious glance sought the tarpaulin-covered boxes on deck and at sight of them his mental thermometer rose at once. In the cabin he found Mr. Gibney and Mc-Guffey playing cribbage. They laid down their hands as Scraggs entered.

"Well, are you all cooled out an' willin' to listen to reason, Scraggsy, old business man?" Gibney greeted him cheerfully.

"None more so, Gib. If you've got a proposition to submit, fire away."

"That's comfortin', Scraggsy. Well, me an' Bart's been chewing over your proposition to buy out our interest in them two Chinks, an' as the upshot of our talk we made up our minds to sell, but not for no measly little five bucks' profit. Now, Scraggsy, you old he-devil, on your honour as between shipmates, you got to admit five dollars ain't hardly worth considerin'. Come down to earth now. You know blamed well you're expectin' to pull out with a neat profit an' that you can afford to boost that five-dollar ante. What would you consider a fair price for a one-third interest? Be honest an' fair, Scraggsy."

Captain Scraggs sat down, beaming. With Mr. Gibney in this frame of mind he knew he could do anything with him. "Well, now, Gib, my *dear* boy, if a man was to get twenty-five dollars for his interest, I should say he oughtn't to have no kick comin'. I know I wouldn't."

"If you was sellin' your interest—imagine, now, that you're me an' I'm you—would you be satisfied to sell for twenty-five dollars?"

"I certainly would, Gib, my boy. Why, that's almost four hundred per cent. profit, an' any man that'd turn up his nose at a four hundred per cent. profit ought to go an' have his head examined by a competent nut doctor."

"Well, if you feel that way about it, all right, Scraggsy," Mr. Gibney replied slowly and put his hand in his pocket. "As I remarked previous, while you're away me an' Bart gets chewin' over the proposition an' decides we'll sell. An' to show you what a funny world this is, while me an' Bart's settin' on deck a-waitin' for you to come back an' close with us, along breezes a fat old Chinaman in an express wagon an' offers to buy them two cases of Oriental goods. He makes me an' Mac what we considers a fair offer for our two-thirds. You ain't around to offer suggestions an' as it's a take-it-or-leave-it proposition an' two-thirds o' the stock is represented in me an' Mac an' accordin' to your rulin' the majority's got the decidin' vote, we ups an' smothers his offer. Lemme see, now," he continued, and got out a stub of lead pencil with which he commenced figuring on the white oilcloth table cover. "We paid twenty dollars for them two derelicts an' a dollar towage. That's twenty-one dollars, an' a third o' twenty-one is seven, an' seven dollars from twenty-five leaves eighteen dollars comin' to you. Here's your eighteen dollars, Scraggsy, you lucky old vagabond—all clear profit on a neat day's work, no expense, no investment, no back-breakin' interest charges or overhead, an' sold out at your own figger."

Captain Scraggs's face was a study in conflicting emotions as he raked in the eighteen dollars. "Thanks, Gib," he said frigidly.

"Me an' Gib's goin' ashore for lunch at the Marigold Café," McGuffey announced presently, in order to break the horrible silence that followed Scraggsy's crushing defeat. "I'm willin' to spend some o' my profits on the deal an' blow you to a lunch with a small bottle o' Dago Red thrown in. How about it, Scraggs?"

"I'm on." Scraggs sought to throw off his gloom and appear sprightly. "What'd you peddle them two cadavers for, Gib?"

Mr. Gibney grinned broadly but did not answer. In effect, his grin informed Scraggs that *that* was none of the latter's business—and Scraggs assimilated the hint. "Well, at any rate, Gib, whatever you soaked him, it was a mighty good sale an' I congratulate you. I think mebbe I might ha' done a little better myself, but then it ain't every day a feller can turn an eighteen-dollar trick on a corpse."

"Comin' to lunch with us?" McGuffey demanded.

"Sure. Wait a minute till I run forward an' see if the lines is all fast."

He stepped out of the cabin and presently Gibney and McGuffey were conscious of a rapid succession of thuds on the deck. Gibney winked at McGuffey.

"'Nother new hat gone to hell," murmured McGuffey.

CHAPTER XVIII

IT WAS fully a week before Captain Scraggs's mental hemorrhage, brought on every time his mind reverted to his loss on the "ginseng" deal, ceased. During all of that period his peregrinations around the *Maggie* were as those of one for whom the sweets of existence had turned to wormwood and vinegar. Mr. Gibney confided to McGuffey that it was a toss-up whether the old man was meditating murder or suicide. In fact, so depressed was Captain Scraggs that he lacked absolutely the ambition to "rag" his associates; observing which Mr. McGuffey vouchsafed the opinion that perhaps Scraggsy was "teched a mite in his head-block."

"Don't you think it," Mr. Gibney warned. "If old Scraggsy's crazy he's crazy like a fox. What's rilin' him is the knowledge that he's stung to the heart an' can't admit it without at the same time admittin' he'd cooked up a deal to double-cross us. He's just a-bustin' with the thoughts that's accumulatin' inside him. Right now he'd drown his sorrers in red liquor if he could afford it."

"He's troubled financially, Gib."

"Well, you know who troubled him, don't you, Bart?"

"I mean about the cost o' them repairs in the engine room. Unless he can come through in thirty days with the balance he owes, the boiler people are goin' to libel the *Maggie* to protect their claim."

Mr. Gibney arched his bushy eyebrows. "How do you know?" he demanded.

"He was a-tellin' me," Mr. McGuffey admitted weakly.

"Well, he wasn't a-tellin' me." Mr. Gibney's tones were ominous; he glared at his friend suspiciously as from the *Maggie's* cabin issued forth Scraggsy's voice raised in song.

"Hello! The old boy's thermometer's gone up, Bart. Listen at him. 'Ever o' thee he's fondly dreamin'.' Somethin's busted the spell an' I'll bet a cooky it was ready cash." He menaced Mr. McGuffey with a rigid index finger. "Bart," he demanded, "did you loan Scraggsy some money?"

The honest McGuffey hung his head. "A little bit," he replied childishly.

"What d'ye call a little bit?"

"Three hundred dollars, Gib."

"Secured?"

'He gimme his note at eight per cent. The savin's bank only pays four."

"Is the note secured by endorsement or collateral?"

"No."

"Hum-m-m! Strange you didn't say nothin' to me about this till I had to pry it out o' you, Bart. How about you?"

"Well, Scraggsy was feelin' so dog-goned blue——"

"The truth," Mr. Gibney insisted firmly, "the truth, Bart."

"Well, Scraggsy asked me not to say anythin' to you about it."

"Sure. He knew I'd kill the deal. He knew better'n to try to nick me for three hundred bucks on his
danged, worthless note. Bart, why'd you do it?"

"Oh, hell, Gib, be a good feller," poor McGuffey
pleaded. "Don't be too hard on ol' Scraggsy."

"We're discussin' *you*, Bart. 'Pears to me you've
sort o' lost confidence in your old shipmate, ain't you?
'Pears that way to me when you act sneaky like."

McGuffey bridled. "I ain't a sneak."

"A rose by any other name'd be just as sweet," Mr.
Gibney quoted. "You poor, misguided simp. If you
ever see that three hundred dollars again you'll be a lot
older'n you are now. However, that ain't none o' my
business. The fact remains, Bart, that you conspired
with Scraggsy to keep things away from me, which
shows you ain't the man I thought you were, so from
now on you go your way an' I'll go mine."

"I got a right to do as I blasted please with my
own money," McGuffey defended hotly. "I ain't no
child to be lectured to."

"Considerin' the fact that you wouldn't have had the
money to lend if it hadn't been for me, I allow I'm in-
sulted when you use the said money to give aid an' com-
fort to my enemy. I'm through."

McGuffey, smothered in guilt, felt nevertheless that
he had to stand by his guns, so to speak. "Stay through,
if you feel like it," he retorted. "Where d'ye get
that chatter? Ain't I free, white, an' twenty-one year
old?"

Mr. Gibney was really hurt. "You poor boob," he
murmured. "It's the old game o' settin' a beggar on
horseback an' seein' him ride to the devil, or slippin' a

gold ring in a pig's nose. An' I figured you was my friend!"

"Well, ain't I?"

"Fooey! Fooey! Don't talk to me. You'd sell out your own mother."

"Them's fightin' words, Gib."

"Shut up."

"Gib, you tryin' to pick a fight with me?"

"No, but I would if I thought I wouldn't git a foot-race instead," Gibney rejoined scathingly. "Cripes, what a double-crossin' I been handed! Honest, Bart, when it comes to that sort o' work Scraggs is in his infancy. You sure take the cake."

"I ain't got the heart to clout you an' make you eat them words," Mr. McGuffey declared sorrowfully.

"You mean you ain't got the guts," Mr. Gibney corrected him. "Bart, I got your number. Good-bye."

Mr. McGuffey had a wild impulse to cast himself upon the Gibney neck and weep, but his honour forbade any such weakness. So he invited Mr. Gibney to betake himself to a region several degrees hotter than the *Maggie's* engine room; then, because he feared to linger and develop a sentimental weakness, he turned his back abruptly and descended to the said engine room.

On his part, Adelbert P. Gibney entered the cabin and glared long and menacingly at Captain Scraggs. "I'll have my time," he growled presently. "Give it to me an' give it quick."

The very intonation of his voice warned Scraggs that the present was not a time for argument or trifling. Silently he paid Mr. Gibney the money due him; in equal silence the navigating officer went to the pilot house, unscrewed his framed certificate from the wall, packed it with his few belongings, and departed for Scab Johnny's boarding house.

"Hello," Scab Johnny saluted him at his entrance. "Quit the *Maggie ?*"

Mr. Gibney nodded.

"Want a trip to the dark blue?"

"Lead me to it," mumbled Mr. Gibney.

"It'll cost you twenty dollars, Gib. Chief mate on the *Rose of Sharon*, bound for the Galapagos Islands sealing."

"I'll take it, Johnny." Mr. Gibney threw over a twenty-dollar bill, went to his room, packed all of his belongings, paid his bill to Scab Johnny, and within the hour was aboard the schooner *Rose of Sharon*. Two hours later they towed out with the tide.

Poor McGuffey was stunned when he heard the news that night from Scab Johnny. When he retailed the information to Scraggs next morning, Scraggs was equally perturbed. He guessed that McGuffey and Gibney had quarrelled and he had the poor judgment to ask McGuffey the cause of the row. Instantly, Mc-Guffey informed him that that was none of his dad-fetched business—and the incident was closed.

The three months that followed were the most harrowing of McGuffey's life. Captain Scraggs knew his engineer would not resign while he, Scraggs, owed him three hundred dollars; wherefore he was not too particular to put a bridle on his tongue when things appeared to go wrong. McGuffey longed to kill him, but dared not. When, eventually, the railroad had been extended sufficiently far down the coast to enable the farmers to haul their goods to the railroad in trucks, the *Maggie* automatically went out of the green-pea trade; simultaneously, Captain Scraggs's note to McGuffey fell due and the engineer demanded payment. Scraggs demurred, pleading poverty, but Mr. McGuffey assumed such a threatening attitude that reluctantly Scraggs paid him a hundred and fifty dollars on account, and McGuffey extended the balance one year—and quit.

"See that you got that hundred and fifty an' the interest in your jeans the next time we meet," he warned Scraggs as he went overside.

Time passed. For a month the *Maggie* plied regularly between Bodega Bay and San Francisco in an endeavour to work up some business in farm and dairy produce, but a gasoline schooner cut in on the run and declared a rate war, whereupon the *Maggie* turned her blunt nose riverward and for a brief period essayed some towing and general freighting on the Sacramento and San Joaquin. It was unprofitable, however, and at last Captain Scraggs was forced to lay his darling little *Maggie* up and take a job as chief officer of the ferry steamer *Encinal*, plying between San Francisco and Oakland. In the meantime, Mr. McGuffey, after two barren months "on the beach," landed a job as second assistant on a Standard Oil tanker running to the West Coast, while thrifty Neils Halvorsen invested the savings of ten years in a bay scow known as the *Willie and Annie*, arrogated to himself the title of captain, and proceeded to freight hay, grain, and paving stones from Petaluma.

The old joyous days of the green-pea trade were gone

forever, and many a night, as Captain Scraggs paced the deck of the ferryboat, watching the ferry tower loom into view, or the scattered lights along the Alameda shore, he thought longingly of the old *Maggie*, laid away, perhaps forever, and slowly rotting in the muddy waters of the Sacramento. And he thought of Mr. Gibney, too, away off under the tropic stars, leading the care-free life of a real sailor at last, and of Bartholomew McGuffey, imbibing "pulque" in the "cantina" of some disreputable café. Captain Scraggs never knew how badly he was going to miss them both until they were gone, and he had nobody to fight with except Mrs. Scraggs; and when Mrs. Scraggs (to quote Captain Scraggs) "slipped her cable" in her forty-third year, Captain Scraggs felt singularly lonesome and in a mood to accept eagerly any deviltry that might offer.

Upon a night, which happened to be Scraggs's night off, and when he was particularly lonely and inclined to drown his sorrows in the Bowhead saloon, he was approached by Scab Johnny, and invited to repair to the latter's dingy office for the purpose of discussing what Scab Johnny guardedly referred to as a "proposition."

Upon arrival at the office, Captain Scraggs was introduced to a small, fierce-looking gentleman of tropical appearance, who owned to the name of Don Manuel Garcia Lopez. Scab Johnny first pledged Captain Scraggs to absolute secrecy, and made him swear by the honour of his mother and the bones of his father not to divulge a word of what he was about to tell him.

Scab Johnny was short and to the point. He stated that as Captain Scraggs was doubtless aware, if he merused the daily papers at all, there was a revolution raging in Mexico. His friend, Señor Lopez, represented the under-dogs in the disturbance, and was anxious to secure a ship and a nervy sea captain to land a shipment of arms in Lower California. It appeared that at a sale of condemned army goods held at the arsenal at Benicia, Señor Lopez had, through Scab Johnny, purchased two thousand single-shot Springfield rifles that had been retired when the militia regiments took up the Krag. The Krag in turn having been replaced by the modern magazine Springfield, the old single-shot Springfields, with one hundred thousand rounds of 45-70 ball cartridges, had been sold to the highest bidder. In addition to the small arms, Lopez had at present in a warehouse three machine guns and four 3 inch breech-loading pieces of field artillery (the kind of guns generally designated as a "jackass battery," for the reason that they can be taken down and transported over rough country on mules)—together with a supply of ammunition for same.

"Now, then," Scab Johnny continued, "the job that confronts us is to get these munitions down to our friends in Mexico. You know, as well as anybody, Scraggs, that while our government makes no bones of selling a lot o' retired rifles an' ammunition, nevertheless it's goin' to develop a heap o' curiosity regardin' what we do with 'em. If we're caught sneakin' 'em into Mexico we'll spend the rest of our lives in a Federal penitentiary for bustin' the neutrality laws. All them rifles an' the ammunition is cased an' in my basement at the present moment—and the government agents knows they're there. But that ain't troubling me. I rent the saloon next door an' I'll cut a hole through the wall from my cellar into the saloon cellar, carry 'em through the saloon into the backyard, an' out into the alley half a block away. I'm watched, but I got the watcher spotted—only he don't know it. Our only trouble is a ship. How about the *Maggie* ?"

"I'd have to spend about two thousand dollars on her to put her in condition for the voyage," Scraggs replied.

"Can do," Scab Johnny answered him briefly, and Señor Lopez nodded acquiescence. "You discharge on a lighter at Descanso Bay about twenty miles below Ensenada. What'll it cost us?"

"Ten thousand dollars, in addition to fixin' up the *Maggie*. Half down and half on delivery. I'm riskin' my hide an' my ticket an' I got to be well paid for it."

Again Señor Lopez nodded. What did he care? It wasn't his money.

"I'll furnish you with our own crew just before you sail," Scab Johnny continued. "Get busy."

"Gimme a thousand for preliminary expenses," Scraggs demanded. "After that Speed is my middle name."

The charming Señor Lopez produced the money in crisp new bills and, perfect gentleman that he was, demanded no receipt. As a matter of fact, Scraggs would not have given him one.

The two weeks that followed were busy ones for Captain Scraggs. The day after his interview with Scab Johnny and Don Manuel he engaged an engineer and a deck hand and went up the Sacramento to bring the *Maggie* down to San Francisco. Upon her arrival she was hauled out on the marine ways at Oakland creek, cleaned, caulked, and some new copper sheathing put on her bottom. She was also given a dash of black paint, had her engines and boilers thoroughly overhauled and repaired, and shipped a new propeller that would add at least a knot to her speed. Also, she had her stern rebuilt. And when everything was ready, she slipped down to the Black Diamond coal bunkers and took on enough fuel to carry her to San Pedro; after which she steamed across the bay to San Francisco and tied up at Fremont Street wharf.

The cargo came down in boxes, variously labelled. There were "agricultural implements," a "cream separator," a "windmill," and half a dozen "sewing-machines," in addition to a considerable number of kegs alleged to contain nails. Most of it came down after five o'clock in the afternoon after the wharfinger had left the dock, and as nothing but a disordered brain would have suspected the steamer *Maggie* of an attempt to break the neutrality laws, the entire cargo was gotten aboard safely and without a jot of suspicion attaching to the vessel.

When all was in readiness, Captain Scraggs incontinently "fired" his deckhand and engineer and inducted aboard a new crew, carefully selected for their filibuster virtues by Scab Johnny himself. Then while the new engineer got up steam, Captain Scraggs went up to Scab Johnny's office for his final instructions and the balance of the first instalment due him.

Briefly, his instructions were as follows: Upon arrival off Point Dume on the southern California coast, he was to stand in close to Dume Cove under cover of darkness and show two green lights on the masthead. A man would come alongside presently in a small boat, and climb aboard. This man would be the supercargo and the confidential envoy of the insurrecto junta in Los Angeles. Captain Scraggs was to look to this man for orders and to obey him implicitly, as upon this depended the success of the expedition. This agent of the insurrecto forces would pay him the balance of five thousand dollars due him immediately upon discharge of the cargo at Descanso Bay. There was a body of insurrecto troops encamped at Megano rancho, a mile from the beach, and they would have a barge and small boats in readiness to lighter the cargo. Scab Johnny explained that he had promised the crew double wages and a bonus of a hundred dollars each for the trip. Don Manuel Garcia Lopez paid over the requisite amount of cash, and half an hour later the *Maggie* was steaming down the bay on her perilous mission.

The sun was setting as they passed out the Golden Gate and swung down the south channel, and with the wind on her beam, the aged *Maggie* did nine knots. Late in the afternoon of the following day she was off the Santa Barbara channel, and about midnight she ran in under the lee of Point Dume and lay to. The mate hung out the green signal lights, and in about an hour Captain Scraggs heard the sound of oars grating in rowlocks. A few minutes later a stentorian voice hailed them out of the darkness. Captain Scraggs had a Jacob's ladder slung over the side and the mate and two deckhands hung over the rail with lanterns, lighting up the surrounding sea feebly for the benefit of the lone adventurer who sat muffled in a great coat in the stern of a small boat rowed by two men. There was a very slight sea running, and presently the men in the small boat, watching their opportunity by the ghostly light of the lanterns, ran their frail craft in under the lee of the *Maggie*. The figure in the stern sheets leaped on the instant, caught the Jacob's ladder, climbed nimbly over the side, and swore heartily in very good English as his feet struck the deck.

"What's the name of this floating coffin?" he demanded in a chain-locker voice. It was quite evident that even in the darkness, where her many defects were mercifully hidden, the *Maggie* did not suit the special envoy of the Mexican insurrectos.

"American steamer *Maggie*," said the skipper frigidly. "Scraggs is my name, sir. And if you don't like my vessel——"

"Scraggsy!" roared the special envoy. "Scraggsy, for a thousand! And the old *Maggie* of all boats! Scraggsy, old tarpot, your fin! Duke me, you doggoned old salamander!"

"Gib, my *dear* boy!" shrieked Captain Scraggs and cast himself into Mr. Gibney's arms in a transport of joy. Mr. Gibney, for it was indeed he, pounded Captain Scraggs on the back with one great hand while with the other he crushed the skipper's fingers to a pulp, the while he called on all the powers of darkness to witness that never in all his life had he received such a pleasant surprise.

It was indeed a happy moment. All the old animosities and differences were swallowed up in the glad handclasp with which Mr. Gibney greeted his old shipmate of the green-pea trade. Scraggs took him below at once and they pledged each other's health in a steaming kettle of grog, while the *Maggie*, once more on her course, rolled south toward Descanso Bay.

"Well, I'll be keel-hauled and skull-dragged!" said Captain Scraggs, producing a box of two-for-a-quarter cigars and handing it to Mr. Gibney. "Gib, my *dear* boy, wherever have you been these last three years?"

"Everywhere," replied Mr. Gibney. "I have been all over, mostly in Panama and the Gold Coast. For two years I've been navigatin' officer on the Colombian gunboat *Bogota*. When I was a young feller I did a hitch in the navy and become a first-class gunner, and then I went to sea in the merchant marine, and got my mate's license, and when I flashed my credentials on the president of the United States of Colombia he give me a job at "dos cienti pesos oro" per. That's Spanish for two hundred bucks gold a month. I've been through two wars and I got a medal for sinkin' a fishin' smack. I talk Spanish just like a native, I don't drink no more to speak of, and I've been savin' my money. Some day when I get the price together I'm goin' back to San Francisco, buy me a nice little schooner, and go tradin' in the South Seas. How they been comin' with you, Scraggsy, old kiddo?"

"Lovely," replied Scraggs. "Just simply grand. I'll pull ten thousand out of this job."

Mr. Gibney whistled shrilly through his teeth.

"That's the ticket for soup," he said admiringly. "I tell you, Scraggs, this soldier of fortune business may be all right, but it don't amount to much compared to being a sailor of fortune, eh, Scraggsy? Just as soon as I

heard there was a revolution in Mexico I quit my job
in the Colombian navy and come north for the pickin's. . . . No, I ain't been in their rotten little
army. . . . D'ye think I want to go around killin'
people? . . . There ain't no pleasure gettin' killed
in the mere shank of a bright and prosperous life . . .
a dead hero don't gather no moss, Scraggsy. Reads
all right in books, but it don't appeal none to me. I'm
for peace every time, so right away as soon as I heard
of the trouble, says I to myself: 'Things has been pretty
quiet in Mexico for twenty years, and they're due to
shift things around pretty much. What them peons
need is a man with an imagination to help 'em out, and
if they've got the money, Adelbert P. Gibney can supply the brains.' So I comes north to Los Angeles, shows
the insurrecto junta my medal and my honourable dis-
charges from every ship I'd ever been in, includin' the
gunboart *Bogota,* and I talked big and swelled around
and told 'em to run in some arms and get busy. I
framed it all up for this filibuster trip you're on, Scraggsy, only I never did hear that they'd picked on you. I
told that coffee-coloured rat of a Lopez man to hunt up
Scab Johnny and he'd set him right, but if anybody had
told me you had the nerve to run the *Maggie* in on this
deal, Scraggsy, I'd a-called him a liar. Scraggs, you're
mucho-bueno—that is, you're all right. I'm so used to
talkin' Spanish that I forget myself. Still, there's one
end of this little deal that I ain't exactly explained to all
hands. If I'd a-known they was charterin' the *Maggie,*
I'd have blocked the game."

"Why?" demanded Captain Scraggs, instantly on
the defensive.

"Not that I'm holdin' any grudge agin you, Scrag-gsy," said Mr. Gibney affably, "but I wouldn't a-had you no more now than I would when we was runnin' in the green-pea trade. It's because you ain't got no imagination, and the *Maggie* ain't big enough for my purpose. Havin' the *Maggie* sort of puts a crimp in my plans."

"Rot," snapped Captain Scraggs. "I've had the *Maggie* overhauled and shipped a new wheel, and she's a mighty smart little boat, I'll tell you. I'll land them arms in Descanso Bay all right."

"I know you will," said Mr. Gibney sadly. "That's just what hurts. You see, Scraggsy, I never intended 'em for Descanso Bay in the first place. There's a nice healthy little revolution fomentin' down in the United States of Colombia, with Adelbert P. Gibney playin' both ends to the middle. And there's a dog-hole down on the Gold Coast where I intended to land this cargo, but now that Scab Johnny's gone to work and sent me a bay scow instead of a sea-goin' steamer, I'm in the nine-hole instead o' dog-hole. I can never get as far as the Gold Coast with the *Maggie*. She can't carry coal enough to last her."

"But I thought these guns and things was for the Mexicans," quavered Captain Scraggs. "Scab Johnny and Lopez told me they was."

Mr. Gibney groaned and hid his face in his hands. "Scraggsy," he said sadly, "it's a cinch you ain't used the past four years to stimulate that imagination of yours. Of course they was purchased for the Mexicans, but what was to prevent me from lettin' the Mexicans pay for them, help out on the charter of the boat, and then have me divert the cargo to the United States of Colombia, where I can sell 'em at a clear profit, the cost bein' nothin' to speak of? Now you got to come buttin' in with the *Maggie*, and what happens? Why, I got to be honest, of course. I got to make good on my bluff, and what's in it for me? Nothin' but glory. Can you hock a chunk of glory for ham and eggs, Phineas Scraggs? Not on your life. If it hadn't been for you buttin' in with your blasted, rotten hulk of a fresh-water skiff, I'd——"

Mr. Gibney paused ominously and savagely bit the end of his cigar. As for Captain Scraggs, every drop of blood in his body was boiling in defense of the ship he loved.

"You're a pirate," he shrilled.

"And you're just as big a hornet as you ever was," replied Mr. Gibney. "Always buzzin' around where you ain't wanted. But still, what's the use of bawlin' over spilt milk? We'll drop into San Diego for a couple of hours and take on coal, and about sunset we'll pull out and make the run down to Descanso Bay in the dark. We might as well forget the past and put this thing through as per program. Only I saw visions of a schooner all my own, Scraggsy, and—well, what's the use? What's the use? Scraggsy, you're a natural-born mar-plot. Always buttin' in, buttin' in, buttin' in, fit for nothin' but the green-pea trade. However, I guess I can turn into my old berth and get some sleep. Put the old girl under a slow bell and save your coal. We'll have to fool away four or five hours in San Diego anyhow and there ain't no sense in crowdin' the old hulk."

"Gib," said Captain Scraggs, "was that really your lay—to steal the cargo, double-cross the insurrecto junta, and sell out to a furrin' country?"

"Of course it was," said Mr. Gibney pettishly. "They all do such things in the banana republics. Why should I be an exception? There's half a dozen different gangs fightin' each other and the government in Mexico, and if I don't deliver these arms, just see all the lives I'll be savin'. And after I got the cargo into Colombia and sold it, I could have peached on the rebels there, and got a reward for it, and saved a lot more lives, and come away rich and respected."

"By the Lord Harry," said Captain Scraggs, "but you've got an imagination, Gib. I'll swear to that. Gib, I take off my hat to you. You're all tight and shipshape and no loose ends bobbin' around *you*. Don't tell me th' scheme's got t' fall through, Gib. Great snakes, don't tell me that. Ain't there some way o' gettin' around it? There *must* be. Why, Gib, my dear boy, I never heard of such a grand lay in my life. It's a absolute winner. Don't give up, Gib. Oil up your imagination and find a way out. Let's get together, Gib, and make a little money. Dang it all, Gib, I been lonesome ever since I seen you last."

"Well," replied Mr. Gibney, "I'll turn in and try to scheme a way out, but I don't hold out no hope. Not a ray of it. I'm afraid, Scraggsy, we've got to be honest."

Saying which, Mr. Gibney hopped up into his berth, stretched his huge legs, and fell asleep with his clothes on. Captain Scraggs looked him over with the closest approach to affection that had ever lightened his cold gray eye, and sighing heavily, presently went on deck. As he passed up the companion-way, the first mate heard him murmur:

"Gib's a fine lad.   I'll be dad burned if he ain't."

CHAPTER XIX

AT SIX o'clock next morning the *Maggie* was rounding Point Loma, heading in for San Diego Bay, and Captain Scraggs went below and awakened Mr. Gibney.

"What's for breakfast, Scraggsy, old kid?" asked Mr. Gibney.

"Fried eggs," said Captain Scraggs, remembering Mr. Gibney's partiality for that form of nutriment in the vanished days of the green-pea trade. "Ham an' fried eggs an' a sizzlin' pot o' coffee. Thought a way out o' our mess, Gib?"

"Not yet," replied Mr. Gibney as he rolled out of bed, "but eggs is always stimulatin', and I don't give up hope on a full stomach."

An hour later they were tied up under the coal bunkers, and at Mr. Gibney's suggestion some twenty tons of sacked coal were piled on top of the fo'castle head and on the main deck for'd, in case of emergency. They lay in the harbour all day until about four o'clock, when Mr. Gibney, by virtue of his authority as supercargo, ordered the lines cast off and the *Maggie* steamed out of the harbour. Off Point Loma they veered to the south, leaving the Coronado Islands on the starboard quarter, ten miles to the west. Mr. Gibney was below with Captain Scraggs, battling with the problem that confronted them, when the mate stuck his head down the companion-way to report a large power schooner coming out from the lee of the Coronados and standing off on a course calculated to intercept the *Maggie* in an hour or two.

Captain Scraggs and Mr. Gibney sprang up on the bridge at once, the latter with Scraggs's long glass up to his eye.

"She was hove to under the lee of the island, and the minute we came out of the harbour and turned south she come nosin' after us," said the mate.

"Hum!" muttered Mr. Gibney. "Gasoline schooner. Two masts and baldheaded. About a hundred and twenty ton, I should say, and showin' a pretty pair of heels. There's somethin' up for'd—yes—let me see— ye-e-es, there's two more—*holy sailor! it's a gunboat!* One of those doggoned gasoline coast patrol boats, and there's the Federal flag flying at the fore."

"Let's put back to San Diego Bay," quavered Captain Scraggs. "I'll be durned if I relish the idee o' losin' the *Maggie*."

"Too late," said the philosophical Gibney. "We're in Mexican waters now, and she can cut us off from the bay. The only thing we can do is to run for it and try to lose her after dark. Tell the engineer to crowd her to the limit. There ain't much wind to speak of, so I guess we can manage to hold our own for a while. Nevertheless, I've got a hunch that we'll be overhauled. Of course, you ain't got no papers to show, Scraggs, and they'll search the cargo, and confiscate us, and shoot the whole bloomin' crowd of us. I bet a dollar to a doughnut that fel ow Lopez sold us out, after the fashion of the country. I can't help thinkin' that

that gunboat was there just a-waitin' for us to show up."

For several minutes Mr. Gibney continued to study the gunboat until there could no longer be any doubt that she intended to overhaul them. He made out that she had a long gun for'd, with a battery of two one-pounders on top of her house and something on her port quarter that looked like a Maxim rapid-fire gun. About twenty men, dressed in white cloth, could be seen on her decks.

Presently Mr. Gibney was interrupted by Captain Scraggs pulling at his sleeve.

"You was a gunner once, wasn't you, Gib?" said Captain Scraggs in a trembling voice.

"You bet I was," replied Mr. Gibney. "My shootin' won the trophy three times in succession when I was on the old *Kearsarge*. If I had one good gun and a half-decent crew, I'd knock that gunboat silly before she knew what had hit her."

"Gib, I've got an idee," said Captain Scraggs.

"Out with it," said Mr. Gibney cheerfully.

"There was four little cannon lowered into the hold the last thing before we put on the main hatch, and the ammunition to load 'em with is stowed in the after hold and very easy to get at."

Mr. Gibney turned a beaming face to the skipper, reached out his arms, and folded Captain Scraggs in an embrace that would have done credit to a grizzly bear. There were genuine tears of admiration in his eyes and in his voice when he could master his emotions sufficiently to speak.

"Scraggsy, old tarpot, you've been a long time comin'

through on the imagination, but you've sure arrived with all sail set. I always thought you had about as much nerve as an oyster, but I take it all back. We'll get out them two little jackass guns and fight a naval battle, and if I don't sink that Mexican gunboat, and save the *Maggie*, feed me to the sharks, for I won't be worthy of the blood that's in me. Pipe all hands and lift off that main hatch. Reeve a block and tackle through that cargo gaff and stand by to heave out the guns."

But Captain Scraggs had repented of his rash suggestion almost the moment he made it. Only the dire necessity of desperate measures to save the *Maggie* had prompted him to put the idea into Mr. Gibney's head, and when he saw the avidity with which the latter set to work clearing for action, his terror knew no bounds.

"Oh, Gib," he wailed, "I'm afraid we better not try to lick that gunboat after all. They might sink us with all hands."

"Rats!" said Mr. Gibney, as he leaped into the hold. "Bear a light here until I can root out the wheels of these guns. Here they are, labelled 'cream separator.' Stand by with that sling to——"

"But, Gib, my *dear* boy," protested Captain Scraggs, "this is *insanity!*"

"I know it," said Mr. Gibney calmly. "Scraggsy, you're perfectly right. But I'd sooner die fightin' than let them stand me up agin a wall in Ensenada. We're filibusters, Scraggsy, and we're caught with the goods. I, for one, am goin' down with the steamer *Maggie*, but I'm goin' down fightin' like a bear."

"Maybe—maybe we can outrun her, Gib," half sobbed Captain Scraggs.

"No hope," replied Mr. Gibney. "Fight and die is the last resort. She's eight miles astern and gainin' every minute, and when she's within two miles she'll open fire. Of course we won't be hit unless they've got a Yankee gunner aboard."

"Let's run up the Stars and Stripes and dare 'em to fire on us," said Captain Scraggs.

"No," said Mr. Gibney firmly, "my old man died for the flag an' I've sailed under it too long to hide behind it when I'm in Dutch. We'll fight. If you was ever navigatin' officer on a Colombian gunboat, Scraggs, you'd realize what it means to run from a Mexican."

Captain Scraggs said nothing further. Perhaps he was a little ashamed of himself in the face of Mr. Gibney's simple faith in his own ability; perhaps in his veins, all unknown, there flowed a taint of the heroic blood of some forgotten sea-dog. Be that as it may, something did swell in his breast when Mr. Gibney spoke of the flag and his scorning to hide behind it, and Scraggs's snaggle teeth came together with a snap.

"All right, Gib, my boy," he said solemnly, "I'm with you. Mrs. Scraggs has slipped her cable and there ain't nobody to mourn for me. But if we can't fight under the Stars and Stripes, by the tail of the Great Sacred Bull, we'll have a flag of our own," and leaving Mr. Gibney and the crew to get the guns on deck, Captain Scraggs ran below. He appeared on deck presently with a long blue burgee on which was emblazoned in white letters the single word *Maggie*. It was his own houseflag, and with trembling hands he ran it to the fore and cast its wrinkled folds to the breeze of heaven.

"Good old dishcloth!" shrieked Mr. Gibney. "She never comes down."

"Damned if she does," said Captain Scraggs profanely.

While all this was going on a deckhand had reeved a block and tackle through the end of the cargo gaff and passed it to the winch. The two guns came out of the hold in jig time, and while Scraggs and one deckhand opened the after hold and got out ammunition for the guns, Mr. Gibney, assisted by the other deckhand, proceeded to put one of the guns together. He was shrewd enough to realize that he would have to do practically all of the work of serving the gun himself, in view of which condition one gun would have to defend the *Maggie*. He had never seen a mountain gun before, but he did not find it difficult to put the simple mechanism together.

"Now, then, Scraggsy," he announced cheerfully when the gun was finally assembled on the carriage, "get a sizeable timber an' spike it to the centre o' the deck. I'll run the trail spade up against that cleat an' that'll keep the recoil from lettin' the gun go backward, clean through the opposite rail and overboard. Gimme a coupler gallons o' distillate an' some waste, somebody. This cosmoline's got to come out o' the tube an' out o' the breech mechanism before we commence shootin'."

The enemy had approached within three miles by the time the piece was ready for action. Under Mr.

Gibney's instructions Captain Scraggs held the fuse
setter in case it should be necessary to adjust with
shrapnel. Mr. Gibney inserted his sights and took a
preliminary squint. "A little different from gun-
pointin' in the navy, but about the same principle," he
declared. "In the army I believe they call this kind
o' shootin' direct fire, because you sight direct on the
target." He scratched his ingenious head and examined the ammunition. "Not a high explosive shell in
the lot," he mourned. "I'll have to use percussion fire
to get the range; then I'll drop back a little an' spray
her with shrapnel. Seems a pity to smash up a fine
schooner like that one with percussion fire. I'd rather
tickle 'em up a bit with shrapnel an' scare 'em into
runnin' away."

He got out the lanyard, slipped a cartridge in the
breech, paused, and scratched his head again. His calm
deliberation was driving Scraggs crazy. He reminded ·
Mr. Gibney with some asperity that they were not attending a strawberry festival and for the love of heaven
to get busy.

"I'm estimatin' the range, you snipe," Gibney retorted. "Looks to be about three miles to me. A little
long, mebbe, for this gun, but—there's nothin' like
tryin'," and he sighted carefully. "Fire," he bawled
as the *Maggie* rested an instant in the trough of the
sea—and a deckhand jerked the lanyard. Instantly
Mr. Gibney clapped the long glass to his eye.

"Good direction—over," he murmured. "I'll lay
on her waterline next time." He jerked open the
breech, ejected the cartridge case, and rammed another
cartridge home. This shot struck the water directly

under the schooner's bow and threw water over her forecastle head. Mr. Gibney smiled, spat overboard, and winked confidently at Captain Scraggs. "Like spearin' fish in a bath tub," he declared. He bent over the fuse setter. "Corrector three zero," he intoned, "four eight hundred." He thrust a cartridge in the fuse setter, twisted it, slammed it in the gun, and fired again. The water broke into tiny waterspouts over a considerable area some two hundred yards short of the schooner, so Mr. Gibney raised his range to five thousand and tried again. "Over," he growled.

Something whined over the *Maggie* and threw up a waterspout half a mile beyond her.

"Dubs," jeered Mr. Gibney, and sighted again. This time his shrapnel burst neatly on the schooner. Almost simultaneously a shell from the schooner dropped into the sacked coal on the forecastle head of the *Maggie* and enveloped her in a black pall of smoke and coal dust. Captain Scraggs screamed.

"Tit for tat," the philosophical Gibney reminded him. "We can't expect to get away with everything, Scraggsy, old kiddo." The words were scarcely out of his mouth before the *Maggie's* mainmast and about ten feet of her ancient railing were trailing alongside. Mr. Gibney whistled softly through his teeth and successfully sprayed the Mexican again. "It breaks my heart to ruin that craft's canvas," he declared, and let her have it once more.

"My *Maggie's* tail is shot away," Captain Scraggs wailed, "an' I only rebuilt it a week ago." Three more shots from the long gun missed them, but the fourth carried away the cabin, leaving the wreck of the pilot house, with the helmsman unscathed, sticking up like a sore thumb.

"Turn her around and head straight for them," the gallant Gibney roared. "She's a smaller target comin' bows on. We're broadside to her now."

"Gib, will you ever sink that Greaser?" Captain Scraggs sobbed hysterically.

"Don't want to sink her," the supercargo retorted. "She's a nice little schooner. I'd rather capture her. Maybe we can use her in our business, Scraggsy," and he continued to shower the enemy with high bursting shrapnel. When the two vessels were less than two miles apart the one-pounders came into action. It was pretty shooting and the wicked little shells ripped through the old *Maggie* like buckshot through a roll of butter. Mr. Gibney slid flat on the deck beside his gun and Captain Scraggs sprawled beside him.

"A feller," Mr. Gibney announced, "has got to take a beatin' while lookin' for an openin' to put over the knockout blow. If the old *Maggie* holds together till we're within a cable's length o' that schooner an' we ain't all killed by that time, I bet I'll make them skunks sing soft an' low."

"How?" Captain Scraggs chattered.

"With muzzle bursts," Mr. Gibney replied. "I'll set my fuse at zero an' at point-blank range I'll just rake everything off that schooner's decks. Guess I'll get half a dozen cartridges set an' ready for the big scene. Up with you, Admiral Scraggs, an' hold the fuse setter steady."

"I'm agin war," Scraggs quavered. "Gib, it's sure hell."

"Rats! It's invigouratin', Scraggsy. There ain't nothin' wrong with war, Scraggsy, unless you happen to get killed. Then it's like cholera. You can cure every case except the first one."

They had come inside the minimum range of the Mexican's long gun now, so that only the one-pounders continued to peck at the *Maggie*. Evidently the Mexican was as eager to get to close quarters as Mr. Gibney, for he held steadily on his course.

"Well, it's time to put over the big stuff," Mr. Gibney remarked presently. "Here's hopin' they don't pot me with rifle fire while I'm extendin' my compliments."

As the first muzzle burst raked the Mexican Captain Scraggs saw that most of the terrible blast of lead had gone too high. Nevertheless, it was effective, for to a man the crews of the one-pounders deserted their posts and tumbled below; seeing which the individual in command lost his nerve. He was satisfied now that the infernal *Maggie* purposed ramming him; he had marvelled that the filibuster should use shrapnel, after she had ranged with shell (he did not know it was percussion shrapnel) and in sudden panic he decided that the *Maggie,* mortally wounded, purposed getting close enough to sink him with shell-fire if she failed to ram him; whereupon the yellow streak came through and he waved his arms frantically above his head in token of surrender.

"She's hauled down her rag," shrieked Scraggs. "Be merciful, Gib. There's men dyin' on that boat."

"Lay alongside that craft," Mr. Gibney shouted to the helmsman. The schooner had hove to and when

the *Maggie* also hove to some thirty yards to windward
of her Mr. Gibney informed the Mexican, in atrocious
Spanish well mixed with English, that if the latter so
much as lifted his little finger he might expect to be
sunk like a dog. "Down below, everybody but the
helmsman, or I'll sweep your decks with another muzzle burst," he thundered.

The Mexican obeyed and Captain Scraggs went up
in the pilot house and laid the terribly battered *Maggie*
alongside the schooner. The instant she touched, Mr.
Gibney sprang aboard, quickly followed by Captain
Scraggs, who had relinquished the helm to his first
mate.

Suddenly Captain Scraggs shouted, "Look, Gib, for
the love of the Lord, look!" and pointed with his finger.
At the head of the little iron-railed companion way
leading down into the engine room a man was standing.
He had a monkey wrench in one hand and a greasy
rag in the other.

Mr. Gibney turned and looked at the man.

"McGuffey, for a thousand," he bellowed, and ran
forward with outstretched hand. Captain Scraggs
was at Gibney's heels, and between them they came
very nearly dislocating Bartholomew McGuffey's arm.

"McGuffey, my *dear* boy," said Captain Scraggs.
"Whatever are you a-doin' on this heathen warship?"

"Me!" ejaculated Mr. McGuffey, with his old-time
deliberation. "Why, I'm the chief engineer of this
craft. I had a good job, too, but I guess it's all off
now, and the Mexican Government'll fire me. Say,
who chucked that buckshot down into my engine
room?"

"Admiral Gibney did it," said Scraggs. "The old *Maggie's* alongside and me and Gib's filibusters. Bear a hand, Mac, and help us clap the hatches on our prisoners."

"Thank God," said Mr. Gibney piously, "I didn't kill you. Come to look into the matter, I didn't kill anybody, though I see half a dozen Mexicans around decks more or less cut up. Where you been all these years, Mac?"

"I been chief engineer in the Mexican navy," replied McGuffey. "Have you captured us in the name of the United States or what?"

"We've captured you in the name of Adelbert P. Gibney," was the reply. "I been huntin' all my life for a ship of my own, and now I've got her. Lord, Mac, she's a beauty, ain't she? All hardwood finish, teak rail, well found, and just the ticket for the island trade. Well, well, well! I'm Captain Gibney at last."

"Where do I come in, Gib?" asked Captain Scraggs modestly.

"Well, seein' as the *Maggie* has two holes through her hull below the waterline, and is generally nicked to pieces, you might quit askin' questions and get back aboard and put the pumps on her. You're lucky if she don't sink on you before we get to Descanso Bay. If she sinks, don't worry. I'll give you a job as my first mate. Mac, you're my engineer, but not at no fancy Mexican price. I'll pay you the union scale and not a blasted cent more or less. Is that fair?"

McGuffey said it was, and went below to tune up his engine. Mr. Gibney took the wheel of the gunboat, and sent Captain Scraggs back aboard the *Maggie*, and in a few minutes both vessels were bowling along toward Descanso Bay. They were off the bay at midnight, and while with Mr. Gibney in command of the federal gunboat Captain Scraggs had nothing to fear, the rapid rise of water in the hold of the *Maggie* was sadly disconcerting. About daylight he made up his mind that she would sink within two hours, and without pausing to whine over his predicament, he promptly beached her. She drove far up the beach, with the slack water breaking around her scarred stern, and when the tide ebbed she lay high and dry. And the rebel soldiers came trooping down from the Megano rancho and falling upon her carcass like so many ants, quickly distributed her cargo amongst them, and disappeared.

Captain Scraggs sent his crew out aboard the captured gunboat to assist Mr. Gibney in rowing his prisoners ashore, and when finally he stood alone beside the wreck of the brave old *Maggie*, piled up at last in the port of missing ships, something snapped within his breast and the big tears rolled in quick succession down his sun-tanned cheeks. The old hulk looked peculiarly pathetic as she lay there, listed over on her beam ends. She had served him well, but she had finished her last voyage, and with some vague idea of saving her old bones from vandal hands, Captain Scraggs, sobbing audibly, scattered the contents of half a dozen cans of kerosene over her decks and in the cabin, lighted fires in three different sections of the wreck, and left her to the consuming flames. Half an hour later he stood on the battered decks of the gunboat beside Gibney and McGuffey and watched the dense clouds of smoke that heralded the passing of the *Maggie*.

"She was a good old hulk," said Mr. Gibney.   "And now, as the special envoy of the Liberal army of Mexico, here's a draft on Los Angeles for five thousand bucks, Scraggsy, which constitutes the balance due you on this here filibuster trip. Of course, I needn't remind you, Scraggsy, that you'd never have earned this money if it hadn't been for Adelbert P. Gibney workin' his imagination overtime. I've made you a chunk of money, and while I couldn't save your ship, I did save your life. As a reward for all this, I don't claim one cent of the money due you, as I could if I wanted to be rotten mean. I'm goin' to keep this fine little power schooner for my share of the loot. She's nicked up some, but that only bears evidence to what a bully good shot I am, and it won't take much to fix her up all ship-shape again. Usin' high bursts shrapnel ain't very destructive. All them bumps an' scratches can be planed down. But we'll have to do some mendin' on her canvas—I'll tell the world. She's called the *Reina Maria*, but I'm going to run her to Panama and change her name. She'll be known as *Maggie II*, out of respect for the old girl that's burnin' up there on the beach."

Captain Scraggs was so touched at this delicate little tribute that he turned away and burst into tears.

"Aw, shut up, Scraggsy, old hunks," said McGuffey consolingly. "You ain't got nothin' to cry about. You're a rich man. Look at me. I ain't a-bawlin', am I? And I don't get so much as a bean out of this mix-up, all on account of me bein' tied up with a lot of hounds that quits fightin' before they're half licked."

"That's so," said Captain Scraggs, wiping his eyes with his grimy fists. "I declare you're out in the cold, McGuffey, and it ain't right. Gib, my boy, us three has had some stirrin' times together and we've had our differences, but I ain't a-goin' to think of them past griefs. The sight o' you, single-handed, meetin' and annihilatin' the pride of the Mexican navy, calm in th' moment o' despair, generous in victory and delicate as blazes to a fallen shipmate, goin' to work an' namin' your vessel after him that way, is somethin' that wipes away all sorrer and welds a friendship that's bound to endoor till death us do part. If McGuffey'd been on our side, we know from past performances that he'd a fit like a tiger, wouldn't you, Mac?" (Here Mr. McGuffey coughed slightly, as much as to say that he would have fought like ten tigers had he only been given the opportunity.)

Captain Scraggs continued: "I should say that a fair valuation of this schooner as she stands is ten thousand dollars. That belongs to Gib. Now I'm willin' to chuck five thousand dollars into the deal, we'll form a close corporation and as a compliment to McGuffey, elect him chief engineer in his own ship and give him say a quarter interest in our layout, as a little testimonial to an old friend, tried and true."

"Scraggsy," said Mr. Gibney, "your fin. We've fought, but we'll let that go. We wipe the slate clean and start in all over again on the *Maggie II*, and I'm free to state, without fear of contradiction, that in the last embroglio you showed up like four aces and a king with the entire company standin' pat. Scraggsy, you're a hero, and what you propose proves that you're considerable of a singed cat—better'n you look. We'll go freebootin' down on the Gold Coast. There's war, red war, breakin' loose down there, and we'll shy in our horseshoe with the strongest side and pry loose a fortune somewhere. I'm for a life of wild adventure, and now that we've got the ship and the funds and the crew, let's go to it. There's a deal of fine liquor in the wardroom, and I suggest that we nominate Phineas Scraggs, late master of the battleship *Maggie*, now second in command of the *Maggie II*, to brew a kettle o' hot grog to celebrate our victory. Mac—Scraggsy—your fins. I'm proud of you both. Shake."

They shook, and as Captain Gibney's eye wandered aloft, First Mate Scraggs and Chief Engineer McGuffey looked up also. From the main topmast of the *Maggie II* floated a long blue burgee, with white lettering on it, and as it whipped out into the breeze the old familiar name stood out against the noonday sun.

"Good old dishcloth!" murmured Mr. Gibney. "She never comes down."

"The *Maggie* forever!" shrieked Scraggs.

"Hooray!" bellowed McGuffey. "An' now, Scraggsy, if you've got all the enthusiasm out of your blood, kick in with a hundred an' fifty dollars an' interest to date. An' don't tell me that note's outlawed, or I'll feed you to the fishes."

Captain Scraggs looked crestfallen, but produced the money.

CHAPTER XX

WELL, Scraggsy, old hunks, this is pleasant, ain't it?" said Mr. Gibney, and spat on the deck of the *Maggie II*.

"Right-o," replied Captain Scraggs cheerily, "though when I was a young feller and first went to sea, it wasn't considered no pleasantry to spit on a nice clean deck. You might cut that out, Gib. It's vulgar."

"Passin' over the fact, Scraggs, that you ain't got no call to jerk me up on sea ettycat, more particular since I'm the master and managin' owner of this here schooner, I'm free to confess, Scraggsy, that your observation does you credit. I just did that to see if you was goin' to take as big an interest in the new *Maggie* as you did in the old *Maggie*, and the fact that you object to me expectoratin' on the deck proves to me that you're leavin' behind you all them bay scow tendencies of the green-pea trade. It leads me to believe that you'll rise to high rank and distinction in the Colombian navy. Your fin, Scraggsy. Expectoratin' on the decks is barred, and the *Maggie II* goes under navy discipline from now on. Am I right?"

"Right as a right whale," said Captain Scraggs. "And now that you've given that old mate of mine the course, and we've temporarily plugged up the holes in this here Mexican gunboat, and everything points to a safe and profitable voyage from now on, suppose you delegate me as a committee of one to brew a scuttle of grog, after which the syndicate holds a meetin' and lays out a course for its future conduct. There's a few questions of rank and privileges that ought to be settled once for all, so there can't be no come-back."

"The point is well taken and it is so ordered," said Mr. Gibney, who had once held office in Harbour 15, Masters and Pilots Association of America, and knew a fragment or two of parliamentary law. "Rustle up the grog, call McGuffey up out of the engine room, and we'll hold the meetin'."

Twenty minutes later Scraggs came on deck to announce the successful concoction of a kettle of whisky punch; whereupon the three adventurers went below and sat down at the cabin table for a conference.

"I move that Gib be appointed president of the syndicate," said Captain Scraggs.

"Second the motion," rumbled McGuffey.

"The motion's carried," said Mr. Gibney, and banged the table with his horny fist. "The meetin' will please come to order. The chair hereby appoints Phineas Scraggs secretary of the syndicate, to keep a record of this and all future meetin's of the board. I will now entertain propositions of any and all natures, and I invite the members of the board to knock the stopper out of their jaw tackle and go to it."

"I move," said Captain Scraggs, "that B. McGuffey, Esquire, be, and he is hereby appointed, chief engineer of the *Maggie II* at a salary not to exceed the wage schedule of the Marine Engineers' Association of the Pacific Coast, and that he be voted a one-fourth interest in the vessel and all subsequent profits."

"Second the motion," said Mr. Gibney, "and not to hamper the business of the meetin', we'll just consider that motion carried unanimous."

B. McGuffey, Esquire, rose, bowed his thanks, and sat down again, apparently very much confused. It was evident that he had something to say, but was having difficulty framing his thoughts in parliamentary language.

"Heave away, Mac," said Mr. Gibney.

"Cast off your lines, McGuffey," chirped Scraggs.

Thus encouraged, McGuffey rose, bowed his thanks once more, moistened his larynx with a gulp of the punch, and spoke:

"Feller members and brothers of the syndicate: In the management of the deck department of this new craft of ourn, my previous knowledge of the worthy president and the unworthy secretary leads me to believe that there's goin' to be trouble. A ship divided agin herself must surely go on her beam ends. Now, Scraggsy here has been master so long that the juice of authority has sorter soaked into his marrer bones. For twenty years it's been 'Howdy do, Captain Scraggs,' 'Have a drink, Captain Scraggs,' 'Captain Scraggs this an' Captain Scraggs that.' I don't mean no offense, gentlemen, when I state that you can't teach an old dog new tricks. No man that's ever been a master makes a good mate. On the other hand, I realize that Gib here has been a-pantin' and a-bellyachin' all his life to get a ship of his own an' have folks call him 'Captain Gibney.' Now that he's gone an' done it, I say he's entitled to it. But the fact of the whole thing is, Gib's the natural leader of the expedition or whatever it's goin' to be, and he can't have his peace of mind wrecked and his plans disturbed a-chasin' sailors around the deck of the *Maggie II.* Gib is sorter what the feller calls the power behind the throne. He's too big a figger for the grade of captain. Therefore, I move you, gentlemen, that Adelbert P. Gibney be, and he is hereby nominated and appointed to the grade of commodore, in full command and supervision of all of the property of the syndicate. And I also move that Phineas Scraggs be appointed chief navigatin' officer of this packet, to retain his title of captain, and to be obeyed and respected as such by every man aboard with the exception of me and Gib. The present mate'll do the navigatin' while Scraggsy's learnin' the deep sea stuff.''

"Second the motion,'' said Captain Scraggs briskly. "McGuffey, your argument does you a heap of credit. It's—it's—dog my cats, McGuffey, it's masterly. It shows a keen appreciation of an old skipper's feelin's, and if the move is agreeable to Gib, I'm willin' to hail him as commodore and fight to maintain his office. I—I dunno, Gib, what I'd do if I didn't have a mate to order around.''

"Gentlemen,'' said Mr. Gibney, beaming, "the motion's carried unanimous. Captain—chief—your fins. Dook me. I'm honoured by the handshake. Now, regarding that crew you brought down from San Francisco on the old *Maggie*, Scraggs, they're a likely lot and will come in handy if times is as lively in Colombia as I figger they will be when we arrive there. Captain Scraggs, you will have your mate pipe the crew to muster and ascertain their feelin's on the subject of takin' a

chance with Commodore Gibney. If they object to goin'
further, we'll land 'em in Panama an' pay 'em off as
agreed. If they feel like followin' the Jolly Roger we'll
give 'em the coast seaman's scale for a deep-water cruise
and a five per cent. bonus in case we turn a big
trick."

Captain Scraggs went at once on deck. Ten minutes later he returned to report that the mate and the
four seamen elected to stick by the ship.

"Bully boys," said the commodore, "bully boys. I
like that mate. He's a smart man and handles a gun
well. While I should hesitate to take advantage of
my prerogative as commodore to interfere with the
normal workin's of the deck department, I trust that
on this special occasion our esteemed navigatin' officer,
Captain Scraggs, will not consider it beneath his dig-
nity or an attack on his office if I suggest to him that
he brew another kettle of grog for the crew."

"Second the motion," replied McGuffey.

"Carried," said Scraggs, and proceeded to heat some
water.

"Anything further?" stated the president.

"How about uniforms?" This from Captain Scraggs.

"We'll leave that to Gib," suggested McGuffey.
"He's been in the Colombian navy and he'll know just
what to get us."

"Well, there's another thing that's got to be settled,"
continued Captain Scraggs. "If I'm to be navigatin'
officer on the flagship of a furrin' fleet, strike me pink
if I'll do any more cookin' in the galley. It's degrad-
in'. I move that we engage some enterprisin' Oriental
for that job."

"Carried," said Mr. Gibney. "Any further business?"

Once more McGuffey stood up. "Gentlemen and brothers of the syndicate," he began, "I'm satisfied that the back-bitin', the scrappin', the petty jealousies and general cussedness that characterized our lives on the old *Maggie* will not be duplicated on the *Maggie II*. Them vicious days is gone forever, I hope, an' from now on the motto of us three should be:

"All for one and one for all—
United we stand, divided we fall."

This earnest little speech, which came straight from the honest McGuffey's heart, brought the tears to the commodore's eyes. Under the inspiration of McGuffey's unselfish words the glasses were refilled and all three pledged their friendship anew. As for Captain Scraggs, he was naturally of a cold and selfish disposition, and McGuffey's toast appealed more to his brain than to his heart. Had he known what was to happen to him in the days to come and what that simple little motto was to mean in his particular case, it is doubtful if he would have tossed off his liquor as gaily as he did.

"There's one thing more that we mustn't neglect," warned Mr. Gibney before the meeting broke up. "We've got to run this little vessel into some dog-hole where there's a nice beach and smooth water, and change her name. I notice that her old name *Reina Maria* is screwed into her bows and across her stern in raised gilt letters, contrary to law and custom. We'll snip 'em off, sandpaper every spot where there's a letter, and repaint it; after which we'll rig up a stagin' over her bows and stern, and cut her new name, '*Maggie II*,' right into her plankin'. Nobody'll ever suspect her name's been changed. I notice that the official letters and numbers cut into her main beam is F-C-P— 9957. I'll change that F to an E, the C to an O, and the P to an R. A handy man with a wood chisel can do lots of things. He can change those nines to eights, the five to a six, and the seven to a nine. I've seen it done before. Then we'll rig a foretopmast and a spinnaker boom on her, and bend a fisherman's staysail. Nothing like it when you're sailing a little off the wind. Scraggs, you have the papers of the old *Maggie,* and we all have our licenses regular enough. Dig up the old papers, Scraggsy, and I'll doctor 'em up to fit the *Maggie II.* As for our armament, we'll dismount the guns and stow 'em away in the hold until we get down on the Colombian coast, and while we're lying in Panama repairing the holes where my shots went through her,and puttin' new planks in her decks where the old plankin' has been scored by shrapnel, those paraqueets will think we're as peaceful as chipmunks. Better look over your supplies, McGuffey, and see if there's any paint aboard. I'd just as lief give the old girl a different dress before we drop anchor in Panama."

"Gib," said Captain Scraggs earnestly, "I'll keelhaul and shull-drag the man that says you ain't got a great head."

"By the lord," supplemented McGuffey, "you have."

The commodore smiled and tapped his frontal bone with his forefinger. "Imagination, my lads, imagination," he said, and reached for the last of the punch.

Exactly three weeks from the date of the naval battle which took place off the Coronado Islands, and whereby Mr. Gibney became commodore and managing owner of the erstwhile Mexican coast patrol schooner *Reina Maria*, that vessel sailed out of the harbour of Panama completely rejuvenated. Not a scar on her shapely lines gave evidence of the sanguinary engagement through which she had passed.

Mr. Gibney had her painted a creamy white with a dark blue waterline. She had had her bottom cleaned and scraped and the copper sheathing overhauled and patched up. Her sails had been overhauled, inspected, and repaired wherever necessary, and in order to be on the safe side, Mr. Gibney, upon motion duly made by him and seconded by McGuffey (to whom the seconding of the Gibney motions had developed into a habit), purchased an extra suit of new sails. The engines were overhauled by the faithful McGuffey and a large store of distillate stored in the hold. Captain Scraggs, with his old-time aversion to expense, made a motion (which was seconded by McGuffey before he had taken time to consider its import) providing for the abolition of the office of chief engineer while the *Maggie II* was under sail, at which time the chief ex-officio was to hold himself under the orders of the commodore and be transferred to the deck department if necessary. Mr Gibney approved the measure and it went into effect. Only on entering or leaving a port, or in case of chase by an enemy, were the engines to be used, and McGuffey was warned to be extremely saving of his distillate.

CHAPTER XXI

MR. GIBNEY had made a splendid job of changing the vessel's name, and as she chugged lazily out of Panama Bay and lifted to the long ground-swell of the Pacific, it is doubtful if even her late Mexican commander would have recognized her. She was indeed a beautiful craft, and Commodore Gibney's heart swelled with pride as he stood aft, conning the man at the wheel, and looked her over. It seemed like a sacrilege now, when he reflected how he had trained the gun of the old *Maggie* on her that day off the Coronados, and it seemed to him now even a greater sacrilege to have brazenly planned to enter her as a privateer in the struggles of the republic of Colombia. The past tense is used advisedly, for that project was now entirely off, much to the secret delight of Captain Scraggs, who, if the hero of one naval engagement, was not anxious to take part in another. In Panama the freebooters of the *Maggie II* learned that during Mr. Gibney's absence on his filibustering trip the Colombian revolutionists had risen and struck their blow. After the fashion of a hot-headed and impetuous people, they had entered the contest absolutely untrained. As a result, the war had lasted just two weeks, the leaders had been incontinently shot, and the white-winged dove of peace had once more spread her pinions along the borders of the Gold Coast.

Commodore Gibney was disgusted beyond measure, and at a special meeting of the syndicate, called in the cabin of the *Maggie II* that same evening, it was finally decided that they should embark on an indefinite trading cruise in the South Seas, or until such time as it seemed their services must be required to free a downtrodden people from a tyrant's yoke.

Captain Scraggs and McGuffey had never been in the South Seas, but they had heard that a fair margin of profit was to be wrung from trade in copra, shell, cocoanuts, and kindred tropical products. They so expressed themselves. To this suggestion, however, Commodore Gibney waved a deprecating paw.

"Legitimate tradin', boys," he said, "is a nice, sane, healthy business, but the profits is slow. What we want is quick profits, and while it ain't set down in black and white, one of the principal objects of this syndicate is to lead a life of wild adventure. In tradin', there ain't no adventure to speak of. We ought to do a little blackbirdin', or raid some of those Jap pearl fisheries off the northern coast of Formosa."

"But we'll be chased by real gunboats if we do that," objected Captain Scraggs. "Those Jap gunboats shoot to kill. Can't you think of somethin' else, Gib?"

"Well," said Mr. Gibney, "for a starter, I can. Suppose we just head straight for Kandavu Island in the Fijis, and scheme around for a cargo of black coral? It's only worth about fifty dollars a pound. Kandavu lays somewhere in latitude 22 south, longitude 178 west, and when I was there last it was fair reekin' with cannibal savages. But there's tons of black coral there, and nobody's ever been able to sneak in and get away with it. Every time a boat used to land at Kandavu, the native niggers would have a white-man stew down on the beach, and it's got so that skippers give the island a wide berth."

"Gib, my *dear* boy," chattered Captain Scraggs, "I'm a man of peace and I—I——"

"Scraggsy, old stick-in-the-mud," said Mr. Gibney, laying an affectionate hand on the skipper's shoulder, "you're nothin' of the sort. You're a fightin' tarantula, and nobody knows it better'n Adelbert P. Gibney. I've seen you in action, Scraggsy. Remember that. It's all right for you to say you're a man of peace and advise me and McGuffey to keep out of the track of trouble, but we know that away down low you're goin' around lookin' for blood, and that once you're up agin the enemy, you never bat an eyelash. Eh, Mc-Guffey?"

McGuffey nodded; whereupon, Captain Scraggs, making but a poor effort to conceal the pleasure which Mr. Gibney's rude compliment afforded him, turned to the rail, glanced seaward, and started to walk away to attend to some trifling detail connected with the boat falls.

"All right, Gib, my lad," he said, affecting to resign himself to the inevitable, "have it your own way. You're a commodore and I'm only a plain captain, but I'll follow wherever you lead. I'll go as far as the next man and we'll glom that black coral if we have to slaughter every man, woman, and child on the island. Only, when we're sizzlin' in a pot don't you up and say I never warned you, because I did. How d'ye propose intimidatin' the natives, Gib?"

"Scraggsy," said the commodore solemnly, "we've waged a private war agin a friendly nation, licked 'em, and helped ourselves to their ship. We've changed her name and rig and her official number and letters and we're sailin' under bogus papers. That makes us pirates, and that old *Maggie* burgee floatin' at the fore ain't nothin' more nor less than the Jolly Roger. All right! Let's be pirates. Who cares? When we slip into M'galao harbour we'll invite the king and his head men aboard for dinner. We'll get 'em drunk, clap 'em in double irons, and surrender 'em to their weepin' subjects when they've filled the hold of the *Maggie II* with black coral. If they refuse to come aboard we'll shell the bush with that long gun and the Maxim rapid-fire guns we've got below decks. That'll scare 'em so they'll leave us alone and we can help ourselves to the coral."

Scraggs's cold blue eyes glistened. "Lord, Gib," he murmured, "you've got a head."

"Like playin' post-office," was McGuffey's comment.

The commodore smiled. "I thought you boys would see it that way. Now to-morrow I'm going ashore to buy three divin' outfits and lay in a big stock of provisions for the voyage. In the meantime, while the carpenters are gettin' the ship into shape, we'll leave the first mate in charge while we go ashore and have a good time. I've seen worse places than Panama."

As a result of this conference Mr. Gibney's suggestions were acted upon, and they contrived to make their brief stay in Panama very agreeable. They inspected the work on the canal, marvelled at the stupendous engineering in the Culebra Cut, drank a little, gambled a little. McGuffey whipped a bartender. He was

ordered arrested, and six spiggoty little policemen, sent
to arrest him, were also thrashed. The reserves were
called out and a riot ensued. Mr. Gibney, following
the motto of the syndicate, i. e.,

> All for one and one for all—
> United we stand, divided we fall,

mixed in the conflict and presently found himself in
durance vile. Captain Scraggs, luckily, forgot the
motto and escaped, but inasmuch as he was on hand
next morning to pay a fine of thirty pesos levied against
each of the culprits, he was instantly forgiven. Mr.
Gibney vowed that if a United States cruiser didn't
happen to be lying in the roadstead, he would have
shelled the town in retaliation.

But eventually the days passed, and the *Maggie II*,
well found and ready for sea, shook out her sails to a
fair breeze and sailed away for Kandavu. She kept
well to the southwest until she struck the southeast
trades, when she swung around on her course, headed
straight for her destination. It was a pleasant voyage,
devoid of incident, and the health of all hands was excellent. Mr. Gibney took daily observations, and was
particular to make daily entries in his log when he,
Scraggs, and McGuffey were not playing cribbage, a
game of which all three were passionately fond.

On the afternoon of the twenty-ninth day after leaving Panama the lookout reported land. Through his
glasses Mr. Gibney made out a cluster of tall palms
at the southerly end of the island, and as the schooner
held lazily on her course he could discern the white

breakers foaming over the reefs that guarded the entrance to the harbour.

"That's Kandavu, all right," announced the commodore. "I was there in '89 with Bull McGinty in the schooner *Dashin' Wave*. There's the entrance to the harbour, with the Esk reefs to the north and the Pearl reefs to the south. The channel's very narrow—not more than three cables, if it's that, but there's plenty of water and a good muddy bottom that'll hold. McGuffey, lad, better run below and tune up your engines. It's too dangerous a passage on an ebb-tide for a sailin' vessel, so we'll run in under the power. Scraggsy, stand by and when I give the word have your crew shorten sail."

Within a few minutes a long white streak opened up in the wake of the schooner, announcing that McGuffey's engines were doing duty, and a nice breeze springing up two points aft the beam, the *Maggie* heeled over and fairly flew through the water. Mr. Gibney smiled an ecstatic smile as he took the wheel and guided the schooner through the channel. He rounded her up in twelve fathoms, and within five minutes every stitch of canvas was clewed down hard and fast. The sun was setting as they dropped anchor, and Mr. Gibney had lanterns hung along the rail so that it would be impossible for any craft to approach the schooner and board her without being seen. Also the watch on deck that night carried Mauser rifles, six-shooters, and cutlasses. Mr. Gibney was taking no chances.

CHAPTER XXII

"NOW, boys," announced Commodore Gibney, as he sat at the head of the officers' mess at breakfast next morning, "there'll be a lot of canoes paddling off to visit us within the hour, so whatever you do, don't allow more than two of these cannibals aboard the schooner at the same time. Make 'em keep their weapons in the canoes with 'em, and at the first sign of trouble shoot 'em down like dogs. It may be that these precautions ain't necessary, but when I was here twenty years ago it was all the rage to kill a white man and eat him. Maybe times has changed, but the harbour and the coast looks just as wild and lonely as they ever did, and I didn't see no sign of missionary when we dropped hook last night. So don't take no chances."

All hands promised that they would take extreme care, to the end that their precious persons might remain intact, so Mr. Gibney finished his cup of coffee at a gulp and went on deck.

The Kandavu aborigines were not long in putting in an appearance. Even as Mr. Gibney came on deck half a dozen canoes shot out from the beach. Mr. Gibney immediately piped all hands on deck, armed them, and nonchalantly awaited the approach of what might or might not turn out to be an enemy.

When the flotilla was within pistol shot of the schooner Mr. Gibney stepped to the rail and motioned them back. Immediately the natives ceased paddling, and a wild-looking fellow stood up in the forward canoe. After the manner of his kind he had all his life soused his head in lime-water when making his savage toilette, and as a result his shock of black hair stood on end and bulged out like a crowded hayrick. He was naked, of course, and in his hand he held a huge war club.

"That feller'd eat a rattlesnake," gasped Captain Scraggs. "Shoot him, Gib, if he bats an eye."

"Shut up," said the commodore, a trifle testily; "that's the number-one nigger, who does the talkin'. Hello, boy."

"Hello, cap'n," replied the savage, and salaamed gravely. "You likee buy chicken, buy pig? Maybe you say come 'board, I talk. Me very good friend white master."

"Bless my sweet-scented soul!" gasped the commodore. "What won't them missionaries do next? Cut off my ears if this nigger ain't civilized!" He beckoned to the canoe and it shot alongside, and its brown crew came climbing over the rail of the *Maggie II*.

Mr. Gibney met the spokesman at the rail and they rubbed noses very solemnly, after the manner of salutation in Kandavu. Captain Scraggs bustled forward, full of importance.

"Interduce me, Gib," he said amiably, and then, while Mr. Gibney favoured him with a sour glance, Captain Scraggs stuck out his hand and shook briskly with the native.

"Happy to make your acquaintance," he said. "Scraggs is my name, sir. Shake hands with McGuffey, our chief engineer. Hope you left all the folks at home well. What'd you say your name was?"

The islander hadn't said his name was anything, but he grinned now and replied that it was Tabu-Tabu.

"Well, my bucko," muttered McGuffey, who always drew the colour line, "I'm glad to hear that. But you ain't the only thing that's taboo around this packet. You can jest check that war club with the first mate, pendin' our better acquaintance. Hand it over, you black beggar, or I'll hit you a swat in the ear that'll hurt all your relations. And hereafter, Scraggsy, just keep your nigger friends to yourself. I ain't waxin' effusive over this savage, and it's agin my principles ever to shake hands with a coloured man. This chap's a damned ugly customer, and you take my word for it."

Tabu-Tabu grinned again, walked to the rail, and tossed his war club down into the canoe.

"Me good missionary boy," he said rather humbly.

"McGuffey, my *dear* boy," protested Captain Scraggs, "don't be so doggone rude. You might hurt this poor lad's feelin's. Of course he's only a simple native nigger, but even a dawg has feelin's. You——"

"A-r-r-rh!" snarled McGuffey.

"You two belay talkin' and snappin' at each other," commanded Mr. Gibney, "an' leave all bargainin' to me. This boy is all right and we'll get along first rate if you two just haul ship and do somethin' useful besides buttin' in on your superior officer. Come along, Tabu-Tabu. Makee little eat down in cabin. You talkee captain."

"Gib, my *dear* boy," sputtered Captain Scraggs,

bursting with curiosity, following the commodore's re-appearance on deck, "whatever's in the wind?"

"Money—fortune," said Mr. Gibney solemnly.

McGuffey edged up and eyed the commodore seriously. "Sure there ain't a little fightin' mixed up in it?" he asked.

"Not a bit of it," replied Mr. Gibney. "You're as safe on Kandavu as if you was in church. This Tabu kid is sort of prime minister to the king, with a heap of influence at court. The crew of a British cruiser stole him for a galley police when he was a kid, and he got civilized and learned to talk English. He was a cannibal in them days, but the chaplain aboard showed him how foolish it was to do such things, and finally Tabu-Tabu got religion and asked as a special favour to be allowed to return to Kandavu to civilize his people. As a result of Tabu-Tabu's efforts, he tells me the king has concluded that when he eats a white man he's flyin' in the face of his own interests, and most generally a gunboat comes along in a few months and shells the bush, and—well, anyhow, there ain't been a barbecue on Kandavu for ten years. It's a capital crime to eat a man now, and punishable by boilin' the offender alive in palm oil."

"Well," rumbled McGuffey, "this Tabu-Tabu don't look much like a preacher, if you ask me. But how about this black coral?"

"Oh, I've ribbed up a deal with him," said Mr. Gibney. "He'll see that we get all the trade we can lug away. We're the first vessel that's touched here in two years, and they have a thunderin' lot of stuff on hand. Tabu's gone ashore to talk the king into doin'

business with us. If he consents, we'll have him and
Tabu-Tabu and three or four of the sub-chiefs aboard
for dinner, or else he'll invite us ashore for a big feed,
and we'll have to go."

"Supposin' this king don't care to have any truck
with us?" inquired McGuffey anxiously.

"In that case, Mac," replied the commodore with a
smile, "we'll just naturally shell him out of house
and home."

"Well, then," said McGuffey, "let's get the guns
ready. Somethin' tells me these people ain't to be
trusted, and I'm tellin' you right now, Gib, I won't
sleep well to-night unless them two quarter gatlings
and the Maxim-Vickers rapid-fire guns is mounted and
ready for business."

"All right, Mac," replied Mr. Gibney, in the tone
one uses when humouring a baby. "Set 'em up if it'll
make you feel more cheerful. Still, I don't see why
you want to go actin' so foolish over nothin'."

"Well, Gib," replied the engineer, "I may be crazy,
but I ain't no fool, and if there's a dead whale around
the ship, I can come pretty near smellin' it. I tell you,
Gib, that Tabu-Tabu nigger had a look in his eye for
all the world like a cur dog lickin' a bone. I ain't
takin' no chances. My old man used to say: 'Bart,
whatever you do, allers have an anchor out to windward.'"

"By the left hind leg of the Great Sacred Bull,"
snapped Captain Scraggs. "if you ain't enough to precipitate war."

"War," replied McGuffey, "is my long suit—particularly war with native niggers. I just naturally

crave to punch the ear of anything darker than a Portugee. Remember how I cleaned out the police department of Panama?"

"Mount the guns if you're goin' to, Mac. If not, for the love of the Lord don't be demoralizin' the crew with this talk of war. All I ask is that you set the guns up after I've finished my business here with Tabu-Tabu. He's been on a war vessel, and knows what guns are, and if he saw you mountin' them it might break up our friendly relations. He'll think we don't trust him."

"Well, we don't," replied McGuffey doggedly.

"Well, we do," snapped Captain Scraggs.

There is always something connected with the use of that pronoun of kings which eats like a canker at the heart of men of the McGuffey breed. That officer now spat on the deck, in defiance of the rules of his superior officers, and glared at Captain Scraggs.

"Speak for yourself, you miserable little wart," he roared. "If you include me on that cannibal's visitin' list, and go to contradictin' me agin, I'll——"

"Mac," interrupted Mr. Gibney angrily, "control yourself. It's agin the rules to have rag-chewin' and backbitin' on the *Maggie II*. Remember our motto: 'All for one and one for all'——"

"Here comes that sneakin' bushy-headed murderer back to the vessel," interrupted McGuffey. "I wonder what devilment he's up to now."

Mr. McGuffey was partly right, for in a few minutes Tabu-Tabu came alongside, climbed aboard, and salaamed. Mr. Gibney, fearful of McGuffey's inability to control his antipathy for the race, beckoned Captain Scraggs and Tabu-Tabu to follow him down into the cabin. Meanwhile, McGuffey contented himself by parading backward and forward across the fo'castle head with a Mauser rifle in the hollow of his arm and his person fairly bristling with pistols and cutlasses. Whenever one of the flotilla of canoes hove to at a respectful distance, showed signs of crossing an imaginary deadline drawn by McGuffey, he would point his rifle at them and swear horribly. He scowled at Tabu-Tabu when that individual finally emerged from the conference with Mr. Gibney and Scraggs and went over the side to his waiting canoe.

"Well, what's in the wind this time?" inquired McGuffey.

"We're invited to a big feed with the king of Kandavu," replied Captain Scraggs, as happy as a boy. "Hop into a clean suit of ducks, Mac, and come along. Gib's goin to broach a little keg of liquor and we'll make a night of it."

"Good lord," groaned McGuffey, "does the man think I'm low enough to *eat* with niggers?"

"Leave him to his own devices," said Mr. Gibney indulgently. "Mac's just as Irish as if he'd been born in Dublin instead of his old man. Nobody yet overcome the prejudice of an Irishman so we'll do the honours ourself, Scraggsy, old skittles, and leave Mac in charge of the ship."

"Mind you're both back at a seasonable hour," warned McGuffey. "If you ain't, I'll suspect mischief and—say! Gib! Well, what's the use talkin' to a man with an imagination? Only if I have to go ashore after you two, those islanders'll date time from my visit, and don't you forget it."

It was nearing four o'clock that afternoon when Commodore Gibney and his navigating officer, Captain Scraggs, both faultlessly arrayed in Panama hats, white ducks, white canvas shoes, cut low, showing pink silk socks, and wearing broad, black silken sashes around their waists, climbed over the side into the whaleboat and were rowed ashore in a manner befitting their rank. McGuffey stood at the rail and jeered them, for his democratic soul could take no cognizance of form or ceremony to a cannibal king, or at least a king but recently delivered from cannibalism.

CHAPTER XXIII

UPON arrival at the beach the two adventurers were met by a contingent of frightful-looking savages bearing long spears. As the procession formed around the two guests of honour and plunged into the bush, bound for the king's wari, two island maidens marched behind the two sea-dogs, waving huge palm-leaf fans, the better to make passage a cool and comfortable one.

"By the gods of war, Gib, my *dear* boy," said the delighted Captain Scraggs, "but this is class, eh, Gib?"

"Every time," responded the commodore. "If that chuckle-headed McGuffey only had the sense to come along he might be enjoyin' himself, too. You must be dignified, Scraggsy, old salamander. Remember that you're bigger an' better'n any king, because you're an American citizen. Be dignified, by all means. These people are sensitive and peculiar, and that's why we haven't taken any weapons with us. If they thought we doubted their hospitality they'd have the court bouncer heave us out of town before you could say Jack Robinson."

"I'd love to see them giving the bounce to McGuffey," said Captain Scraggs musingly. Mr. Gibney had a swift mental picture of such a proceeding and chuckled happily. Had he been permitted a glance at McGuffey at that moment he might have observed that worthy sweltering in the heat of the forward hold of the *Maggie II*, for he was busy getting his guns on deck. From which it will readily be deduced that B. McGuffey, Esquire, was following the advice of his paternal ancestor and getting an anchor out to windward.

One might go on at great length and describe the triumphal entry of Commodore Gibney and Captain Scraggs into the capitol of Kandavu; of how the king, an undersized, shrivelled old savage, stuck his bushy head out the window of his bungalow when he saw the procession coming; of how a minute later he advanced into the space in the centre of his wari, where in the olden days the populace was wont to gather for its cannibal orgies; how he greeted his distinguished visitors with the most prodigious rubbing of noses seen in those parts for many a day; of the feast that followed; of the fowls and pigs that garnished the festive board, not omitting the keg of Three Star thoughtfully provided by Mr. Gibney.

Tabu-Tabu acted as interpreter and everything went swimmingly until Tabu-Tabu, his hospitality doubtless strengthened by frequent libations of the Elixir of Life, begged Mr. Gibney to invite the remainder of his crew ashore for the feast. Mr. Gibney, himself rather illuminated by this time, thought it might not be a bad idea.

"It's a rotten shame, Scraggsy," he said, "to think of that fool McGuffey not bein' here to enjoy himself. I'm goin' to send a note out to him by one of Tabu-Tabu's boys, askin' him once more to come ashore, or to let the first mate and one or two of the seamen come if Mac still refuses to be civil."

"Good idea, Gib," said Captain Scraggs, his mouth full of roast chicken and yams. So Mr. Gibney tore a leaf out of his pocket memorandum book, scrawled a note to McGuffey, and handed it to Tabu-Tabu, who at once dispatched a messenger with it to the *Maggie II.*

Within half an hour the messenger returned. He was wildly excited and poured a torrent of native gibberish into the attentive ears of Tabu-Tabu and the king. He pointed several times to the point of his jaw, rubbed the small of his back, and once he touched his nose; whereupon Mr. Gibney was aware that the said organ had a slight list to port, and he so informed Captain Scraggs. Neither of the gentlemen had the slightest trouble in arriving at the correct solution of the mystery. The royal messenger had been incontinently kicked overboard by B. McGuffey, Esquire.

Tabu-Tabu's wild eyes glittered and grew wilder and wilder as the messenger reported the indignity thus heaped upon him. The king scowled at Captain Scraggs, and Mr. Gibney was suddenly aware that goose-flesh was breaking out on the backs of his sturdy legs. He had a haunting sensation that not only had he crawled into a hole, but he had pulled the entire aperture in after him. For the first time he began to fear that he had been too precipitate, and with the thought it occurred to the gallant commodore that he would be much safer back on the decks of the *Maggie II.* Always crafty and imaginative, however, Mr. Gibney came quickly to the front with an excuse for getting back to the ship. He stepped quickly toward the little group around the outraged royal ambassador, and inquired the cause of the disturbance. Quivering with rage, Tabu-Tabu informed him of what had occurred.

Mr. Gibney's rage, of course, knew no bounds. Nevertheless, he did not have to simulate his rage, for he was truly furious. When he could control his emotions, he requested Tabu-Tabu to inform the king that he, Gibney, accompanied by Captain Scraggs, would forthwith repair to the schooner and then and there flay the offending McGuffey within an inch of his life. Suiting the action to the word, Mr. Gibney called to Captain Scraggs to follow him, and started for the beach.

As Captain Scraggs arose, a trifle unsteadily, from his seat, a black hand reached around him from the rear and closed over his mouth. Now, Captain Scraggs was well versed in the rough-and-tumble tactics of the San Francisco waterfront; hence, when he felt a long pair of arms crossing over his neck from the rear, he merely stooped and whirled his opponent over his head. In that instant his mouth was free, and clear above the shouting and the tumult rose his frenzied shriek for help. Mr. Gibney whirled with the speed and agility of a panther just in time to dodge a blow from a war club. His fist collided with the jaw of Tabu-Tabu, and down went that savage as if pole-axed.

Pandemonium broke loose at once. Captain Scraggs, after his single shriek for help, broke from the circle of savages and fled like a frightened rabbit for the beach. One of the natives hurled a rock at him. The missile took Scraggs in the back of the head, and he instantly curled up in a heap.

"Scraggsy's dead," thought the horrified Gibney, and sprang at the king. In that moment it came to

"*Captain Scraggs. . .
broke from the circle of
savages . . . and fled
for the beach*"

Mr. Gibney to sell out dearly, and if he could dispose of the king, he felt that Scraggs's death would be avenged. In an instant the commodore's great arms had closed around the king, and with the helpless monarch in his grizzly bear grip Mr. Gibney backed up against the nearest bungalow. A fringe of spears threatened him in front, but for the moment he was safe behind, and the king's body protected him. Whenever one of the savages made a jab at Mr. Gibney, Mr. Gibney gave the king a boa-constrictor squeeze, and the monarch howled.

"I'll squeeze him to death," panted Mr. Gibney to Tabu-Tabu when that individual had managed to pick himself up. "Let me go, or I'll kill your king."

The answer was an earthenware pot which crashed down on Mr. Gibney's head from a window in the bungalow behind him. He sagged forward and fell on his face with the gasping king in his arms.

CHAPTER XXIV

ON BOARD the *Maggie II* B. McGuffey, Esquire, had just gotten into position the Maxim-Vickers "pom-pom" gun on top of the house. The last bolt that held it in place had just been screwed tight when clear and shrill over the tops of the jungle and across the still surface of the little bay there floated to McGuffey's ears the single word:

"Help!"

McGuffey leaned against the gun, and for the moment he was as weak as a child. "Gawd," he muttered, "that was Scraggsy and they're a-goin' to eat him up. Oh, Gib, Gib, old man, why wouldn't you listen to me? Now they've got you, and what in blazes I'm going to do to get you back, dead or alive, I dunno."

McGuffey could hear the cries and general uproar from the wari, though he could not see what was taking place. In a minute or two, however, all was once more silent, silence having descended on the scene simultaneously with the descent of the earthenware pot on Mr. Gibney's head.

"It's all over," said McGuffey sadly to the mate. "They've killed 'em both." Whereupon B. McGuffey, Esquire, sat down on the cabin ventilator, pulled out a bandana handkerchief and wept into it, for his honest Irish heart was breaking.

It was fully half an hour before poor McGuffey could

pull himself together, and when he did, his grief was
superseded by a fit of rage that was terrible to behold.

"Step lively, you blasted scum of the seas," he bawled
to the mate, and the crew gathered around the gun.
"Lug up a case of ammunition and we'll shell that bush
until even a parrot won't be left alive in it."

"Aye, aye, sir," responded the crew to a man, and
sprang to their task.

"I'm an old navy gunner," said the first mate quietly.
"I'll handle the gun. With a 'pom-pom' gun it's just
like playing a garden hose on them, only it's high-ex-
plosive shell instead of water. I can search out every
nook and cranny in the coast of this island. Those guns
are sighted up to 4,000 yards."

"Kill 'em all," raved McGuffey, "kill all the blasted
niggers."

When Mr. Gibney fell under the impact of the earthenware pot he was only partially stunned. As he tried
to struggle to his feet half a dozen hands were laid on
him and in a trice he was lifted and carried back of the
wari to a clear space where a dozen heavy teakwood
posts stood in a row about four feet apart. Mr. Gibney was quickly stripped of his clothing and bound hand
and foot to one of these posts. Three minutes later
another delegation of cannibals arrived, bearing the
limp, naked body of Captain Scraggs, whom they bound
in similar fashion to the post beside Mr. Gibney.
Scraggs was very white and bloody, but conscious, and
his pale-blue eyes were flickering like a snake's.

"What's—what's—the meanin' of this, Gib?" he
gasped.

"It means," replied the commodore, "that it's all off but the shouting with me and you, Scraggsy. This fellow Tabu-Tabu is a damned traitor, and his people are still cannibals. He's the decoy to get white men ashore. They schemed to treat us nice and be friendly until they could get the whole crew ashore, or enough of them to leave the ship helpless, and then—O Gawd, Scraggsy, old man, can you ever forgive me for gettin' you into this?"

Captain Scraggs hung his head and quivered like a hooked fish.

"Will they—eat—us?" he quavered, finally.

Mr. Gibney did not answer, only Captain Scraggs looked into his horrified eyes and read the verdict.

"Die game, Scraggsy," was all Mr. Gibney could say. "Don't show the white feather."

"D'ye think McGuffey could hear us from here if we was to yell for help?" inquired Captain Scraggs hopefully.

"Don't yelp, for Gawd's sake," implored Mr. Gibney. "We got ourselves into this, so let's pay the fiddler ourselves. If we let out one yip and McGuffey hears it, he'll come ashore with his crew and tackle this outfit, even if he knows he'll get killed. And that's just what will happen to him if he comes. Let poor Mac stay aboard. When we don't come back, he'll know it's all off, and if he has time to think over it he'll realize it would be foolish to try to do anything. But right now Mac's mad as a wet hen, and if we holler for help— Scraggsy, please don't holler. Die game."

Captain Scraggs turned his terrified glance on Mr. Gibney's tortured face. Scraggs was certainly a coward

at heart, but there was something in Mr. Gibney's un-
selfishness that touched a spot in his hard nature—a
something he never knew he possessed. He bowed his
head and two big tears stole down his weatherbeaten
face.

"God bless you, Gib, my *dear* boy," he said brokenly.
"You're a man."

At this juncture the king came up and thoughtfully
felt of Captain Scraggs in the short ribs, while Tabu-
Tabu calculated the precise amount of luscious tissue
on Mr. Gibney's well-upholstered frame.

"Bimeby we eat white man," said Tabu-Tabu cheerfully.

"If you eat me, you bloody-handed beggar," snapped
Captain Scraggs, "I'll pizen you. I've chawed tobacco
all my life, and my meat's as bitter as wormwood."

It was too funny to hear Scraggs jesting with death.
Mr. Gibney forgot his own mental agony and roared
with laughter in Tabu-Tabu's face. The cannibal stood
off a few feet and looked searchingly in the commodore's
eyes. He was not used to the brand of white man who
could laugh under such circumstances, and he suspected
treachery of some kind. He hurried over to join the
king and the two held a hurried conversation. As a result of their conference, a huge savage was called over
and given some instructions. Tabu-Tabu handed him
a war club and Mr. Gibney, rightly conjecturing that
this was the official executioner, bowed his head and
waited for the blow.

It came sooner than he expected. The earth seemed
to rise up and smite Adelbert P. Gibney across the face.
There was a roar, as of an explosion in his ears, and he

fell forward on his face.   He had a confused notion that when he fell the post came with him.

For nearly a minute he lay there, semi-conscious, and then something warm, dripping across his face, roused him.   He moved, and found that his feet were free, though his hands were still bound to the post, which lay extended along his back.   He rolled over and glanced up.   Captain Scraggs was shrieking.   By degrees the bells quit ringing in the commodore's ears, and this is what he heard Captain Scraggs yelling:

"Oh, you McGuffey. Oh, you bully Irish terrier. Soak it to 'em, Mac. Kill the beggars. You've got a dozen of 'em already. Plug away, you good old hunk of Irish bacon."

Mr. Gibney was now himself once more.   He struggled to his feet, and as he did, something burst ten feet away and a little fleecy cloud of smoke obscured his vision for a moment.   Then he understood.   McGuffey had a rapid-fire gun trained on the wari, and the savages, with frightful yells, were fleeing madly from the little shells.   Half a dozen of them lay dead and wounded close by.

"Hooray," yelled Mr. Gibney, and dashed at the post which held Captain Scraggs prisoner.   He struck it a powerful blow with his shoulder and Scraggs and the post crashed to the ground.   In an instant Mr. Gibney was on his knees, tearing at Scraggs's rope shackles with his teeth.   Five minutes later, Captain Scraggs's hands were free.   Then Scraggs did a like service for Gibney.

All the time the shells from the *Maggie II* were bursting around them every second or two, and it seemed as if they must be killed before they could make their escape.

"Beat it, Scraggsy," yelled Mr. Gibney. He stood and picked up a war club. "Arm yourself, Scraggsy. Take a spear. We may have a little fighting to do on the beach," he yelled. Captain Scraggs helped himself to a loose spear, and side by side they raced through the jungle for the beach.

As they tore along through the jungle path Mr. Gibney's good right eye (his left was obscured) detected two savages crouching behind a clump of cocoa-palms.

"There's the king and Tabu-Tabu," yelled Scraggs. "Let's round the beggars up."

"Sure," responded the commodore. "We'll need 'em for hostages if we're to get that black coral. We'll turn 'em over to McGuffey."

"I'd better ease up a minute, sir," said the mate to Mr. McGuffey. "The gun's getting fearful hot."

"Let her melt," raved McGuffey, "but keep her workin' for all she's worth. I'll have revenge for Gib's death, or—*sufferin' mackerel !*"

McGuffey once more sat down on the cabin ventilator. He pointed dumbly to the beach, and there, paddling off to the *Maggie II,* were two naked cannibals and two naked white men in a canoe. Five minutes later they came alongside. McGuffey met them at the rail, and he smiled and licked his lower lip as the trembling monarch and his prime minister, in response to a severe application of Mr. Gibney's hands and feet, came flying over the rail. Mr. Gibney and Captain Scraggs followed.

"I'm much obliged to you, Mac," said Mr. Gibney, striving bravely to appear jaunty. "One of your first shots came between my legs and cut the rope that held me, and banged me and the post I was tied to all over the lot. A fragment of the shell appears to have taken away part of my ear, but I guess I'll recover. We're pretty well shook up, Mac, old socks, and a jolt of whisky would be in order after you've put the irons on these two cannibals."

"You're two nice bloody-lookin' villains, ain't you?" was McGuffey's comment, as he surveyed the late arrivals.

"Which two do you mean?" inquired Mr. Gibney, with a touch of asperity in his tones.

"I dunno," replied McGuffey. "It's pretty hard to distinguish between niggers and folks that goes to work an' eats with 'em."

"Mac," said Captain Scraggs severely, "you're prejudiced."

CHAPTER XXV

AT 6:30 o'clock of the morning of the day following the frightful experience of Commodore Gibney and Captain Scraggs with the cannibals of Kandavu, the members of the *Maggie II* Syndicate faced each other across the breakfast table with appetites in no wise diminished by the exciting events of the preceding day. Captain Scraggs appeared with a lump on the back of his head as big as a goose egg. The doughty commodore had a cut over his right eye, and the top of his sinful head was so sore, where the earthenware pot had struck him, that even the simple operation of winking his bloodshot eyes was productive of pain. About a teaspoonful of Kandavu real estate had also been blown into Mr. Gibney's classic features when the shells from the Maxim-Vickers gun exploded in his immediate neighbourhood, and as he naïvely remarked to Bartholomew McGuffey, he was in luck to be alive.

McGuffey surveyed his superior officers, cursed them bitterly, and remarked, with tears of joy in his honest eyes, that both gentlemen had evaded their just deserts when they escaped with their lives. "If it hadn't been for the mate," said McGuffey severely, "I'd 'a' let you two boobies suffer the penalty for your foolishness. Any man that goes to work and fraternizes with a cannibal ain't got no kick comin' if he's made up into chicken curry with rice. The minute I hear old Scraggsy yippin' for help, says I to myself, 'let the beggars fight their own way out of the mess.' But the mate comes a-runnin' up and says he's pretty sure he can come near plantin' a mess of shells in the centre of the disturbance, even if we can't see the wari on account of the jungle. 'It's all off with the commodore and the skipper anyhow,' says the mate, 'so we might just as well have vengeance on their murderers.' So, of course, when he put it that way I give my consent——"

At this juncture the mate, passing around McGuffey on his way to the deck, winked solemnly at Mr. Gibney, who hung his war-worn head in simulated shame. When the mate had left the cabin the commodore pounded with his fork on the cabin table and announced a special meeting of the *Maggie II* Syndicate.

"The first business before the meeting," said Mr. Gibney, "is to readjust the ownership in the syndicate. Me and Scraggsy's had our heads together, Mac, and we've agreed that you've shot your way into a full one-third interest, instead of a quarter as heretofore. From now on, Mac, you're an equal owner with me and Scraggsy, and now that that matter's settled, you can quit rippin' it into us on the race question and suggest what's to be done in the case of Tabu-Tabu and this cannibal king that almost lures me and the navigatin' officer to our destruction."

"I have the villains in double irons and chained to the mainmast," replied McGuffey, "and as a testimonial of my gratitude for the increased interest in the syndicate which you and Scraggs has just voted me, I will scheme up a fittin' form of vengeance on them two tar babies. However, only an extraordinary sentence can fit such an extraordinary crime, so I must have time to think it over. These two bucks is mine to do what I please with and I'll take any interference as unneighbourly and unworthy of a shipmate."

"Take 'em," said Captain Scraggs vehemently. "For my part I only ask one thing. If you can see your way clear, Mac, to give me the king's scalp for a tobacco pouch, I'll be obliged."

"And I," added the commodore, "would like Tabu-Tabu's shin bone for a clarionet. Pendin' McGuffey's reflections on the hamperin' of crime in Kandavu, however, we'll turn our attention to the prime object of the expedition. We've had our little fun and it's high time we got down to business. It will be low tide at nine o'clock, so I suggest, Scraggs, that you order the mate and two seamen out in the big whaleboat, together with the divin' apparatus, and we'll go after pearl oysters and black coral. As for you, Mac, suppose you take the other boat and Tabu-Tabu and the king, and help the mate. Take a rifle along with you, and make them captives dive for pearl oysters until they're black in the face——"

"Huh!" muttered the single-minded McGuffey. "What are they now? Sky blue?"

"Of course," continued the commodore, "if a tiger shark happens along and picks the niggers up, it ain't none of our business. As for me and Scraggsy, we'll sit on deck and smoke. My head aches and I guess Scraggsy's in a similar fix."

"Anythin' to be agreeable," acquiesced McGuffey.

After breakfast Commodore Gibney ordered that the prisoners be brought before him. The cook served them with breakfast, and as they ate, the commodore reminded them that it was only through his personal efforts and his natural disinclination to return blow for blow that they were at that moment enjoying a square meal instead of swinging in the rigging.

"I'm goin' to give you two yeggs a chance to reform," concluded Mr. Gibney, addressing Tabu-Tabu. "If you show us where we can get a cargo of black coral and work hard and faithful helpin' us to get it aboard, it may help you to comb a few gray hairs. I'm goin' to take the irons off now, but remember! At the first sign of the double-cross you're both shark meat."

On behalf of himself and the king, Tabu-Tabu promised to behave, and McGuffey kicked them both into the small boat. The mate and two seamen followed in another boat, in which the air-pump and diving apparatus was carried, and Tabu-Tabu piloted them to a patch of still water just inside the reef. The water was so clear that McGuffey was enabled to make out vast marine gardens thickly sprinkled with the precious black coral.

"Over you go, you two smokes," rasped McGuffey, menacing the captives with his rifle. "Dive deep, my hearties, and bring up what you can find, and if a shark comes along and takes a nip out of your hind leg, don't expect no help from B. McGuffey, Esquire—because you won't get any."

Thus encouraged, the two cannibals dove overboard. McGuffey could see them pawing around on the bottom of the little bay, and after half a minute each came up with a magnificent spray of coral. They hung to the side of the boat until they could get their breath, then repeated the performance. In the meantime, the mate had sent his two divers below to loosen the coral; with the result that when both boats returned to the *Maggie II* at noon Captain Scraggs fairly gurgled with delight at the results of the morning's work, and Mr. Gibney declared that his headache was gone. He and Captain Scraggs had spent the morning seated on deck under an awning, watching the beach for signs of a sortie on the part of the natives of Kandavu to recapture their king. Apparently, however, the destructive fire from the pom-pom gun the night before had so terrified them that the entire population had emigrated to the northern end of the island, leaving the invaders in undisputed possession of the bay and its hidden treasures of coral and pearl and shell.

For nearly two weeks the *Maggie II* lay at anchor, while her crew laboured daily in the gardens of the deep. Vast quantities of pearl oysters were brought to the surface, and these Mr. Gibney stewed personally in a great iron pot on the beach. The shell was stored away in the hold and the pearls went into a chamois pouch which never for an instant was out of the commodore's possession. The coast at that point being now deserted, frequent visits ashore were made, and the crew feasted on young pig, chicken, yams, and other delicacies. Captain Scraggs was almost delirious with joy. He announced that he had not been so happy since Mrs. Scraggs "slipped her cable."

At the end of two weeks Mr. Gibney decided that there was "loot" enough ashore to complete the

246 THE GREEN-PEA PIRATES

schooner's cargo, and at a meeting of the syndicate held
one lovely moonlight night on deck he announced his
plans to Captain Scraggs and McGuffey.

"Better leave the island alone," counselled McGuffey.
"Them niggers may be a-layin' there ten thousand
strong, waitin' for a boat's crew to come prowlin' up
into the bush so they can nab 'em."

"I've thought of that, Mac," said the commodore a
trifle coldly, "and if I made a sucker of myself once it
don't stand to reason that I'm apt to do it again. Remember, Mac, a burnt child dreads the fire. To-morrow morning, right after breakfast, we'll turn the guns
loose and pepper the bush for a mile or two in every
direction. If there's a native within range he'll have
business in the next county and we won't be disturbed
none."

Mr. Gibney's programme was duly put through and
capital of Kandavu looted of the trade accumulations
the of years. And when the hatches were finally bat-
tened down, the tanks refilled with fresh water, and
everything in readiness to leave Kandavu for the run to
Honolulu, Mr. Gibney announced to the syndicate
that the profits of the expedition would figure close up
to a hundred thousand dollars. Captain Scraggs
gasped and fell limply against the mainmast.

"Gib, my *dear* boy," he sputtered, "are you sure it
ain't all a dream and that we'll wake up some day and
find that we're still in the green-pea trade; that all these
months we've been asleep under a cabbage leaf, com-
munin' with potato bugs?"

"Not for a minute," replied the commodore. "Why,
I got a dozen matched pearls here that's fit for a queen.

Big, red, pear-shaped boys—regular bleedin' hearts. There's ten thousand each in them alone."

"Well, I'll—I'll brew some grog," gasped Captain Scraggs, and departed forthwith to the galley. Fifteen minutes later he returned with a kettle of his favourite nepenthe and all three adventurers drank to a bon voyage home. At the conclusion of the toast Mr. McGuffey set down his glass, wiped his mouth with the back of his hairy hand, and thus addressed the syndicate.

"In leavin' this paradise of the South Pacific," he began, "we find that we have accumulated other wealth besides the loot below decks. I refer to His Royal Highness, the king of Kandavu, and his prime minister, Tabu-Tabu. When these two outlaws was first captured, I informed the syndicate that I would scheme out a punishment befittin' their crime, to-wit—murderin' an' eatin' you two boys. It's been a big job and it's taken some time, me not bein' blessed with quite as fine an imagination as our friend, Gib. However, I pride myself that hard work always brings success, and I am ready to announce what disposition shall be made of these two interestin' specimens of aboriginal life. I beg to announce, gentlemen, that I have invented a punishment fittin' the crime."

"Impossible," said Captain Scraggs.

"Shut up, Scraggs," struck in Commodore Gibney. "Out with it, Mac. What's the programme?"

"I move you, members of the syndicate, that the schooner *Maggie II* proceed to some barren, uninhabited island, and that upon arrival there this savage king and his still more savage subject be taken ashore in a small boat. I also move you, gentlemen of the syndicate, that inasmuch as the two aggrieved parties, A. P. Gibney and P. Scraggs, having in a sperrit of mercy refrained from layin' their hands on said prisoners for fear of invalidin' them at a time when their services was of importance to the expedition, be given an opportunity to take out their grudge on the persons of said savages. Now, I notice that the king is a miserable, skimpy, sawed-off, and hammered-down old cove. By all the rules of the prize ring he's in Scraggsy's class." (Here Mr. McGuffey flashed a lightning wink to the commodore. It was an appeal for Mr. Gibney's moral support in the engineer's scheme to put up a job on Captain Scraggs, and thus relieve the tedium of the homeward trip. Mr. Gibney instantly telegraphed his approbation, and McGuffey continued.) "I notice also that if I was to hunt the universe over, I couldn't find a better match for Gib than Tabu-Tabu. And as we are all agreed that the white race is superior to any race on earth, and it'll do us all good to see a fine mill before we leave the country, I move you, gentlemen of the syndicate, that we pull off a finish fight between Scraggsy and the king, and Gib and Tabu-Tabu. I'll referee both contests and at the conclusion of the mixup we'll leave these two murderers marooned on the island and then——"

"Rats," snapped Captain Scraggs. "That ain't no business at all. You shouldn't consider nothin' short of capital punishment. Why, that's only a petty larceny form of——"

"Quit buttin' in on my prerogatives," roared McGuffey. "That ain't the finish by no means."

"What is the finish, then?"

"Why, these two cannibals, bein' left alone on the desert island, naturally bumps up agin the old question of the survival of the fittest. They get scrappin' among themselves, and one eats the other up."

"By the toe-nails of Moses," muttered Mr. Gibney in genuine admiration, "but you *have* got an imagination after all, Mac. The point is well taken and the programme will go through as outlined. Scraggs, you'll fight the king. No buckin' and grumblin'. You'll fight the king. You're outvoted two to one, the thing's been done regular, and you can't kick. I'll fight Tabu-Tabu, so you see you're not gettin' any the worst of it. We'll proceed to an island in the Friendly Group called Tuvana-tholo. It lies right in our homeward course, and there ain't enough grub on the confounded island to last two men a week. And I know there ain't no water there. So, now that that matter is all settled, we will proceed to heave the anchor and scoot for home. Mac, tune up your engines and we'll get out of here a-whoopin' and a-flyin'."

Ten minutes later the anchor was hanging at the hawsepipe, and under her power the *Maggie II* swung slowly in the lagoon, pointed her sharp bow for the opening in the reef, and bounded away for the open sea. Captain Scraggs jammed on all of her lower sails and within two hours the island of Kandavu had faded forever from their vision.

It was an eight-hundred-mile run up to Tuvana-tholo, but the weather held good and the trade-winds never slackened. Ten days from the date of leaving Kandavu they hove to off the island. It was a long, low, sandy atoll, with a few cocoanut-palms growing in the centre of it, and with the exception of a vast colony of seabirds that apparently made it their headquarters, the island was devoid of life.

The bloodthirsty McGuffey stood at the break of the poop, and as he gazed shoreward he chuckled and rubbed his hands together.

"Great, great," he murmured. "I couldn't have gotten a better island if I'd had one built to order." He called aft to the navigating officer: "Scraggsy, there's the ring. Nothin' else to do now but get the contestants into it. Along in the late afternoon, when the heat of the day is over, we'll go ashore and pull off the fight. And, by George, Scraggs, if that old king succeeds in lambastin' you, I'll set the rascal free."

"I'll lick him with one hand tied and the other paralyzed," retorted Captain Scraggs with fine nonchalance. "No need o' waitin' on my account. Heat or no heat, I'm just naturally pinin' to beat up the royal person."

"If this ain't the best idea I ever heard of, I'm a Dutchman," replied McGuffey. "A happy combination of business and pleasure. Who fights first, Gib? You or Scraggs?"

"I guess I'd better open the festivities," said Mr. Gibney amiably. "I ain't no kill-joy and I want Scraggsy to get some fun out of this frolic. If I fight first the old kiddo can look on in peace and enjoy the sight, and if him and the king fights first perhaps he won't be in no condition to appreciate the spectacle that me and Tabu-Tabu puts up."

"That's logic," assented McGuffey solemnly; "that's logic."

Seeing that there was no escape, Captain Scraggs decided to bluff the matter through. "Let's go ashore and have it over with," he said carelessly. "I'm a man of peace, but when there's fightin' to be done, I say go to it and no tomfoolery."

Mr. Gibney winked slyly at McGuffey. They each knew Scraggs little relished the prospect before him, though to do him justice he was mean enough to fight and fight well, if he thought he had half a chance to get the decision. But he knew the king was as hard as tacks, and was more than his match in a rough and tumble, and while he spoke bravely enough, his words did not deceive his shipmates, and inwardly they shook with laughter.

"Clear away the big whaleboat with two men to pull us ashore," said Mr. Gibney to the mate. Five minutes later the members of the syndicate, accompanied by the captives, climbed into the whaleboat and shoved off, leaving the *Maggie II* in charge of the mate. "We'll be back in half an hour," called the commodore, as they rowed away from the schooner. "Just ratch back and forth and keep heavin' the lead."

They negotiated the fringe of breakers to the north of the island successfully, pulled the boat up on the beach, and proceeded at once to business. Mr. Gibney explained to Tabu-Tabu what was expected of him, and Tabu-Tabu in turn explained to the king. It was not the habit of white men, so Mr. Gibney explained, to kill their prisoners in cold blood, and he had decided to give them an opportunity to fight their way out of a sad predicament with their naked fists. If they won, they would be taken back aboard the schooner and later dropped at some inhabited island. If they lost, they must make their home for the future on Tuvana-tholo.

"Let 'er go," called McGuffey, and Mr. Gibney squared off and made a bear-like pass at Tabu-Tabu. To the amazement of all present Tabu-Tabu sprang lightly backward and avoided the blow. His footwork was excellent and McGuffey remarked as much to Captain Scraggs. But when Tabu-Tabu put up his hands after the most approved method of self-defense and dropped into a "crouch," McGuffey could no longer contain himself.

"The beggar can fight, the beggar can fight," he croaked, wild with joy. "Scraggs, old man, this'll be a rare mill, I promise you. He's been aboard a British man-o'-war and learned how to box. Steady, Gib. Upper-cut him, upper—*wow!*"

Tabu-Tabu had stepped in and planted a mighty right in the centre of Mr. Gibney's physiognomy, following it up with a hard left to the commodore's ear. Mr. Gibney rocked a moment on his sturdy legs, stepped back out of range, dropped both hands, and stared at Tabu-Tabu.

"I do believe the nigger'll lick you, Gib," said McGuffey anxiously. "He's got a horrible reach and a mule kick in each mit. Close with him, or he's due for a full pardon."

"In a minute," said the commodore faintly. "He's so good I hate to hurt him. But I'll infight him to a finish."

Which Mr. Gibney forthwith proceeded to do. He rushed his opponent and clinched, though not until his right eye was in mourning and a stiff jolt in the short

"*Tabu Tabu . . .
planted a mighty
right in the centre
of Mr. Gibney's
physiognomy*"

ribs had caused him to grunt in most ignoble fashion. But few men could withstand Mr. Gibney once he got to close quarters. Tabu-Tabu wrapped his long arms around the commodore and endeavoured to smother his blows, but Mr. Gibney would not be denied. His great fist shot upward from the hip and connected with the cannibal's chin. Tabu-Tabu relaxed his hold, Mr. Gibney followed with left and right to the head in quick succession, and McGuffey was counting the fatal ten over the fallen warrior.

Mr. Gibney grinned rather foolishly, spat, and spoke to McGuffey, *soto voce:* "By George, the joke ain't all on Scraggsy," he said. Then turning to Captain Scraggs: "Help yourself to the mustard, Scraggsy, old tarpot."

Captain Scraggs took off his hat, rolled up his sleeves, and made a dive for the royal presence. His majesty, lacking the scientific training of his prime minister, seized a handful of the Scraggs mane and tore at it cruelly. A well-directed kick in the shins, however, caused him to let go, and a moment later he was flying up the beach with the angry Scraggs in full cry after him. McGuffey headed the king off and rounded him up so Scraggs could get at him, and the latter at once "dug in" like a terrier. After five minutes of mauling and tearing Captain Scraggs was out of breath, so he let go and stood off a few feet to size up the situation. The wicked McGuffey was laughing immoderately, but to Scraggs it was no laughing matter. The fact of the matter was the king was dangerous and Scraggs had glutted himself with revenge.

"I don't want to beat an old man to death," he

gasped finally. "I'll let the scoundrel go. He's had enough and he won't fight. Let's mosey along back to the schooner and leave them here to amuse themselves the best way they know how."

"Right-O," said Mr. Gibney, and turned to walk down the beach to the boat. A second later a hoarse scream of rage and terror broke from his lips.

"What's up?" cried McGuffey, the laughter dying out of his voice, for there was a hint of death in Mr. Gibney's cry.

"Marooned!" said the commodore hoarsely. "Those two sailors have pulled back to the schooner, and—there—look, Mac! My Gawd!"

McGuffey looked, and his face went whiter than the foaming breakers beyond which he could see the *Maggie II*, under full sail, headed for the open sea. The small boat had been picked up, and there was no doubt that at her present rate of speed the schooner would be hull down on the horizon by sunset.

"The murderin' hound," whispered McGuffey, and sagged down on the sands. "Oh, the murderin' hound of a mate!"

"It's—it's mutiny," gulped Captain Scraggs in a hard, strained voice. "That bloody fiend of a mate! The sly sneak-thief, whith his pleasant smile and his winnin' ways! Saw a chance to steal the *Maggie* and her rich cargo, and he is leavin' us here, marooned on a desert island, with *two cannibals*."

Captain Scraggs fairly shrieked the last two words and burst into tears. "Lord, Gib, old man," he raved, "whatever will we do?"

Thus appealed to, the doughty commodore permitted

his two unmatched optics to rest mournfully upon his shipmates. For nearly a minute he gazed at them, the while he struggled to stifle the awful fear within him. In the Gibney veins there flowed not a drop of craven blood, but the hideous prospect before him was almost more than the brave commodore could bear. Death, quick and bloody, had no terrors for him, but a finish like this—a slow finish—thirst, starvation, heat——

He gulped and thoughtfully rubbed the knuckles of his right hand where the skin was barked off. He thought of the silly joke he and McGuffey had thought to perpetrate on Captain Scraggs by leading him up against a beating at the hands of a cannibal king, and with the thought came a grim, hard chuckle, though there was the look of a thousand devils in his eyes.

"Well, boys," he said huskily, "who's looney now?"

"What's to be done?" asked McGuffey.

"Well, Mac, old sporty boy, I guess there ain't much to do except to make up our minds to die like gentlemen. If I was ever fooled by a man in my life, I was fooled by that doggone mate. I thought he'd tote square with the syndicate. I sure did."

For a long time McGuffey gazed seaward. He was slower than his shipmates in making up his mind that the mate had really deserted them and sailed away with the fortunes of the syndicate. Of the three, however, the stoical engineer accepted the situation with the best grace. He spurned the white sand with his foot and faced Mr. Gibney and Captain Scraggs with just the suspicion of a grin on his homely face.

"I make a motion," he said, "that the syndicate pass a resolution condemnin' the action of the mate."

It was a forlorn hope, and the jest went over the heads of the deck department.   Said Mr. Gibney sadly:

"There ain't no more *Maggie II* Syndicate."

"Well, let's form a Robinson Crusoe Syndicate," suggested McGuffey.   "We've got the island, and there's a quorum present for all meetin's."

Mr. Gibney smiled feebly.   "We can appoint Tabu-Tabu the man Friday."

"Sure," responded McGuffey, "and the king can be the goat.   Robinson Crusoe had a billy goat, didn't he, Gib?"

But Captain Scraggs refused to be heartened by this airy persiflage.   "I'm all het up after my fight with the king," he quavered presently.   "I wonder if there's any water on this island."

"There is," announced Mr. Gibney pleasantly; "there is, Scraggsy.   There's water in just one spot, but it's there in abundance."

"Where's that spot?" inquired Scraggs eagerly.

Mr. Gibney removed his old Panama hat, and with his index finger pointed downward to where the hair was beginning to disappear, leaving a small bald spot on the crown of his ingenious head.

"There," he said, "right there, Scraggsy, old top. The only water on this island is on the brain of Adelbert P. Gibney."

CHAPTER XXVI

NEILS HALVORSEN often wondered what had
become of the *Maggie* and Captain Scraggs.
Mr. Gibney and Bartholomew McGuffey he
knew had turned their sun-tanned faces toward deep
water some years before Captain Scraggs and the *Maggie* disappeared from the environs of San Francisco
Bay, and Neils Halvorsen was wise enough to waste no
time wondering what had become of *them*. These two
worthies might be anywhere, and every conceivable
thing under the sun might have happened to them;
hence, in his idle moments, Neils Halvorsen did not
disturb his gray matter speculating on their whereabouts and their then condition of servitude.

But the continued absence of Captain Scraggs from
his old haunts created quite a little gossip along the
waterfront, and in the course of time rumours of his
demise by sundry and devious routes came to the ears
of Neils Halvorsen. Now, Neils had sailed too long
with Captain Scraggs not to realize that the erstwhile
green-pea trader would be the last man to take a chance
in any hazardous enterprise unless forced thereto by
the weight of circumstance; also there was affection
enough in his simple Scandinavian heart to cause him
to feel just a little worried when two weeks passed
and Captain Scraggs failed to show up. He had disappeared in some mysterious manner from San Fran-

cisco Bay and the old *Maggie* had never been heard
from again.

Hence Neils Halvorsen was puzzled. In fact, to
such an extent was Neils puzzled, that one perfectly
calm, clear night while beating down San Pablo Bay
in his bay scow, the *Willie and Annie*, he so far forgot
himself and his own affairs as to concentrate all his
attention on the problem of the ultimate finish of Captain Scraggs. So engrossed was Neils in this vain
speculation that he neglected to observe toward the
rules of the ocean highways that nicety of attention
which is highly requisite, even in the skipper of a bay
scow, if the fulsome title of captain is to be retained for
any definite period. As a result, Neils became confused regarding the exact number of blasts from the
siren of a river steamer desiring to pass him to port.
Consequently the *Willie and Annie* received such a
severe butting from the river steamer in question as
to cause her to career and fill. Being, unfortunately,
loaded with gravel on this particular trip, she subsided
incontinently to the bottom of San Pablo Bay, while
Neils and his crew of two men sought refuge on a
plank.

Without attempting to go further into the details of
the misfortunes of Neils Halvorsen, be it known that
the destruction of the *Willie and Annie* proved to be
such a severe shock to Neil's reputation as a safe and
sane bay scow skipper that he was ultimately forced to
seek other and more virgin fields. With the fragments
of his meagre fortune, the ambitious Swede purchased a
course in a local nautical school from which he duly
managed to emerge with sufficient courage to appear

before the United States Local Inspectors of Hulls and Boilers and take his examination for a second mate's certificate. To his unutterable surprise the license was granted; whereupon he shipped as quartermaster on the steamer *Alameda*, running to Honolulu, and what with the lesson taught him in the loss of the *Willie and Annie* and the exacting duties of his office aboard the liner, he forgot that he had ever known Captain Scraggs.

Judge of Neils Halvorsen's surprise, therefore, upon the occasion of his first trip to Honolulu, when he saw something which brought the whole matter back to mind. They were standing in toward Diamond Head and the *Alameda* lay hove to taking on the pilot. It was early morning and the purple mists hung over the entrance to the harbour. Neils Halvorsen stood at the gangway enjoying the sunrise over the Punch-bowl, and glancing longingly toward the vivid green of the hills beyond the city, when he was aware of a "put," "put," "put," to starboard of the *Alameda*. Neils turned at the sound just in time to see a beautiful gasoline schooner of about a hundred and thirty tons heading in toward the bay. She was so close that Neils was enabled to make out that her name was *Maggie II*.

"Vell, aye be dam," muttered Neils, and scratched his head, for the name revived old memories. An hour later, when the *Alameda* loafed into her berth at Brewer's dock, Neils noticed that the schooner lay at anchor off the quarantine station.

That night Neils Halvorsen went ashore for those forms of enjoyment peculiar to his calling, and in the

Pantheon saloon, whither his pathway led him, he filled himself with beer and gossip. It was here that Neils came across an item in an afternoon paper which challenged his instant attention. It was just a squib in the shipping news, but Neils Halvorsen read it with amazement and joy:

> The power schooner *Maggie II* arrived this morning, ten days from the Friendly Islands. The little schooner came into port with her hold bursting with the most valuable cargo that has entered Honolulu in many years. It consists for the most part of black coral.
>
> The *Maggie II* is commanded by Captain Phineas Scraggs, and after taking on provisions and water to-day will proceed to San Francisco, to-morrow, for discharge of cargo.

"By yiminy," quoth Neils Halvorsen, "aye bat you that bane de ole man so sure as you bane alive. And aye bat new hat he skall be glad to see Neils Halvorsen. I guess aye hire Kanaka boy an' he bane pull me out to see de ole man."

Which is exactly what Neils Halvorsen proceeded to do. Ten minutes later he was at the foot of Fort Street, bargaining with a Kanaka fisherman to paddle him off to the schooner *Maggie II*. It was a beautiful moonlight night, and as Neils sat in the stern of the canoe, listening to the sound of the sad, sweet falsetto singing of half a dozen *waheenies* fishing on the wharf, he actually waxed sentimental. His honest Scandinavian heart throbbed with anticipated pleasure as he conjured up a mental picture of the surprise and delight of Captain Scraggs at this unexpected meeting with his old deckhand.

A Jacob's ladder was hanging over the side of the schooner as the canoe shot in under her lee quarter, and half a minute later the expectant Neils stepped upon her deck. A tall dark man, wearing an ancient palmleaf hat, sat smoking on the hatch coaming, and him Neils Halvorsen addressed.

"Aye bane want to see Cap'n Scraggs," he said.

The tall dark man stood erect and cast a quick, questioning look at Neils Halvorsen. He hesitated before he made answer.

"What do you want?" he asked deliberately, and there was a subtle menace in his tones. As for Neils Halvorsen, thinking only of the surprise he had in store for his old employer, he replied evasively:

"Aye bane want job."

"Well, I'm Captain Scraggs, and I haven't any job for you. Get off my boat and wait until you're invited before you come aboard again."

For nearly half a minute Neils Halvorsen stared open-mouthed at the spurious Captain Scraggs, while slowly there sifted through his brain the notion that he had happened across the track of a deep and bloody mystery of the seas. There was "something rotten in Denmark." Of that Neils Halvorsen was certain. More he could not be certain of until he had paved the way for a complete investigation, and as a preliminary step toward that end he clinched his fist and sprang swiftly toward the bogus skipper.

"Aye tank you bane damn liar," he muttered, and struck home, straight and true, to the point of the jaw. The man went down, and in an instant Neils was on top of him. Off came the sailor's belt, the hands of the half-stunned man were quickly tied behind him, and before he had time to realize what had happened Neils had cut a length of cord from a trailing halyard and tied his feet securely, after which he gagged him with his bandana handkerchief.

A quick circuit of the ship convinced Neils Halvorsen that the remainder of the dastard crew were evidently ashore, so he descended to the cabin in search of further evidence of crime. He was quite prepared to find Captain Scraggs's master's certificate in its familiar oaken frame, hanging on the cabin wall, but he was dumfounded to observe, hanging on the wall in a similar and equally familiar frame, the certificate of Adelbert P. Gibney as first mate of steam or sail, any ocean and any tonnage. But still a third framed certificate hung on the wall, and Neils again scratched his head when he read the wording that set forth the legal qualifications of Bartholomew McGuffey to hold down a job as chief engineer of coastwise vessels up to 1,200 tons net register.

It was patent, even to the dull-witted Swede, that there had been foul play somewhere, and the schooner's log, lying open on the table, seemed to offer the first means at hand for a solution of the mystery. Eagerly Neils turned to the last entry. It was not in Captain Scraggs's handwriting, and contained nothing more interesting than the stereotyped reports of daily observations, currents, weather conditions, etc., including a notation of arrival that day at Honolulu. Slowly Halvorsen turned the leaves backward, until at last he was rewarded by a glimpse of a different handwriting.

It was the last entry under that particular handwriting, and read as follows:

June 21, 19—. Took an observation at noon, and find that we are in 20—48 S., 178-4 W. At this rate should lift Tuvana-tholo early this afternoon. All hands well and looking forward to the fun at Tuvana. Bent a new flying jib this morning and had the king and Tabu-Tabu holystone the deck.

A. P. GIBNEY.

Neils Halvorsen sat down to think, and after several minutes of this unusual exercise it appeared to the Swede that he had stumbled upon a clue to the situation. The last entry in the log kept by Mr. Gibney was under date of June 21st—just eleven days ago, and on that date Mr. Gibney had been looking forward to some fun at Tuvana-tholo. Now where was that island and what kind of a place was it?

Neils searched through the cabin until he came across the book that is the bible of every South Sea trading vessel—the British Admiralty Reports. Down the index went the old deckhand's calloused finger and paused at "Friendly islands—page 177"; whereupon Neils opened the book at page 177 and after a five-minute search discovered that Tuvana-tholo was a barren, uninhabited island in latitude 21-2 south, longitude 178-49 west.

Ten days from the Friendly Islands, the paper said. That meant under power and sail with the trades abaft the beam. It would take nearer fifteen days for the run from Honolulu to that desert island, and Neils Halvorsen wondered whether the marooned men would still be alive by the time aid could reach them. For by some sixth sailor sense Neils Halvorsen became convinced that his old friends of the vegetable trade were marooned. They had gone ashore for some kind of a frolic, and the crew had stolen the schooner and left them to their fate, believing that the castaways would never be heard from and that dead men tell no tales.

"Yumpin' yiminy," groaned Neils. "I must get a wiggle on if aye bane steal this schooner."

He rushed on deck, carried his prisoner down into the cabin, and locked the door on him. A minute later he was clinging to the Jacob's ladder, the canoe shot in to the side of the vessel at his gruff command and passed on shoreward without missing a stroke of the paddle. An hour later, accompanied by three Kanaka sailors picked up at random along the waterfront, Neils Halvorsen was pulled out to the *Maggie II*. Her crew had not returned and the bogus captain was still triced hard and fast in the cabin.

The Swede did not bother to investigate in detail the food and water supply. A hasty round of the schooner convinced him that she had at least a month's supply of food and water. Only one thought surged . through his mind, and that was the awful necessity for haste. The anchor came in with a rush, the Kanaka boys chanting a song that sounded to Neils like a funeral dirge, and Neils went below and turned the gasoline engines wide open. The *Maggie II* swung around and with a long streak of opalescent foam trailing behind her swung down the bay and faded at last in the ghostly moonlight beyond Diamond Head; after which Neils Halvorsen, with murder in his eye and a tarred rope's end in his horny fist, went down into the cabin and talked to the man who posed as Captain Scraggs. In the end he got a confession. Fifteen minutes later he emerged, smiling grimly, gave the Kanaka boy at the wheel the course, and turned in to sleep the sleep of the conscience-free and the weary.

CHAPTER XXVII

DARKNESS was creeping over the beach at Tuvana-tholo before Mr. Gibney could smother the despair in his heart sufficient to spur his jaded imagination into working order. For nearly an hour the three castaways had sat on the beach in dumb horror, gazing seaward. They were not alone in this, for a little further up the beach the two Fiji Islanders sat huddled on their haunches, gazing stupidly first at the horizon and then at their white captors. It was the sight of these two worthies that spurred Mr. Gibney's torpid brain to action.

"Didn't you say, Mac, that when we left these two cannibals alone on this island that it would develop into a case of dog eat dog or somethin' of that nature?"

Captain Scraggs sprang to his feet, his face white with a new terror. However, he had endured so much since embarking with Mr. Gibney on a life of wild adventure that his nerves had become rather inured to impending death, and presently his fear gave way to an overmastering rage. He hurled his hat on the sands and jumped on it until it was a mere shapeless rag.

"By the tail of the Great Sacred Bull," he gasped, "if they don't start in on us first I'm a Dutchman. Of all the idiots, thieves, crimps, thugs, and pirates, Bart

McGuffey, you're the worst. Gib, you hulkin' swine, whatever did you listen to him for? It was a crazy idea, this talk of fight. Why didn't we just drop the critters overboard and be done with it? We got to kill 'em now with sticks and stones in order to protect ourselves."

"Forgive me, Scraggsy, old scout," said Mr. Gibney humbly. "The fat's in the fire now, and there ain't no use howlin' over spilt milk."

"Shut up, you murderer," shrilled Captain Scraggs and danced once more on his battered hat.

"Let's call a meetin' of the Robinson Crusoe Syndicate," said Mr. Gibney.

"Second the motion," rumbled McGuffey.

"Carried," said the commodore. "The first business before the meetin' is the organization of a expedition to chase these two cannibals to the other end of the island. I ain't got the heart to kill 'em, so let's chase 'em away before they get fresh with us."

"Good idea," responded McGuffey, whereupon he picked up a rock and threw it at the king. Mr. Gibney followed with two rocks, Captain Scraggs screamed defiance at the enemy, and the enemy fled in wild disorder, pursued by the syndicate. After a chase of half a mile Mr. Gibney led his cohorts back to the beach.

"Let's build a fire—not that we need it, but just for company—and sleep till mornin'. By that time my imagination'll be in workin' order and I'll scheme a breakfast out of this God-forsaken hole."

At the first hint of dawn Mr. Gibney, true to his promise, was up and scouting for breakfast He found some gooneys asleep on a rocky crag and killed half a

dozen of them with a club. On his way back to camp
he discovered a few handfuls of sea salt in a crevice
between some rocks, and the syndicate breakfasted
an hour later on roast gooney. It was oily and fishy
but an excellent substitute for nothing at all, and the
syndicate was grateful. The breakfast would have been
cheerful, in fact, if Captain Scraggs had not made repeated reference to his excessive thirst. McGuffey
lost patience before the meal was over, and cuffed
Captain Scraggs, who thereupon subsided with tears
in his eyes. This hurt McGuffey. It was like salt
in a fresh wound, so he patted the skipper on the back
and humbly asked his pardon. Captain Scraggs for-
gave him and murmured something about death making them all equal.

"The next business before the syndicate," announced
Mr. Gibney, anxious to preserve peace, "is a search of
this island for water."

They searched all forenoon. At intervals they caught
glimpses of the two cannibals skulking behind sand-
dunes, but they found no water. Toward the centre
of the island, however, the soil was less barren, and
here a grove of cocoa-palms lifted their tufted crests
invitingly.

"We will camp in this grove," said the commodore,
"and keep guard over these green cocoanuts. There
must be nearly a hundred of them and I notice a little
taro root here and there. As those cocoanuts are full
of milk, that insures us life for a week or two if we
go on a short ration. By bathin' several times a
day we can keep down our thirst some and perhaps it'll
rain."

"What if it does?" snapped Captain Scraggs bitterly. "We ain't got nothin' but our hats to catch it in."

"Well, then, Scraggsy, old stick-in-the-mud," replied the commodore quizzically, "it's a cinch you'll go thirsty. Your hat looks like a cullender."

Captain Scraggs choked with rage, and Mr. Gibney, springing at the nearest palm, shinned to the top of it in the most approved sailor fashion. A moment later, instead of cocoanuts, rich, unctuous curses began to descend on McGuffey and Scraggs.

"Gib, my *dear* boy," inquired Scraggs, "whatever *is* the matter of you?"

"That hound Tabu-Tabu's been strippin' our cocoanut grove," roared the commodore. "He must have spent half the night up in these trees."

"Thank the Lord they didn't take 'em all," said McGuffey piously. "Chuck me down a nut, Gib," said Captain Scraggs. "I'm famished."

In conformity with the commodore's plans, the castaways made camp in the grove. For a week they subsisted on gooneys, taro root, cocoanuts and cocoanut milk, and a sea-turtle which Scraggs found wandering on the beach. This suggested turtle eggs to Mr. Gibney, and a change of diet resulted. Nevertheless, the unaccustomed food, poorly cooked as it was, and the lack of water, told cruelly on them, and their strength failed rapidly. Realizing that in a few days he would not have the strength to climb cocoanut trees, Mr. Gibney spent nearly half a day aloft and threw down every cocoanut he could find, which was not a great many. They had their sheath knives and consequently had little fear from an attack by Tabu-Tabu and the king. These latter kept well to the other side of the island and subsisted in much the same manner as their white neighbours.

At the end of a week, all hands were troubled with indigestion and McGuffey developed a low fever. They had lost much flesh and were a white, haggard-looking trio. On the afternoon of the tenth day on the island the sky clouded up and Mr. Gibney predicted a williwaw. Captain Scraggs inquired feebly if it was good to eat.

That night it rained, and to the great joy of the ma-rooned mariners Mr. Gibney discovered, in the centre of a big sandstone rock, a natural reservoir that held about ten gallons of water. They drank to repletion and felt their strength return a thousand-fold. Tabu-Tabu and the king came into camp about this time, and pleaded for a ration of water. Mr. Gibney, swearing horribly at them, granted their request, and the king, in his gratitude, threw himself at the commodore's feet and kissed them. But Mr. Gibney was not to be de-ceived, and after furnishing them with a supply of water in cocoanut calabashes, he ordered them to their own side of the island.

On the eighteenth day the last drop of water was gone, and on the twenty-second day the last of the cocoanuts disappeared. The prospects of more rain were not bright. The gooneys were becoming shy and distrustful and the syndicate was experiencing more and more difficulty, not only in killing them, but in eat-ing them. McGuffey, who had borne up uncomplain-ingly, was shaking with fever and hardly able to stagger down the beach to look for turtle eggs. The syndicate was sick, weak, and emaciated almost beyond recognition, and on the twenty-fifth day Captain Scraggs fainted twice. On the twenty-sixth day McGuffey crawled into the shadow of a stunted mimosa bush and started to pray!

To Mr. Gibney this was an infallible sign that Mc-Guffey was now delirious. In the shadow of a neighbouring bush Captain Scraggs babbled of steam beer in the Bowhead saloon, and the commodore, stifling his own agony, watched his comrades until their lips and tongues, parched with thirst, refused longer to produce even a moan, and silence settled over the dismal camp.

It was the finish. The commodore knew it, and sat with bowed head in his gaunt arms, wondering, wondering. Slowly his body began to sway; he muttered something, slid forward on his face, and lay still. And as he lay there on the threshold of the unknown he dreamed that the *Maggie II* came into view around the headland, a bone in her teeth and every stitch of canvas flying. He saw her luff up into the wind and hang there shivering; a moment later her sails came down by the run, and he saw a little splash under her port bow as her hook took bottom. There was a commotion on decks, and then to Mr. Gibney's dying ears came faintly the shouts and songs of the black boys as a whaleboat shot into the breakers and pulled swiftly toward the beach. Mr. Gibney dreamed that a white man sat in the stern sheets of this whaleboat, and as the boat touched the beach it seemed to Mr. Gibney that this man sprang ashore and ran swiftly toward him. And—Mr. Gibney twisted his suffering lips into a wry smile as he realized the oddities of this mirage—it seemed to him that this visionary white man bore a striking resemblance to Neils Halvorsen. Neils Halvorsen, of all men! Old Neils, "the squarehead" deckhand of the green-pea trade! Dull, bowlegged Neils, with his lost dog smile and his——

Mr. Gibney rubbed his eyes feebly and half staggered to his feet. What was that? A shout? Without doubt he had heard a sound that was not the moaning of their remorseless prison-keeper, the sea. And——

"Hands off," shrieked Mr. Gibney and struck feebly at the imaginary figure rushing toward him. No use. He felt himself swept into strong arms and carried an immeasurable distance down the beach. Then somebody threw water in his face and pressed a drink of brandy and sweet water to his parched lips. His swimming senses rallied a moment, and he discovered that he was lying in the bottom of a whaleboat. McGuffey lay beside him, and on a thwart in front of him sat good old Neils Halvorsen with Captain Scraggs's head on his knees. As Mr. Gibney looked at this strange tableau Captain Scraggs opened his eyes, glanced up at Neils Halvorsen, and spoke:

"Why if it ain't old squarehead Neils," he muttered wonderingly. "If it ain't Neils, I'll go to hades or some other seaport." He closed his eyes again and subsided into a sort of lethargy, for he was content. He knew he was saved.

Mr. Gibney rolled over, and, struggling to his knees, leaned over McGuffey and peered into his drawn face.

"Mac, old shipmate! Mac, speak to me. Are you alive?"

B. McGuffey, Esquire, opened a pair of glazed eyes and stared at the commodore.

"Did we lick 'em?" he whispered. "The last I remember the king was puttin' it all over Scraggsy. And that Tabu boy—was—no slouch." McGuffey paused, and glanced warily around the boat, while a dawning horror appeared in his sunken eyes. "Go back, Neils—go back—for God's sake. There's two niggers—still—on the—island. Bring—'em some—water. They're cannibals—Neils, but never—mind. Get them—aboard—the poor devils—if they're living. I—wouldn't leave a—crocodile on that—hell hole, if I could—help it."

An hour later the Robinson Crusoe Syndicate, including the man Friday and the Goat, were safe aboard the *Maggie II*, and Neils Halvorsen, with the tears streaming down his bronzed cheeks, was sparingly doling out to them a mixture of brandy and water. And when the syndicate was strong enough to be allowed all the water it wanted, Neils Halvorsen propped them up on deck and told the story. When he had finished, Captain Scraggs turned to Mr. Gibney.

"Gib, my *dear* boy," he said, "make a motion."

"I move," said the commodore, "that we set Tabu-Tabu and the king down on the first inhabited island we can find. They've suffered enough. And I further move that we readjust the ownership of the *Maggie II* Syndicate and cut the best Swede on earth in on a quarter of the profits."

"Second the motion," said McGuffey.

"Carried," said Captain Scraggs.

CHAPTER XXVIII

THE lookout on the power schooner *Maggie II* had sighted Diamond Head before Commodore Adelbert P. Gibney, Captain Phineas P. Scraggs, and Engineer Bartholomew McGuffey were enabled to declare, in all sincerity (or at least with as much sincerity as one might reasonably expect from this band of roving rascals), that they had entirely recovered from their harrowing experiences on the desert island of Tuvanatholo, in the Friendly group.

At the shout of "Land, ho!" Mr. McGuffey yawned, stretched himself, and sat up in the wicker lounging chair where he had sprawled for days with Mr. Gibney and Captain Scraggs, under the awning on top of the house. He flexed his biceps reflectively, while his companions, stretched at full length in their respective chairs, watched him lazily.

"As a member o' the *Maggie* Syndicate an' ownin' an' votin' a quarter interest," boomed the engineer, "I hereby call a meetin' o' the said syndicate for the purpose o' transactin' any an' all business that may properly come before the meetin'."

"Pass the word for Neils Halvorsen," suggested Mr. Gibney. "Bless his squarehead soul," he added.

"We got a quorum without him, an' besides this business is just between us three."

"Meetin'll come to order." The commodore tap-

274

ped the hot deck with his bare heel twice. "Haul away,
Mac."

"I move you, gentlemen, that it be the sense o' this
meetin' that B. McGuffey, Esquire, be an' he is hereby
app'inted a committee o' one to lam the everlastin'
daylights out o' that sinful former chief mate o' ourn
for abandonin' the syndicate to a horrible death on that
there desert island. Do I hear a second to that motion?"

"Second the motion," chirped Captain Scraggs.

"The motion's denied," announced Mr. Gibney
firmly.

"Now, looky here, Gib, that ain't fair. Didn't
you fight Tabu-Tabu an' didn't Scraggsy fight the king
o' Kandavu? I ain't had no fightin' this entire v'yage
an' I did cal'late to lick that doggone mate."

"Mac, it can't be done nohow."

"Oh, it can't, eh? Well, I'll just bet you two boys
my interest in the syndicate——"

"It ain't that, Mac, it ain't that. Nobody's doubtin'
your natural ability to mop him up. But it ain't policy. You wasn't sore agin them cannibal savages, was
you? You made Neils go back an' save 'em, an' it took
us two days to beat up to the first inhabited island an'
drop 'em off——"

"But a cannibal's like a dumb beast, Gib. He ain't
responsible. This mate knows better. He's as fly as
they make 'em."

"Ah!" Mr. Gibney levelled a horny forefinger at the
engineer. "That's where you hit the nail on the head.
He's too fly, and there's only two ways to keep him from
flyin' away with us. The first is to feed him to the

sharks and the second is to treat him like a long-lost
brother. I know he ought to be hove overboard, but
I ain't got the heart to kill him in cold blood. Consequently, we got to let the villain live, an' if you go to
beatin' him up, Mac, you'll make him sore an' he'll
peach on us when we get to Honolulu. If us three
could get back to San Francisco with clean hands, I'd
say lick the beggar an' lick him for fair. But we got
to remember that this mate was one o' the original
filibuster crew o' the old *Maggie I*. The day we tackled
the Mexican navy an' took this power schooner away
from 'em, we put ourselves forty fathom plumb outside the law, an' this mate was present an' knows it.
We've changed the vessel's name an' rig, an' doctored
up the old *Maggie's* papers to suit the *Maggie II*, an'
we've give her a new dress. But at that, it's hard to
disguise a ship in a live port, an' the secret service
agents o' the Mexican government may be a-layin' for
us in San Francisco; and with this here mate agin us
an' ready to turn state's evidence, we're pirates under
the law, an' it don't take much imagination to see three
pirates swingin' from the same yard-arm. No, sir,
Mac. I ain't got no wish, now that we're fixed nice
an' comfortable with the world's goods, to be hung
for a pirate in the mere shank o' my youth. Why, I
ain't fifty year old yet."

"By the tail o' the Great Sacred Bull," chattered
Scraggs. "Gib's right."

McGuffey was plainly disappointed. "I hadn't
thought o' that at all, Gib. I been cherishin' the thought
o' lammin' the whey out'n that mate, but if you say
so I'll give up the idee. But if bringin' the *Maggie II*

into home waters is invitin' death, what in blue blazes're we goin' to do with her?"

Mr. Gibney smiled—an arch, cunning smile. "We'll give her to that murderin' mate, free gratis."

Captain Scraggs bounded out of his chair, struck the hot deck with his bare feet, cursed, and hopped back into the chair again. McGuffey stared incredulously.

"Gib, my *dear* boy," quavered Scraggs, "say that agin."

"Yes," continued the commodore placidly, "we'll just get shet o' her peaceable like by givin' her to this mate. Don't forget, Scraggsy, old tarpot, that this mate's been passin' himself off for you in Honolulu, an' if there's ever an investigation, the trail leads to the *Maggie II*. This mate's admitted being Captain Scraggs, an' if he's found with the schooner in his possession it'll take a heap o' evidence for him to prove that he ain't Captain Scraggs. We'll just keep this here mate in the brig while we're disposing of our black coral, pearl, shell, and copra in Honolulu, an' then, when we've cleaned up, an' got our passages booked for San Francisco——"

"But who says we're goin' back to San Francisco?" cut in McGuffey.

"Why, where else would men with money in their pockets head for, you oil-soaked piece of ignorance? Ain't you had enough adventure to do you a spell?" demanded Captain Scraggs. "Me an' Gib's for goin' back to San Francisco, so shut up. If you got any objection, you're outvoted two to one in the syndicate."

McGuffey subsided, growling, and Mr. Gibney continued:

"When we're ready to leave Honolulu, we'll bring this mate on deck, make him a kind Christian talk an' give him the *Maggie II* with the compliments o' the syndicate. He'll think our sufferin's on that island has touched us with religion an' he'll be so tickled he'll keep his mouth shut. Then, with all three of us safe an' out o' the mess, an' the evidence off our hands, we'll clear out for Gawd's country an' look around for some sort of a profitable investment."

"What you figurin' on, Gib?" demanded Captain Scraggs. "I hope it's a steamboat. This wild adventure is all right when you get away with it, but I like steamboatin' on the bay an' up the river."

"Oh, nothin' particular, Scraggsy. We'll just hold the syndicate together an' when somethin' good bobs up we'll smother it. In the meantime, we'll continue our life o' wild adventure."

"But there ain't no wild adventures around San Francisco Bay," protested McGuffey.

"That shows your ignorance, Mac. Adventure lurks in every nook an' slough an' doghole on the bay. You walk along the Embarcadero, only reasonably drunk, an' adventure's liable to hit you a swipe in the face like a loose rope-end bangin' around in a gale. Adventure an' profits goes hand in hand——"

"Then why give the *Maggie II* to this hound of a mate?" demanded the single-minded McGuffey.

The commodore sighed. "She's a love of a boat an' it breaks my heart to give up the only command I've ever had, but the fact is, Mac, her possession by us is dangerous, an' we don't need her, an' we can't sell her because her record's got blurs on it. We can't convey

a clean an' satisfactory title.   Anyhow, she didn't cost
us a cent an' there ain't no real financial loss if we give
her to this mate.   He'd be glad to get her if she had
yellow jack aboard, an' if he's caught with her he'll
have to do the explainin'.   When you're caught with
the goods in your possession, Mac, it makes the explainin' all the harder.   Besides, we're three to one,
an' if it comes to a show-down later we can outswear
the mate."

Captain Scraggs picked his snaggle teeth with
the little blade of his jack-knife and cogitated a minute.

"Well," he announced presently, "far be it from me
to fly in the face o' a felon's death.   I've made a heap
o' money, follerin' Gib's advice, an' bust my bob-stay
if I don't stay put on this.   Gib, it's your lead."

"Well, I'll follow suit.   Gib's got all the trumps,"
acquiesced the engineer.   "We got plenty o' dough
an' no board bills comin' due, so we'll loaf alongshore
until Gib digs up somethin' good.

Mr. Gibney smiled his approval of these sentiments.
"Thank you, boys.   I ain't quite sure yet whether we'll
quit the sea an' go into the chicken business, build a
fast sea-goin' launch an' smuggle Chinamen in from
Mexico, buy a stern-wheel steamer an' do bay an'
river freightin', or just live at a swell hotel an' scheme
out a fortune by our wits.   But whatever I do, as the
leadin' sperrit o' this syndicate, the motto o' the syndicate will ever be my inspiration:

> "All for one an' one for all
> United we stand, divided we fall."

"How about Neils?" queried Captain Scraggs. "Do we continue to let that ex-deckhand in on our fortunes?"

"If Neils Halvorsen had asked *you* that question when he come to rescue you the day you lay a-dyin' o' thirst on that desert island, wouldn't you have said yes?"

"Sure pop."

"Then don't ask no questions that's unworthy of you," said Mr. Gibney severely. "I don't want to see none o' them green-pea trade ethics croppin' up in you, Scraggsy. If it wasn't for that Swede the sea-gulls'd be pickin' our bones now. Neils Halvorsen is included in this syndicate for good."

"Amen." This from the honest McGuffey.

"Meetin's adjourned," said Captain Scraggs icily.

CHAPTER XXIX

UNDER the direction of the crafty commodore, the valuable cargo of the *Maggie II* was disposed of in Honolulu. During the period while the schooner lay at the dock discharging Captain Scraggs and McGuffey prudently remained in the cabin with the perfidious mate, in order that, should an investigation be undertaken later by the Treasury Department, no man might swear that the real Phineas Scraggs, filibuster, had been in Honolulu on a certain date. The Kanaka crew of the schooner Mr. Gibney managed to ship with an old shipmaster friend bound for New Guinea, so their testimony was out of the way for a while, at least.

When the *Maggie II* was finally discharged and the proceeds of her rich cargo nestled, in crisp bills of large denomination, in a money belt under Mr. Gibney's armpits and next his rascally skin, he purchased tickets under assumed names for himself, Scraggs, McGuffey, and Halvorsen on the liner *Hilonian*, due to sail at noon next day.

These details attended to, the *Maggie II* backed away from the dock under her own power and cast anchor off the quarantine station. The mate was then brought on deck and made to confront the syndicate.

"It appears, my man," the commodore began, "that you was too anxious to horn in on the profits o' this expedition, so in a moment o' human weakness you did your employers an evil deed. We had it all figgered out to feed you to the sharks on the way home, because dead men tell no tales, but our sufferin's on that island has caused us all to look with a milder eye on mere human shortcomin's. The Good Book says: 'Forgive us our trespasses as we forgive those what trespass agin us,' an' I ain't ashamed to admit that you owe your wicked life to the fact that Scraggsy's got religion an' McGuffey ain't much better. But we got all the money we need an' we're goin' to Europe to enjoy it, so before we go we're goin' to pass sentence upon you. It is the verdict o' the court that we present you with the power schooner *Maggie II* free gratis, an' that you accept the same in the same friendly sperrit in which it is tendered. Havin' a schooner o' your own from now on, you won't be tempted to steal one an' commit wholesale murder a-doin' it. You're forgiven, my man. Take the *Maggie II* with our blessin', organize a comp'ny, an' go back to Kandavu an' make some money for yourself. Scraggsy, are you a-willin' to prove that you've given this errin' mate complete forgiveness by shakin' hands with him?"

"I forgive him freely," said Captain Scraggs, "an' here's my fin on it."

The unfortunate mate hung his head. He was much moved.

"You don't mean it, sir, do you?" he faltered.

"I hope I may never see the back o' my neck if I don't," replied the skipper.

"Surest thing you know, brother," shouted Mr. McGuffey and swatted the deluded mate between the shoulders. "Take her with our compliments. You was a good brave mate until you went wrong. I ain't forgot how you sprayed the hillsides with lead the day Gib an' Scraggsy was took by them cannibals. No, sir-ee! I ain't holdin' no grudge. It's human to commit crime. I've committed one or two myself. Good luck to you, matey. Hope you make a barrel o' money with the old girl."

"Thanks," the mate mumbled. "I ain't deservin' o' this nohow," and he commenced to snivel a little.

Mr. Gibney forgot that he was playing a hypocrite's part, and his generous nature overcame him.

"Dog my cats," he blustered, "what's the use givin' him the vessel if we don't give him some spondulicks to outfit her with grub an' supplies? Poor devil! I bet he ain't got a cent to bless himself with. Scraggsy, old tarpot, if we're goin' to turn over a new leaf an' be Christians, let's sail under a full cloud o' canvas."

"By Neptune, that's so, Gib. This feller did us an awful dirty trick, but at the same time there ain't a cowardly bone in his hull carcass. I ain't forgot how he stood to the guns that day off the Coronados when we was attacked by the Mexicans."

"Stake the feller, Gib," advised McGuffey, and wiped away a vagrant tear. He was quite overcome at his own generosity and the manner in which it had touched the hard heart of the iniquitous mate.

Mr. Gibney laid five one-hundred-dollar bills in the mate's palm.

"Good-bye," he said gently, "an' see if you can't be as much of a man an' as good a sport hereafter as them you've wronged an' who's forgive you fully and freely."

One by one the three freebooters of the green-pea trade pumped the stricken mate's hand, tossed him a scrap of advice, and went overside into the small boat which was to take them ashore. It was a solemn parting and Mr. Gibney and McGuffey were snuffling audibly. Captain Scraggs, however, was made of sterner stuff.

"'Pears to me, Gib," he remarked when they were clear of the schooner, "that you're a little mite generous with the funds o' the syndicate, ain't you?"

Mr. Gibney picked up a paddle and threatened Scraggs with it.

"Dang your cold heart, Scraggs," he hissed, "you're un-Christ'an, that's what you are."

"Quit yer beefin', you shrimp," bellowed McGuffey. "Them cannibals would have et you if it wasn't for that poor devil of a mate."

Captain Scraggs snarled and remained discreetly silent. Nevertheless, he was in a fine rage. As he remarked *sotto voce* to Neils Halvorsen, five hundred dollars wasn't picked up in the street every day.

The next day, as the *Hilonian* steamed out of the harbour, bearing the syndicate back to San Francisco, they looked across at the little *Maggie II* for the last time, and observed that the mate was on deck, superintending three Kanaka sailors who were hoisting supplies aboard from a bumboat.

Commodore Gibney bade his first command a misty farewell.

"Good-bye, little ship," he yelled and waved his hand. "Gawd! You was a witch in a light wind."

"He'll be flyin' outer the harbour an' bound south by

sunset," rumbled McGuffey.   "I suppose that lovely
gas engine o' mine'll go to hell now."

Captain Scraggs sighed dismally.   "It costs like
sixty to be a Christian, Gib, but what's the odds as
long as we're safe an' homeward bound?   Holy sailor!
But I'm hungry for a smell o' Channel creek at low tide.
I tell you, Gib, rovin' and wild adventure's all right,
but the old green-pea trade wasn't so durned bad, after
all."

"You bet!"   McGuffey's response was very fervid.

"Them was the happy days," supplemented the
commodore.   He was as joyous as a schoolboy.   Four
long years had he been roving and now, with his pockets
lined with greenbacks, he was homeward bound to his
dear old San Francisco—back to steam beer, to all of
his old cronies of the Embarcadero, to moving picture
shows—to Life!   And he was glad to get back with a
whole skin.

Seven days after leaving Honolulu, the *Hilonian*
steamed into San Francisco Bay.   The syndicate could
not wait until she had tied up at her dock, and the minute the steamer had passed quarantine Mr. Gibney
hailed a passing launch.   Bag and baggage the happy
quartette descended to the launch and landed at Meiggs
wharf.   Mr. Gibney stepped into the wharfinger's office
and requested permission to use the telephone.

"What's up, Gib?" demanded Captain Scraggs.

"I want to 'phone for a automobile to come down an'
snake us up town in style.   This syndicate ain't a-goin'
to come rampin' home to Gawd's country lookin' like
a lot o' Eyetalian peddlers.   We're goin' to the best
hotel an' we're goin' in *style*."

McGuffey nudged Captain Scraggs, and Neils Halvorsen nudged Mr. McGuffey.

"Hay bane a sport, hay bane," rumbled the honest Neils.

"You bet he bane," McGuffey retorted. "Ain't he the old kiddo, Scraggsy? Ain't he? This feller Adelbert P. Gibney's a farmer, I guess."

With the assistance of the wharfinger an automobile was summoned, and in due course the members of the syndicate found themselves ensconced in a fashionable suite in San Francisco's most fashionable hotel. Mr. Gibney stored the syndicate's pearls in the hotel safe, deposited an emergency roll with the hotel clerk, and banked the balance of the company funds in the names of all four; after which the syndicate gave itself up to a period of joy unconfined.

At the end of a week of riot and revelry Mr. Gibney revived sufficiently to muster all hands and lead them to a Turkish bath. Two days in the bath restored them wonderfully, and when the worthy commodore eventually got them back to the hotel he announced that henceforth the lid was on—and on tight. Captain Scraggs, who was hard to manage in his cups and the most prodigal of prodigals with steam up to a certain pressure, demurred at this.

"No more sky-larkin', Scraggsy, you old cut-up," Mr. Gibney ordered. "We had our good time comin' after all that we've been through but it's time to get down to business agin. Riches has wings, Scraggsy, old salamander, an' even if we are ashore, I'm still the commodore. Now, set around an' we'll hold a meetin'."

He banged the chiffonier with his great fist. "Meetin' o' the *Maggie* Syndicate," he announced. "Meet-in'll come to order. The first business before the meetin' is a call for volunteers to furnish a money-makin' idee for the syndicate."

Neils Halvorsen shook his sorrel head. He had no ideas. B. McGuffey, Esquire, shook his head also. Captain Scraggs wanted to sing.

"I see it's up to me to suggest somethin'." Mr. Gibney smiled benignly, as if a money-making idea was the easiest thing on earth to produce. "The last thing I remember before we went to that Turkish bath was us four visitin' a fortune teller an' havin' our fortunes told, past, present, an' future, for a dollar a throw. Anybody here remember what his fortune was?"

It appeared that no one remembered, not even Mr. Gibney. He therefore continued:

"The chair will app'int Mr. McGuffey an' himself a committee o' two to wait on one o' these here clair-voyants and have their fortunes told agin."

McGuffey, who was as superstitious as a negro, seconded the motion heartily and the committee forth-with sallied forth to consult the clairvoyant. Within the hour they returned.

"Members o' the syndicate," the commodore an-nounced, "we got an idea. Not a heluva good one, but fair to middlin'. Me an' Mac calls on this Madame de What-you-may-call-her an' the minute she gets a lamp at my mit (it is worthy of remark here that Mr. Gibney had a starfish tattooed on the back of his left hand, a full-rigged ship across his breast, and a gor-geous picture of a lady climbing a ladder adorned the inner side of his brawny right fore-arm. The feet of the lady in question hung down below the fringe of Mr. Gibney's shirt sleeve) she up an' says: 'My friend, you're makin' a grave mistake remainin' ashore. Your fortune lies at sea.' Then she threw a fit an' mumbled something about a light-haired man that was' goin' to cross my path. I guess she must have meant Scraggsy or Neils, both bein' blondes—an' she come out of her trance shiverin' an' shakin'.

"'Your fortune lies at sea, my friend,' she kept on sayin'. 'Go forth an' seek it.'

"'Gimme the longitude an' latitude, ma'am,' I says, 'an' I'll light out.'

"'Look in the shippin' news in the papers to-morrower,' she pipes up. 'Five dollars, please.'

"You didn't give her five dollars, did you?" gasped Captain Scraggs. "Why, Gib my *dear* boy, I thought you was sober."

"So I was."

"Then, Gib, all I got to say is that you're a sucker. You want to consult the rest of us before you go throwin' away the funds o' the syndicate on such tom-fool idees as——"

McGuffey saw a storm gathering on Mr. Gibney's brows, and hastened to intervene.

"Meetin's adjourned," he announced, "pendin' the issue o' the papers to-morrow mornin'. Scraggsy, you oughter j'ine the Band o' Hope. You're ugly when you got a drink in you."

Neils Halvorsen interfered to beg a cigar of Mr. Gibney and the affair passed over.

At six o'clock the following morning the members of the syndicate were awakened by a prodigious pounding at their respective doors.   Answering the summons, they found Mr. Gibney in undress uniform and the morning paper clutched in his hand.

"Meetin' o' the *Maggie* Syndicate in my room," he bawled.   "I've found our fortune."

The meeting came to order without the formality of dressing, and the commodore, spreading the paper on his knee, read aloud:

For Sale Cheap

The stern-wheel steamer *Victor*, well found, staunch and newly painted.   Boilers and engines in excellent shape.   Vessel must be sold to close out an estate.   Address John Coakley, Jackson Street wharf.

"How d'ye know she's a fortune, Gib?" McGuffey demanded.   "Lemme look at her engines before you get excited."

"I ain't sayin' she is," Mr. Gibney retorted testily. "Lemme finish readin!"   He continued:

REPORTS PASSING DERELICT

The steam schooner *Arethusa*, Grays Harbour to Oakland Long wharf, reports passing a derelict schooner twenty miles off Point Reyes at six o'clock last night.   The derelict was down by the head, and her rail just showed above the water.   It was impossible to learn her identity.

The presence of this derelict in the steamer lanes to North Pacific ports is a distinct menace to navigation, and it is probable that a revenue cutter will be dispatched to-day to search for the derelict and either tow her into port or destroy her.

"Gentlemen o' the syndicate, them's the only two items in the shippin' page that looks likely.   The question is, in which lies our fortune?"

Neils Halvorsen spoke up, giving it as his opinion that the fortune-telling lady probably knew her business and that their fortune really lay at sea. The derelict was at sea. How else, then, could the prophecy be interpreted?

"Well, this steamer *Victor* ain't exactly travelling overland," McGuffey suggested. He had a secret hankering to mess around some real engines again, and gave it as his opinion that fortune was more likely to lurk in a solid stern-wheel steamer with good engines and boilers than in a battered hulk at sea. Captain Scraggs agreed with him most heartily and a tie vote resulted, Mr. Gibney inclining toward the derelict.

"What're we goin' to do about it, Gib?" Captain Scraggs demanded.

"When in doubt, Scraggsy, old tarpot, always play trumps. In order to make no mistake, right after breakfast you an' McGuffey go down to Jackson Street wharf an' interview this man Coakley about his steamer *Victor*. You been goin' to sea long enough to know a good hull when you see it, an' if we can't trust Mac to know a good set of inner works we'd better dissolve the syndicate. If you two think she's a bargain, buy her in for the syndicate. As for me an' Neils, we'll go down to the Front an' charter a tug an' chase out after that there derelict before the revenue cutter gets her an' blows her out o' the path o' commerce with a stick o' dynamite."

Forthwith Mr. Gibney and Neils, after snatching a hasty breakfast, departed for the waterfront, where they chartered a tug for three days and put to sea. At about ten o'clock Captain Scraggs and McGuffey strol-

led leisurely down to Jackson Street wharf to inspect
the *Victor*. By noon they had completed a most satisfactory inspection of the steamer's hull and boilers, and
bought her in for seven thousand dollars. Captain
Scraggs was delighted. He said she was worth ten
thousand. Already he had decided that heavy and
profitable freights awaited the syndicate along the Sacramento River, where the farmers and orchardists had
been for years the victims of a monopoly and a gentlemen's agreement between the two steamboat lines that
plied between Sacramento, Stockton, and San Francisco.

On the afternoon of the third day Mr. Gibney and
Neils Halvorsen returned from sea. They were unut-
terably weary and hollow-eyed for lack of sleep.

"Well, I suppose you two suckers found that derelict," challenged McGuffey.

"Yep. Found her an' got a line aboard an' towed
her in, an' it was a tough job. She's layin' over on the
Berkeley tide flats, an' at lowtide to-morrow we'll
go over an' find out what we've got. Don't even know
her name yet. She's practically submerged."

"I think you was awful foolish, Gib, buyin' a pig
in a poke that way. I don't believe in goin' it blind.
Me an' Mac's bought a real ship. We own the *Victor*."

"I'm dead on my feet," growled the commodore, and
jumping into bed he refused to discuss the matter further and was sound asleep in a jiffy.

Mr. Gibney was up bright and early and aroused the
syndicate to action. The tide would be at its lowest
ebb at nine thirty-one and the commodore figured
that his fortune would be lying well exposed on the
Berkeley tide flats. He engaged a diver and a small

gasoline launch, and after an early breakfast in a chop-house on the Embarcadero they started for the wreck.

They were within half a mile of it, heading right into the eye of the wind, when Captain Scraggs and McGuffey stood erect in the launch simultaneously and sniffed like a pair of—well, sea-dogs.

"Dead whale," suggested McGuffey.

"I hope it ain't Gib's fortune," replied Scraggs drily.

"Shut up," bellowed Mr. Gibney. He was sniffing himself by this time, for as the launch swiftly approached the derelict the unpleasant odour became more pronounced.

"Betcher that schooner was in collision with a steamer," Captain Scraggs announced. "She was cut down right through the fo'castle with the watch below sound asleep, an' this here fragrance appeals to me as a sure sign of a job for the coroner."

The commodore shuddered. He was filled with vague misgivings, but Neils Halvorsen grinned cheerfully. McGuffey got out a cologne-scented handkerchief and clamped it across his nose.

"Well, if that's Gib's fortune, it must be filthy lucre," he mumbled through the handkerchief. "Gib, what *have* you hooked on to? A public dump?"

Mr. Gibney's eyes flashed, but he made no reply. They had rounded the schooner's stern now, and her name was visible.

"Schooner *Kadiak*, Seattle," read Scraggs. "Little old three sticker a thousand years old an' cut clear through just abaft the foremast. McGuffey, you don't s'pose this here's a pirate craft an' just bulgin' with gold."

"Sure," retorted the engineer with a slow wink, "tainted wealth."

Mr. Gibney could stand their heckling no longer. "Looky here, you two," he bawled angrily. "I got a hunch I picked up a lemon, but I'm a-willin' to tackle the deal with Neils if you two think I didn't do right by the syndicate a-runnin' up a bill of expense towing this craft into port. I ain't goin' to stand for no kiddin', even if we are in a five-hundred-dollar towage bill. Man is human an' bound to make mistakes."

"Don't kid the commodore, Scraggsy. This aromer o' roses is more'n a strong man can stand, so cut out the josh."

"All right, Mac. I guess the commodore's foot slipped this time, but I ain't squawkin' yet."

"No. Not *yet*," cried Mr. Gibney bitterly, "but soon."

"I ain't, nuther," Captain Scraggs assumed an air of injured virtue. "I'm a-willin' to go through with you, Gib, at a loss, for nothin' else except to convince you o' the folly o' makin' this a one-man syndicate. I ain't a-kickin', but I'm free to confess that I'd like to be consulted *oncet* in a while."

"That's logic," rumbled the single-minded McGuffey.

"You dirty welchers," roared the commodore. "I ain't askin' you two to take chances with *me*. Me an' Neils'll take this deal over independent o' the syndicate."

"Well, let's dress this here diver," retorted the cautious Scraggs, "an' send him into the hold for a look around before we make up our minds." Captain Scraggs was not a man to take chances.

They moored the launch to the wreck and commenced operations. Mr. Gibney worked the air pump while the diver, ax in hand, dropped into the murky depths of the flooded hold. He was down half an hour before he signalled to be pulled up. All hands sprang to the line to haul him back to daylight, and the instant he popped clear of the water Mr. Gibney unburdened himself of an agonized curse.

In his hands the diver held a large decayed codfish!

Captain Scraggs turned a sneering glance upon the unhappy commodore while McGuffey sat down on the damp rail of the derelict and laughed until the tears coursed down his honest face.

"A dirty little codfishin' schooner," raved Captain Scraggs, "an' you a-sinkin' the time an' money o' the syndicate in rotten codfish on the say-so of a clairvoyant you ain't even been interduced to. Gib, if that's business, all I got to say is: 'Excuse *me*'."

Mr. Gibney seized the defunct fish from the diver's hand, tore it in half, slapped Captain Scraggs with one awful fragment and hurled the other at McGuffey.

"I'm outer the syndicate," he raved, beside himself with anger. "Here I go to work an' make a fortune for a pair of short sports an' pikers an' you get to squealin' at the first five-hundred-dollar loss. I know you of old, Phineas Scraggs, an' the leopard can't change his spots." He raised his right hand to heaven. "I'm through for keeps. We'll sell the pearls to-day, divvy up, an' dissolve. I'm through."

"Glad of it," growled McGuffey. "I don't want no more o' that codfish, an' as soon as we git fightin' room I'll prove to you that no near-sailor can insult

me an' git away with it. Me an' Scraggsy's got some
rights. You can walk on Scraggsy, Gib, but it takes a
man to walk on the McGuffey family."

Nothing but the lack of sea-room prevented a battle
royal. Mr. Gibney stood glaring at his late partners.
His great ham-like fists were opening and closing automatically.

"You're right, Mac," he said presently, endeavour-
ing to control his anger and chagrin. "We'll settle
this later. Take that helmet off the diver an' let's
hear what he's got to report."

With the helmet removed the diver spoke:

"As near as I can make out, boss, there ain't a thing
o' value in this hulk but a couple o' hundred tons o'
codfish. She was cut in two just for'd o' the bulkhead
an' her anchors carried away on the section that was cut
off. She ain't worth the cost o' towin' her in on the
flats."

"So that codfish has some value," sneered Captain
Scraggs.

"Great grief, Scraggsy! Don't tell me it's sp'iled,"
cried McGuffey, simulating horror.

"No, not quite, Mac, not quite. Just *slightly*.
I s'pose Gib'll tack a sign to the stub o' the main mast:
'Slightly spoiled codfish for sale. Apply to A. P. Gib-
ney, on the premises. Special rates on Friday.'"

Mr. Gibney quivered, but made no reply. He carefully examined that portion of the derelict above water
and discovered that by an additional expenditure of
about fifty dollars he might recover an equal amount
in brass fittings. The *Kadiak's* house was gone and her
decks completely gutted. Nothing remained but the

amputated hull and the foul cargo below her battered decks.

In majestic silence the commodore motioned all hands into the launch. In silence they returned to the city. Arrived here, Mr. Gibney paid off the launch man and the diver and accompanied by his associates repaired to a prominent jeweller's shop with the pearls they had accumulated in the South Seas. The entire lot was sold for thirty thousand dollars. An hour later they had adjusted their accounts, divided the fortune of the syndicate equally, and then dissolved. At parting, Mr. Gibney spoke for the first time when it had not been absolutely necessary.

"Put a beggar on horseback an' he'll ride to the devil," he said. "When you two swabs was poor you was content to let me lead you into a fortune, but now that you're well-heeled, you think you're business men. All right! I ain't got a word to say except this: Before I get through with you two beachcombers I'll have all your money and you'll be a-beggin' me for a job. I apologize for soakin' you two with that diseased codfish, an' for old sake's sake we won't fight. We're still friends, but business associates no longer, for I'm too big a figger in this syndicate to stand for any criticism on my handlin' o' the joint finances. Hereafter, Scraggsy, old kiddo, you an' Mac can go it alone with your sternwheel steamer. Me an' The Squarehead legs it together an' takes our chances. You don't hear that poor untootered Swede makin' no holler at the way I've handled the syndicate——"

"But, Gib, my *dear* boy," chattered Captain Scraggs, "will you just listen to re——"

"Enough! Too much is plenty. Let's shake hands an' part friends. We just can't get along in business together, that's all."

"Well, I'm sorry, Gib," mumbled McGuffey, very much crestfallen, "but then you hove that dog-gone fish at me an'——"

"That was fortune hittin' you a belt in the face, Mac, an' you was too self-conceited to recognize it. Remember that, both of you two. Fortune hit you in the face to-day an' you didn't know it."

"I'd ruther die poor, Gib," wailed McGuffey.

The commodore shook hands cordially and departed, followed by the faithful Neils Halvorsen. The moment the door closed behind them Scraggs turned to the engineer.

"Mac," he said earnestly, "Gib's up to somethin'. He's got that imagination o' his workin'. I can tell it every time; he gets a foggy look in his eyes. We made a mistake kiddin' him to-day. Gib's a sensitive boy some ways an' I reckon we hurt his feelin's without intendin' it."

"He thrun a dead codfish at me," protested McGuffey. "I love old Gib like a brother, but that's carryin' things with a mighty high hand."

"Well, I'll apologize to him," declared Captain Scraggs and started for the door to follow Mr. Gibney. McGuffey barred his way.

"You apologize without my consent an' you gotta buy me out o' the *Victor*. I won't be no engineer with a skipper that lacks backbone."

"Oh, very well, Mac." Captain Scraggs realized too well the value of McGuffey in the engine room.

He knew he could never be happy with anybody else. "We'll complete the deal with the *Victor*, ship a crew, get down to business, an' leave Gib to his codfish. An' let's pay our bill an' get outer here. It's too high-toned for me—an' expensive."

For two weeks Captain Scraggs and McGuffey saw no more of Mr. Gibney and Neils Halvorsen. In the meantime, they had commenced running the *Victor* regularly up river, soliciting business in opposition to the regular steamboat lines. While the *Victor* was running with light freights and consequently at a loss, the prospect for ultimate good business was very bright and Scraggs and McGuffey were not at all worried about the future.

Judge of their surprise, therefore, when one morning who should appear at the door of Scraggs's cabin but Mr. Gibney.

"Mornin', Gib," began Scraggs cheerily. "I s'pose you been rolled for your money as per usual, an' you're around lookin' for a job as mate."

Mr. Gibney ignored this veiled insult. "Not yet, Scraggsy, I got about five hundred tons o' freight to send up to Dunnigan's Landin' an' I want a lump sum figger for doin' the job. We parted friends an' for the sake o' old times I thought I'd give you a chance to figger on the business."

"Thanky, Gib. I'll be glad to. Where's your freight an' what does it consist of?"

"Agricultural stuff. It's crated, an' I deliver it here on the steamer's dock within reach o' her tackles. No heavy pieces. Two men can handle every piece easy."

"Turnin' farmer, Gib?"

"Thinkin' about it a little," the commodore admitted. "What's your rate on this freight? It ain't perishable goods, so get down to brass tacks."

"A dollar a ton," declared the greedy Scraggs, naming a figure fully forty cents higher than he would have been willing to accept. "Five hundred dollars for the lot."

"Suits me." The commodore nonchalantly handed Scraggs five hundred dollars. "Gimme a receipt," he said.

So Captain Scraggs gave him a receipted freight bill and Mr. Gibney departed. An hour later a barge was bunted alongside the *Victor* and Neils Halvorsen appeared in Scraggs's cabin to inform him that the five hundred tons of freight was ready to be taken aboard.

"All right, Neils. I'll put a gang to work right off." He came out on deck, paused, tilted his nose, and sniffed. He was still sniffing when McGuffey bounced up out of the engine room.

"Holy Sailor!" he shouted. "Who uncorked that atter o' violets?"

"You dog-gone 'squarehead," shrieked Captain Scraggs. "You been monkeyin' around that codfish again."

"What smells?" demanded the mate, poking his nose out of his room.

"That tainted wealth I picked up at sea," shouted a voice from the dock, and turning, Scraggs and Mc-Guffey observed Mr. Gibney standing on a stringer smiling at them.

"Gib, my *dear* boy," quavered Captain Scraggs, "you can't mean to say you've unloaded them gosh-awful codfish——"

"No, not yet—but soon, Scraggsy, old tarpot."

Captain Scraggs removed his near-Panama hat, cast it on the deck, and pranced upon it in a terrible rage.

"I won't receive your rotten freight, you scum of the docks," he raved. "You'll run me outer house an' home with that horrible stuff."

"Oh, you'll freight it for me, all right," the commodore retorted blithely. "Or I'll libel your old sternwheel packet for you. I've paid the freight in advance an' I got the receipt."

Captain Scraggs was on the verge of tears. "But, Gib! My *dear* boy! This freight'll foul the *Victor* up for a month o' Fridays— *an' I just took out a passenger license!*"

"I'm sorry, Scraggsy, but business is business. You've took my money an' you got to perform."

"You lied to me. You said it was agricultural stuff an' I thought it was plows an' harrers an' sich——"

"It's fertilizer—an' if that ain't agricultural stuff I hope my teeth may drop out an' roll in the ocean. An' it ain't perishable. It perished long ago. I ain't deceived you. An' if you don't like the scent o' dead codfish on your decks, you can swab 'em down with Florida water for a month."

Captain Scraggs's mate came around the corner of the house and addressed himself to Captain Scraggs.

"You can give me my time, sir. I'm a steamboat mate, not a grave digger or a coroner's assistant, or an undertaker, an' I can't stand to handle this here freight."

Mr. McGuffey tossed his silken engineer's cap over to Scraggs.

"Hop on that, Scraggsy. Your own hat is ground to powder. Ain't it strange, Gib, what little imagination Scraggsy's got? He'll stand there a-screamin' an' a-cussin' an' a-prancin'—Scraggsy! Ain't you got no pride, makin' such a spectacle o' yourself? We don't have to handle this freight o' Gib's at all. We'll just hook onto that barge *an' tow it up river*."

"You won't do nothin' o' the sort, Mac, because that's my barge an' I ain't a-goin' to let it out o' my sight. I've delivered my freight alongside your steamer and prepaid the freight an' it's up to you to handle it."

"Gib!"

"That's the programme!"

"Adelbert," crooned Mr. McGuffey, "ain't you got no heart? You know I got a half interest in the *Victor*——"

"O-oo-oh!" Captain Scraggs groaned, and his groan was that of a seasick passenger. When he could look up again his face was ghastly with misery.

"Gib," he pleaded sadly, "you got us where the hair is short. Don't invoke the law an' make us handle that codfish, Gib! It ain't right. Gimme leave to tow that barge—anything to keep your freight off the *Victor*, an' we'll pull it up river for you——"

"Be a good feller, Gib. You usen'ter be hard an' spiteful like that," urged McGuffey.

"I'll tow the barge free," wailed Scraggs.

Mr. Gibney sat calmly down on the stringer and lit a cigar. Nature had blessed him with a strong constitution amidships and the contiguity of his tainted fortune bothered him but little. He squinted over the tip of the cigar at Captain Scraggs.

"You're just the same old Scraggsy you was in the green-pea trade. All you need is a ring in yer nose, Scraggsy, to make you a human hog. Here you goes to work an' soaks me a dollar a ton when you'd be tickled to death to do the job for half o' that, an' then you got the gall to stand there appealin' to my friend-ship! So you'll tow the barge up free, eh? Well, just to make the transaction legal, I'll give you a dollar for the job an' let you have the barge. Skip to it, Scraggsy, an' draw up a new bill, guaranteein' to tow the barge for one dollar. Then gimme back $499.00 an' I'll hand you back this receipted freight bill."

Captain Scraggs darted into his cabin, dashed off the necessary document, and returning to the deck, presented it, together with the requisite refund, to Mr. Gibney, who, in the meantime, had come aboard.

"Whatever are you a-goin' to do with this awful cod-fish, Gib?" he demanded.

Mr. Gibney cocked his hat over one ear and blew a cloud of smoke in the skipper's face.

"Well, boys, I'll tell you. Salted codfish that's been under water a long time gets most o' the salt took out of it, an' even at sea, if it's left long enough, it'll get so durned ripe that it's what you might call offensive. But it makes good fertilizer. There ain't nothin' in the world to equal a dead codfish, medium ripe, for fer-tilizer. I've rigged up a deal with a orchard comp'ny that's layin' out a couple o' thousand acres o' young trees up in the delta lands o' the Sacramento. I've sold 'em the lot, after first buyin' it from the owners o' the schooner for a hundred dollars. Every time these orchard fellers dig a hole to plant a young fruit tree they aims to heave a codfish in the bottom o' the hole first, for fertilizer. There was upwards o' two hundred thousand codfish in that schooner an' I've sold 'em for five cents each, delivered at Dunnigan's Landin'. I figger on cleanin' up about seven thousand net on the deal. I thought me an' Neils was stuck at first, but I got my imagination workin'——"

Captain Scraggs sank limply into McGuffey's arms and the two stared at the doughty commodore.

"Hit in the face with a fortune an' didn't know it," gasped poor McGuffey. "Gib, I'm sure glad you got out whole on that deal."

"Thanks to a lack o' imagination in you an' Scraggsy I'm about two hundred an' fifty dollars ahead o' my estimate now, on account o' the free tow o' that barge. Me an' Neils certainly makes a nice little split on account o' this here codfish deal."

"Gib," chattered Scraggs, "what's the matter with reorganizin' the syndicate?"

"Be a good feller, Adelbert," pleaded McGuffey.

Mr. Gibney was never so vulnerable as when one he really loved called him by his Christian name. He drew an arm across the shoulders of McGuffey and Scraggs, while Neils Halvorsen stood by, his yellow fangs flashing with pleasure under his walrus moustache.

"So you two boys're finally willin' to admit that I'm the white-haired boy, eh?"

"Gib, you got an imagination an' a half."

"One hundred an' fifty per cent. efficient," McGuffey declared.

Neils Halvorsen said nothing, but grinned like the

head of an old fiddle. Mr. Gibney appeared to swell visibly, after the manner of a turkey gobbler.

"Thanks, Scraggsy—an' you, too, Bart. So you're willin' to admit that though that there seeress might have helped some the game would have been deader than it is if it hadn't been for my imagination?"

Captain Scraggs nodded and Mr. McGuffey slapped the commodore on the back affectionately. "Aye bane buy drink in the Bowhead saloon," The Squarehead announced.

"Scraggsy! Mac! Your fins! We'll reorganize the syndicate, an' the minute me an' Neils finds ourselves with a bill o' sale for a one quarter interest in the *Victor*, based on the actual cost price, we'll tow this here barge——"

"An' split the profits on the codfish?" Scraggs queried eagerly.

"Certainly not. Me an' Neils splits that fifty-fifty. A quarter o' them profits is too high a price to pay for your friendship, Scraggsy, old deceitful. Remember, I made that profit after you an' Mac had pulled out o' the syndicate."

"That's logic," McGuffey declared.

"It's highway robbery," Scraggs snarled. "I won't sell no quarter interest to you or The Squarehead, Gib. Not on them terms."

"Then you'll load them codfish aboard, or pay demurrage on that barge for every day they hang around; an' if the Board o' Health condemns 'em an' chucks 'em overboard I'll sue you an' Mac for my lost profits, git a judgment agin you, an' take over the *Victor* to satisfy the judgment."

"You're a sea lawyer, Gib," Scraggs retorted sarcastically.

"You do what Gib says," McGuffey ordered threateningly. "Remember, I got a half interest in any jedgment he gits agin us—an' what's more, I object to them codfish clutterin' up my half interest."

"You bullied me on the old *Maggie*," Scraggs screeched, "but I won't be bullied no more. If you want to tow that barge, Mac, you buy me out, lock, stock, and barrel. An' the price for my half interest is five thousand dollars."

"You've sold somethin, Scraggsy," Mr. McGuffey flashed back at him, obeying a wink from Mr. Gibney. "An' here's a hundred dollars to bind the bargain. Balance on delivery of proper bill-o'-sale."

While Scraggs was counting the money Mr. Gibney was writing a receipt in his note book. Scraggs, still furious, signed the receipt.

"Now, then, Scraggsy," said Mr. Gibney affably, "hustle up to the Custom House, get a formal bill-o'-sale blank, fill her in, an' hustle back agin for your check. An' see to it you don't change your mind, because it won't do you any good. If you don't come through now I can sue you an' force you to."

"Oh! So you're buyin' my interest, eh?"

"Well, I'm lendin' Mac the money, an' I got a hunch he'll sell the interest to me an' Neils without figgerin' on a profit. You're a jarrin' note in the syndicate, Scraggsy, an' I've come to that time o' life where I want peace. An' there won't be no peace on the *Victor* unless I skipper her."

Captain Scraggs departed to draw up the formal bill

of sale and Mr. Gibney, drawing The Squarehead and
McGuffey to him, favoured each with a searching glance
and said:

"Gentlemen, did it ever occur to you that there's
money in the chicken business?"

It had! Both McGuffey and Neils admitted it.
There are few men in this world who have not, at some
period of their lives, held the same view, albeit the
majority of those who have endeavoured to demonstrate that fact have subsequently changed their
minds.

"I thought as much," the commodore grinned. "If
I was to let you two out o' my sight for a day you'd both
be flat busted the day after. So we won't buy no farm
an' go in for chickens. We'll sell the *Victor* an' buy a
little tradin' schooner. Then we'll go back to the South
Seas an' earn a legitimate livin'."

"But why'll we sell the *Victor?*" McGuffey demanded. "Gib, she's a love of a boat."

"Because I've just had a talk with the owners o' the
two opposition lines an' they, knowin' me to be chummy
with you an' Scraggsy, give me the tip to tell you two
that you could have your choice o' two propositions—
a rate war or a sale o' the *Victor* for ten thousand dollars. That gets you out clean an' saves your original
capital, an' it gits Scraggsy out the same way, while
nettin' me an' Neils five hundred each."

"A rate war would ruin us," McGuffey agreed. "In
addition to sourin' Scraggsy's disposition until he
wouldn't be fit to live with. Gib, you're a wonder."

"I know it," Mr. Gibney replied.

Within two hours Captain Scraggs's half interest had

passed into the hands of McGuffey, and half an hour
later the *Victor* had passed into the hands of the opposition lines, to be operated for the joint profit of the latter.   Later in the day all four members of the syndicate
met in the Bowhead saloon, where Mr. Gibney explained the deal to Captain Scraggs.   The latter was
dumfounded.

"I had to fox you into selling," the commodore confessed.

"But how about them defunct codfish, Gib?"

"I got the new owners to agree to tow 'em up at a
reasonable figger.   When I've cleaned up that deal,
we'll buy a schooner an' run South again."

"You'll run without me, Gib," Scraggs declared
emphatically.   "I've had a-plenty o' the dark blue for
mine.   I got a little stake now, so I'm going to look
around an' invest in a——"

"A chicken ranch," McGuffey interrupted.

"Right-O, Bart.   How'd you guess it?"

"Imagination," quoth McGuffey, tapping his fore-
head, "imagination, Scraggsy."

Something told Mr. Gibney that it would be just as
well if he did not insist upon having Scraggs as a
member of his crew.   So he did not insist.   In the
afternoon of life Mr. Gibney was acquiring common
sense.

Three weeks later Mr. Gibney had purchased, for
account of his now abbreviated syndicate, the kind of
power schooner he desired, and the Inspectors gave him
a ticket as master.   With The Squarehead as mate and
Mr. McGuffey as engineer and general utility man, the
little schooner cleared for Pago Pago on a day when

Captain Scraggs' was too busy buying incubators to come down to the dock and see them off.

And for aught the chronicler of this tale knows to the contrary, the syndicate may be sailing in that self-same schooner to this very day.

THE END

www.ingramcontent.com/pod-product-compliance
Lightning Source LLC
Chambersburg PA
CBHW031157020726
47499CB00002B/403